Mrs. Perivale and the Dragon Prince

By Dash Hoffman

Mrs. Perivale and the Dragon Prince

Written by Dash Hoffman

Published by Paris Publishing
Copyright 2020 Dash Hoffman

With Special Thanks To

@broodingYAhero
And
@Dinuriel
For inspiring this book series in the first place!

@broodingYAhero published a post that read: "It's amazing how many prophecies involve teens. You'd think they'd pick more emotionally stable people, with more free time. Like grandmas."

To which @Dinuriel replied:
"…I would read the hell out of a series of a chosen eighty-five-year-old woman who goes on epic journeys throughout a dangerous and magical land, armed only with a cane and her stab-tastic knitting needles, accompanied by her six cats and a skittish-yet-devoted orderly who makes sure she takes her pills on time.

Wish Granted…

Dedications

For Mehrzad,
Renee, Nichole,
Courtney, and Kjirsten
WITH MUCH GRATITUDE AND LOVE

For those intrepid adventurers
WHO HAVE LOVED Coreve AND WISHED
TO GO BACK

Table of Contents

Prelude ~ 1

Chapter One ~ Dragon Storm 5

Chapter Two ~ The Land of Dragons 25

Chapter Three ~ And Alice Makes Three 56

Chapter Four ~ A Twist in the Tail 86

Chapter Five ~ This Way and That 102

Chapter Six ~ Beyond Expectations 118

Chapter Seven ~ Matters of the Heart 144

Chapter Eight ~ Alice to the Rescue 157

Chapter Nine ~ The Calm Before the Storm 174

Chapter Ten ~ Risk, Sacrifice, Love 190

Chapter Eleven ~ The Dragon King 226

Chapter Twelve ~ Home Again 236

CHIPPA MARI

PRELUDE

Listless ashen smoke emanated from deep crevices within blackened, rough-hewn rock, wreathing the base of a massive ebony fortress which seemed more a deadly claw reaching up out of the top of the mountain, than a castle set at its peak.

The broad foothold rose into three solid towers at the back, and one guards' tower at the front, overlooking a steep wasteland of scorched ground and widespread stone rubble that almost met the timberline far beyond it.

Nearly scraping the clouds above, the smoldering mountain-head was densely skirted from the timberline to the foothills far below with variant trees and growth. Every green and living thing looked to be running from the crest and from the recent resident in command there, where the mountain's burning heart had ruptured and slowly bled fire.

She strode the great, dark halls of the looming citadel; her two clawed-feet striking the flagstone floor loudly, as her long tail hovered slightly over it. More sheen and light reflected off of her thick amphibious skin; gray and speckled with small beige spots, than from her lusterless blood-red eyes.

There was no hair on her body, but miniscule fibers all over her quivered, sensing electric current from approaching beings.

"Someone is here. Open the door." Her cold voice echoed through the great hall though she did not speak with volume. Shooting out three feet from between her jagged teeth, her forked tongue tasted the air to detect every hint of information in it.

A squat, dull green goblin hustled toward the door, his pointed nose and ears shivering slightly as he reached for the rope at the side of it. Giving a hard pull, the rope slid through old metal rings and slowly drew the enormous barrier inward.

Two creatures entered. One spoke, and the other remained silent. "Sorceress Baliste, you've summoned me, and I have come at your bidding. How may I serve you?"

Baliste's sanguine eyes pierced him. "I have tried to capture and hold the dragon Diovalo, and twice he has escaped me. With your service, I have taken all of the fire dragons, and yet this one, the most important one of them, eludes me! I want him found and caught! I want him brought here to me, and I want it done immediately!"

She began to pace; her seven foot form, slender and lithe, save for the bumpy ridge along her back, twisting as she turned here and there. Her arms were held still at her sides until she lifted one, jabbing the claw at the end of it toward her minions.

"Fail me not; it would not bode well for you, Wurm."

Each claw resembled the shape of her home; three wide fingers and a thumb, tipped with razor sharp points. They were dangerous, but they were nothing compared to the long, tapered tail that swept out behind her, ending in a spiked club bigger than her head. The goblins around her backed off quickly, staring at the weapon she bore.

"He was rescued last time by the warrior of the prophecy of the Blue Fire Crystal." The servant replied pointedly. "He disappeared after that."

"Diovalo did not disappear. He was last seen by my servants in the desert of Aridan. He must be found. The warrior... Alice... is gone. She is no longer in Corevé. The prophecy is complete, so there should be no more hinderance." Baliste spat bitterly.

An old mystic, sitting on a woven mat upon the floor before a wall, stared straight ahead with glowing white eyes, and spoke. "The prophecy is not fulfilled. It was only begun. Alice is returning."

A deafening shriek erupted from Baliste, and the goblins clamped their gnarled fingers over their ears.

"You should have told me that the first time! Do not parse out what you know in bits and pieces! Tell me all of it now! I want no surprises, and no mistakes!"

The mystic only continued to stare straight ahead into nothing, though the glow faded from her ancient eyes.

Baliste turned in place and glared at the visiting servants before her. "Bring me Diovalo, and I shall bestow upon you great power in return for it. I know what you want, and you shall have it, so long as I get what I want! Now go!"

Her minions bowed low to her. "Yes, my queen." The one who spoke replied, and they both turned and left the fortress.

Baliste raised her voice slightly. "Mendax!"

Behind her, a short man with a large rounded belly bound up in a sapphire blue sash, a dark moustache over his mouth, golden robes drifting from his shoulders, and a red turban twisted upon his head, floated a few feet above the floor. He inclined his chin somewhat to the sorceress.

"I am here."

"Did you bring what I asked you for?"

"Yes, oh Dark One. They are waiting for you in the next room." The djinn answered evenly.

"Be gone until I call for you again." Baliste snapped at him, flinging her tail behind her, narrowly missing hitting Mendax with it. She stomped toward an adjoining room, and once she was inside it, she slammed the door behind her.

Three human women sat on a long bench beside a table. They faced her.

Baliste narrowed her eyes at them and an icy tone flooded her voice. "All right, Alice, I want to know everything about you!"

CHAPTER ONE

DRAGON STORM

Late afternoon sun trimmed the edges of dark clouds closing in around the skies over Notting Hill in London. Beneath them, a seventy-three-year-old woman knelt on a cushion beside a colorful flowerbed.

Not far from her, laying in what little warm light there was left, an Abyssinian cat gazed at her from behind hooded eyes. Within the stems of flowers growing in the garden, a small, fuzzy, orange kitten stalked a bug; his big green eyes locked on it with laser beam focus.

Beside the white-haired woman, a twelve-year-old boy held a tube of superglue in one hand, and a teacup saucer in the other.

"Just squeeze a good amount out there around the ring inside the saucer." She instructed him.

He squeezed the tube, spreading superglue gel.

Just then an old man shuffled up alongside them and bent over, furrowing his bushy gray brows and peering through his thick eyeglasses at the boy's hands.

"Hello there, Mrs. Perivale. What are you working at today?" He asked, trying to figure it out. His mouth formed an O, and his eyes appeared enormous through his spectacles.

Alice Perivale smiled at him and spoke loudly. "Hello there, Murray. How nice to see you. Eddie, this is my neighbor, Murray. Murray, this is my grandson, Eddie."

Murray gave the boy a nod, but he was distracted with the project.

Eddie flashed him a bright smile and, taking a cue from his grandmother, spoke with a louder voice. "It's nice to meet you, Mr. Murray."

The old man waved his hand lightly. "Oh, it's not Mr. Murray, thank you. It's just Murray. I like to keep things simple. Good to meet you as well, Freddie. Or do you go by Fred? Now… what are you doing here? I can't make it out!" He waggled a wrinkled, crooked finger at the saucer and the glue.

Alice's eyes twinkled at her grandson. "Would you like to tell him?"

Eddie's chin lifted and his chest puffed out a little. "We're making a teacup garden!"

Murray frowned and spoke up more. "A what now?"

Alice held up one of the finished versions they'd already completed. It was a teacup glued to a matching saucer, which was glued to the top of a wooden stake about two feet long. Murray took it in his hands and examined it.

"What's it for?" He boomed, and handed it back to Alice.

She pointed to the flowerbed, which was already dotted with three of the teacup-saucer stakes, firmly planted into the ground. The cups and saucers, held fast to the top of the stakes, ranged in heights of a foot to a foot and a half from the earth.

"It's a teacup garden! We fill the cups with water, unless it rains and then that happens on its own. That way the birds, butterflies, bees, and other visitors we have to the flowers can get a sip!" Alice beamed.

Murray chuckled. "A dip? Oh! I see now. Birdbath. Well, you mentioned yesterday that you had been out at the charity shops looking for old teacup sets, and I had an extra one that I never use, so I brought it for you. Didn't realize you were going to put it in your garden!"

He chuckled as he reached into his pocket and pulled out a pretty cup and saucer, handing it to her.

"Oh how lucky! We have another stake we can use. That works out nicely. Thank you, Murray!" Alice took it and set it beside her in the soil.

"It's good of you to help her with this, Freddie!" Murray gave Eddie a pat on the shoulder.

"I'm glad to do it!" Eddie smiled warmly at his grandmother. "I'm staying with her for the weekend while my parents are out of town."

Alice's attention was snared by a chubby young woman with a sour expression who was marching up the way at a brisk pace. In her hand she held a covered pan.

She stopped before Alice, Eddie, and Murray; her mouth closed in a tight line. After eyeing the flowerbed and teacups, she gave Alice a curt nod.

"Well, I'm pleased to see that you're finally doing something that people your age *should* be doing, rather than going to extremes and joining groups they have no business joining."

The young woman, referring to Alice having joined the local Widows of War group against her advisement, glared down her nose at Alice. Her clothes were rumpled and unkempt, and her mousy brown hair was pulled up into a sloppy bun at the back of her head.

Alice sighed. "Hello, Deborah. They've let you out, have they?" Alice got to her feet with Eddie's help and planted her hands on her hips.

"Deborah, you'd better be careful. If that mind of yours gets any smaller, it might just roll right out of your head, and then what will you do?"

Eddie swiftly covered his mouth with his hand and tried to muffle a snicker.

Alice took a step toward the younger woman and leveled a stern gaze at her. "Am I nothing more than a living ghost in your eyes? So simply ignored and forgotten because I'm older? Would you have me set back on a shelf to collect dust as my colors fade? Nothing more than a transparent memory so familiar that I become unseen! Well I'm not about to allow that! You cannot begin to comprehend the depths in me; the far reaching sea of experience and knowledge! As we grow older, we learn to listen and watch more, and speak less, and that only adds to the exponential largeness inside of us!"

Alice shook her head. "You'll have it too, one day, but for now you are blinded and deafened by the blazing flames of freedom and hunger in your young adulthood, so concerned with what you're bringing *to the world* that you have forgotten what it means to be very young and you cannot see what a treasure it is to be very old. Those two ages; the very young and very old are the same; they are the ones who are enraptured by what the world brings *to them*! They cherish one another because they listen to each other, they have so much to share, and they are not burdened or distracted with the worries which are beyond them. They have the freedom of eagles, soaring like kings above every dominion, unfettered, wild, willful, and spilling over with life! It's those pesky years in the middle when grown-ups forget how to live that way that's the trouble. That's where you are, Deborah. You're in the middle where you can't see much further than the end of that upturned nose of yours. You'll be here one day, in my shoes, and only then will you see it all clearly! No matter how hard you try, I'm not going to let you put me on a shelf. I'm going to keep right on living and being useful to everyone who needs me!"

Deborah scowled severely. "I didn't come here to be told off! I just came to bring these berry butter puffs that you purchased from the bake sale because I was ordered to!"

The front door opened and a tall, thin man in a black suit and white button up shirt emerged and came lightly down the front steps of Alice's townhouse. He was Alice's devoted butler.

"Henderson! Good. I'm glad you're out here." Alice nodded to him and he nodded in answer, giving Deborah a cool stare.

Alice took the pan of puffs and handed them to Henderson. "Please give one of these to Murray to take home, and make sure to wrap them up so Bailey doesn't see them." She glanced over at Murray then, who was smiling with anticipation.

"Bailey is my calico cat. He just loves pastries, but he shouldn't have them. We'll have to put them away so he doesn't go looking for them!"

Deborah drew her head back, giving herself a double chin, and shot a haughty look at Alice from over the top of the squared glasses that sat perched at the end of her sharp nose.

"Did you say *he*?"

Alice turned to her and blinked. "Yes. Bailey is a male calico."

Deborah gave her head a slight shake and spoke with a withering tone. "Mrs. Perivale, there's no such thing as a male calico cat. All calico cats are female!"

The corner of Alice's mouth twitched. "As a matter of fact, Deborah, there *are* male calico cats. They're just very rare. You see, there's a chromosomal aberration in them; they have two X chromosomes and one Y chromosome, which produces a male, and definitely explains a lot about Bailey. Granted, they are extremely rare; only one in every three thousand or so, but I promise you, just because you haven't heard of them doesn't mean they don't exist. As a matter of fact, I've seen quite a few things you'd be surprised to know exist."

Deborah's cheeks turned red and she huffed. "I can't stand here and listen to this. I have to leave. I've already been here too long."

"There you go, you're finally right about something. Thank you for bringing the puffs. Good day." Alice waved her hand dismissively, and just as Deborah turned to leave, the water from all of the teacups whisked up into the air and splashed down the young woman's back.

Deborah spun on her heel and gasped, furious with Alice. "You! You!" She sputtered, not seeming to be able to say anything else.

Murray stepped in and raised his hand to pause the imminent explosion. "Now wait a moment, I saw what happened. Mrs. Perivale didn't do a thing. She was standing here with me the whole time. There was a wind that came and took the water up!"

Deborah clenched her fists and her teeth. "There isn't any wind!"

She flipped around and lock-stepped down the street, growling and muttering under her breath about wind and calico cats.

Alice chuckled and Henderson returned, carrying a pretty plate with a wrap over the pastry on it.

"Thank you, Murray. That was very nice of you to step in like that. Here, have a berry butter puff." Alice took the plate from Henderson and handed it to Murray. He blushed and nodded.

"Thank you! This looks wonderful!"

Alice sighed and turned to Eddie, who stood up beside her. "I'm sorry, dear. Sometimes people can get under our skin and pinch us where we are most sensitive. We have to be aware of it and react in the best way possible. I… might not have handled that quite the way I should have."

Alice had no trouble telling Deborah just what she thought, but she wasn't keen to do it in front of her grandson.

Eddie frowned sharply. "I'm glad you said something. I didn't like the way she was speaking to you, and I was about to say something myself."

Alice gave his shoulder a squeeze. "Thank you, darling. Aren't you sweet. She's no match for me, though, so it's best if you keep your front row seat."

An older man and woman happened by just then, and they stopped to admire the flower garden and teacups.

"Hello, Alice! How are you doing today? Are you having a garden party out here?" The kind woman grinned and reached down to pet the Abyssinian cat on his head. "Hello, Marlowe." She greeted him. He purred happily.

Alice gave her a warm hug. "Eddie, these are my neighbors from just down the way. This is James, and his lovely wife, Elaine." She turned to them proudly. "This is my grandson, Eddie. He's with me for the weekend."

"It's very nice to meet you, young man!" James gave the boy a hearty handshake.

"I'm pleased to meet you too, sir." Eddie answered pleasantly.

Elaine bent and took a good look at the teacup garden, enthralled with it. "James! Look at this! Isn't this charming!"

Alice handed one of the finished but unplanted teacup stakes to James and Elaine so they could have a closer look.

"I'll be doing a workshop on how to make these at the Widows of War group next week. You might like to come to that. I'd be so glad to have you both there." Alice offered with a hopeful smile.

James and Elaine shared an excited nod, and Elaine replied. "Oh, yes please! That sounds fine! We've been looking for something nice to spruce up our own garden, and this is just the thing! I'll call the group and sign up for the class. Thank you!"

Alice was pleased. "I look forward to seeing you there."

James and Elaine strolled away hand in hand, talking with each other about the teacups and their own garden, and all the possibilities they might explore.

"Tea is ready Madame. It's nearly four o'clock." Henderson announced quietly. Bailey, the fat calico cat whom Alice had been speaking of earlier, stood expectantly at Henderson's feet, meowing loudly at him in hopes of being fed early and extra.

Murray bid them farewell and headed home delighted with his plate of puffs. Eddie hurried inside to get washed up for tea, and the sun disappeared altogether as heavy drops of rain began to splatter on the pavement.

Henderson gathered the remains of the teacup project and took them inside, following Alice up the stairs and into the door.

With a tender tone, Henderson caught Alice's eye and spoke. "Madame, I wanted to say that I saw what happened with the water and the teacups when the young woman from the Widows of War group was leaving."

Alice sighed in exasperation. "I didn't mean to let her annoy me, but she did, and then... I don't know what happened!"

"Madame, I suspect it's the powers that Bayless Grand Mari gave you when we were in Corevé." Henderson gazed at her earnestly.

"Yes, I think you might be right. I don't really have any idea what kind of powers he gave me, or what I can do with them. There was no booklet of instructions, and of course Chippa's not here so there's no one in *this* world to teach me. I'm on my own with it, I suppose. Honestly, I don't know if the water splashing that girl happened because of me or not, but if it did, I didn't mean for it to. I just have no control over it."

Chippa Mari was the powerful little Inkling that had come from the magical world of Corevé to collect Alice, telling her she was the Chosen One. He had taken her, as well as Henderson and all seven of her cats, back to his beautiful land so she could save it, and she had saved it from complete destruction. In gratitude, Bayless Grand Mari, the chief of Chippa's Inking tribe, had bestowed upon Alice the same powers that the Inklings had to control, protect, and use the elements. He'd done it just before she left to return to London, and she knew nothing about her new gifts.

Henderson pursed his lips thoughtfully. "Chippa was still learning how to handle his own when we met him. You'll learn too."

Eddie stepped into the room with them just then and he cocked an eyebrow at them both. "Who's Chippa?"

The rain began to pour hard against the street outside, and the townhouse. Alice and Henderson shared a smiled.

"He's a friend we met recently." Alice answered with a soft, sentimental voice. She blinked then and drew in a quick breath. "Do you know, I just realized that it was only two days ago!"

Henderson's brows rose as his eyes widened, and he nodded. "Indeed, Madame. It was. Time passes so… swiftly."

Henderson led them into the library and Alice looked through the window at the skies drenching the world outside. She went to her chair by the fireplace and picked up a knitted scarf, then handed it to Eddie with a wide smile. It was navy blue with a light gray stripe running down the center.

"Good knitting will protect you against the cold, and knitting needles are good for protection as well!" She chuckled pensively. She'd successfully defeated a terrible villain with hers earlier that week.

"Thank you, grandma. This means a lot to me." Eddie ran his hands over the scarf and lifted it to his nose, breathing in its scent deeply. "It smells like you. Good."

He hugged her tightly for a long minute, and then finally let her go, looking away as he blinked back some emotion.

They sat down to tea and Alice eyed her grandson curiously. "I'm so glad that we were able to have dinner with your parents last night, and I'm doubly glad that you're here with me now, but I must admit, I was a little surprised by your request to stay with me while they went out of town. You love going to Margate, but you were so adamant to stay with me, instead of heading off with your parents. Why is that?"

Eddie lifted his teacup to his mouth and sipped, turning his eyes toward the six cats lined up at their bowls enjoying their teatime treats.

He didn't answer her until he set the cup back down, but his eyes stayed on the cats. "I just really wanted to see you. That's all."

Alice knew better, but she could tell that he wasn't going to say more than that. She suspected that he would open up to her in his own time. Instead of pressing him further, she changed the subject entirely.

"Shall we have a rousing chess match after tea? Do you think you're up for the challenge?" She raised a brow, taunting him.

Eddie sat up straighter in his chair and his face broke into a wide grin. "Yes! Definitely! I've been practicing, grandma! I joined the chess club at school, and I've learned a lot since you showed me how to play! I bet I could take you this time!"

"Well, we'll just have to see about that!" Alice laughed. "You know I won't hand it to you! You're going to have to figure it out on your own!"

"You're on, grandma!" Eddie laughed.

They finished their tea, and in no time they were both bent across the chessboard from one another; each of them focused intently on the match.

It seemed merely moments to her before he moved his queen for the last time and thrust his hand up into the air excitedly.

"Checkmate!"

Alice groaned and leaned back in her chair. "I should never have showed you how to play this game."

Eddie laughed and stood up from his chair, stretching. He stopped short suddenly, and frowned, peering at his grandmother's roll-top desk in the corner of the room against the rain-soaked window.

"What... what is that thing? It's glowing!"

Before Alice could stop Eddie, he hurried across the room and picked up a spherical glass bottle that just fit into his hands. It was sheathed in a kind of chainmail all around, and inside it, a dark red liquid had begun to glow brightly.

Henderson, who was about to light a fire in the fireplace, shared a worried look with Alice.

"Oh no... it's happening again." Alice murmured as Eddie brought the vial to her, turning it over and over in his hands as he examined it.

Henderson let out a long breath. "It's been happening on and off since shortly after we got back, but it's much brighter than any of the other times it's glowed."

"It's warm!" Eddie blinked in awe, and handed the bottle to Alice.

Her eyes went wide, and she stared at Henderson. "It hasn't gotten warm before."

"Madame... I don't think that we-" He began, but she shook her head.

"We have to go!" Alice insisted.

"What about Eddie?" Henderson pressed.

"Yes, what about me?" Eddie interjected persistently. "And what's in that bottle? You're not going anywhere without me, grandma!"

He took her hand in his and held it tightly.

Alice was surprised, but she gave him a nod and turned to Henderson. "Well, he'll just have to go. There's nothing for it."

Facing Eddie once more she gave him a half smile. "I'll explain about the bottle soon, but for now, you need to hurry and go pack your bag. All of it. Everything you brought. And make sure you have a good jacket, and good shoes. And grab that scarf I made you."

Eddie rushed off to do as he was told, and Henderson sighed. "I'll go pack as well. Do you need anything?"

Alice shook her head. "I can get my own bag, thank you for offering. At least this time we have a much better idea of what we need."

Henderson groaned. "Yes. A much bigger medical kit."

"And ginger chews." Alice added with a tender smile. "All of the ginger chews that we have."

A soft chuckle escaped her butler. "Yes, I'll be sure to get them."

Alice looked down at all six of her cats, who were staring up at her wide-eyed. Tao the Siamese, who was so balanced and meditative. Sophie, the princess with her carefully groomed long white fur and her diamond collar with a monocle hanging from it. Bailey, the fat calico who until that moment had been sniffing the other cat's bowls. Oscar the kitten, whose fluffy orange hair stuck out in every direction, making him look as if he'd just come out of the dryer. Jynx, the sleek black cat who watched over Oscar all the time, and Marlowe the Abyssinian, who watched over Alice all the time.

"Well my darlings, it looks as if it's time we were going back to Corevé. I know you can understand me, so do what you need to before we have to go, and meet me by the door in a few minutes."

A couple of them meowed at her, and Oscar the kitten ran for the litter box. Alice rushed to her room and packed her big black handbag, as well as a second, smaller bag.

As she came back past the library, she nipped in quickly to the knitting basket beside her chair, and grabbed all the knitting needles she had.

"Can't forget these beauties!" She shoved them down into her purse, and headed for the front door. All of the cats were there waiting for her.

Eddie came a moment later, followed closely by Henderson, who was turning up the collar on his raincoat.

"Madame, how are we going to get there without Chippa?" He reached for his umbrella, and handed an extra one to Eddie.

Alice lifted the bottle in her hand; glowing even brighter red than it was before. "He will come to me anywhere. That's what this does. It's a blood bond."

Eddie's eyes grew wide. "That's blood?"

"But, he certainly won't fit in the park down the lane." Alice added, ignoring her grandson's question.

Henderson's brows rose as he agreed. "Not a chance."

She hurried out of the door and down the steps.

"Where are we going?" Eddie called out loudly to her over the splash and rush of the rain.

"We're going to have to go to Hyde Park so Diovalo will have room to land!" Alice called out to Henderson.

Just then a voice called out to her. "Alice!"

She turned and saw Murray coming toward her. He held out the empty plate. "Quite a good plate of puffs! Thank you! Thought I'd bring this back to you." He eyed them thoughtfully and tipped his head.

"Where are you all off to?"

Alice spoke up loudly. "We have to get to Hyde Park!"

Murray nodded and held up his keys. "I'll drive you!"

Alice's mouth fell open and she shook her head adamantly. "No! No, good heavens, thank you, but no."

Henderson held his hand up. "That's all right, Murray, I'll drive."

Alice stopped him. "Wait… Henderson, we don't know how long we're going to be gone! If you drive, there's no telling how long we'll be leaving the car there!"

Henderson's eyes squinted with worry, and Alice groaned, realizing there was no other choice.

"Murray, I'm afraid we're going to have to take you up on your offer. Thank you."

Murray beamed and hustled off to his car with the group of them; Alice, Henderson, Eddie, and all six cats, following. Alice tucked Eddie into the back seat with a stern warning.

"You put your seatbelt on and cross your fingers that we make it there alive. Murray is not a good driver."

Eddie nodded and tightened his belt across his lap. Henderson and Alice did the same. Old Murray whipped out onto the street and took off through the dark afternoon sending walls of water spraying over everything he passed.

In no time at all, he came to a shuddering halt in Hyde Park, and everyone clamored out, gasping for air and praying for solid ground.

Alice waved and called out her thanks to Murray, and then closed the car door. She turned and rushed through the downpour holding her hat to her head, her bag swinging on her arm as Eddie and Henderson followed closely behind her, carrying the bags. The cats darted from the shelter of one tree to the next, zig-zagging across the green, keeping up.

They came to a wide open space and Alice finally stopped, looking around her wildly. "Oh good, there's no one else about. Can't have people seeing him! Lucky it's dinnertime and it's raining so hard. No one wants to be out right now."

"That's certainly true." Henderson groaned and rolled his eyes just a little.

"Grandma, what are we *doing* out here, and what's in that bottle? Why are we standing in the middle of the park in the rain at night with our bags and *all the cats*?" Eddie was done waiting for answers.

Alice chewed at her lower lip a moment and glanced at Henderson, who was not happy about going.

"Uh… dearest…" Alice began uncertainly, "well… this is   this is dragon's blood."

Eddie laughed so hard he had to catch his breath, but then he saw that neither his grandmother nor Henderson were laughing with him.

"Oh no…" Eddie grew serious and his mouth fell open slightly. "Oh grandma. Should… should you be on medication or something? Should I… call someone?"

"I have all of her medication." Henderson mentioned evenly. "And none of it will help us with this."

"Eddie, now I know this might be difficult for you to believe, but… you're about to see a dragon. A real dragon. I don't want you to be afraid. This dragon, Diovalo, he's a friend of ours."

Eddie began to breathe faster, and he held his hand out to Alice, taking her arm in his, and searching her eyes.

"Are you dizzy? Does your chest hurt? What's happening? I think I'd better… I better call someone!

Henderson," He turned swiftly to the butler, "Henderson we have to call someone! Grandma isn't well!"

Henderson shook his head stoically. "She is better than she's been in a long time, young master. Unfortunately, everything she's telling you is quite true."

"But… but… that can't…" Eddie clamped his hands on his head and scowled.

Alice raised the brilliantly glowing vial high up in the air, feeling it getting warmer still in her hand. She drew in a deep breath and called out as loudly as she could.

"DIOVALO!"

The contents of the bottle blazed like a star, and a bolt of red electric current shot straight up from it into the clouds. A deafening clap of thunder shook the trees and the ground around them as the rain fell even harder.

Eddie tugged on Alice's sleeve and tried to pull her arm back down, yelling above the storm to her. "Grandma! What's wrong with you? There's no such thing as dra-"

His words were cut short and his jaw dropped as the form of a great beast took shape in the clouds and fog just above them. It had massive wings that spread so far to either side that no one could see the ends of them. The blast of thunder struck again, and it became clear that it wasn't thunder, it was the creature's mighty wings beating against the air.

Even in the darkness, its ruby red body was radiant; scarlet all down his sides and wings, all over his back, and his legs, while his front and underside were gold and orange. His enormous feet ended in claws bigger than a bus. His entire body might just barely have fit into the field of a stadium.

"Well, Madame, you were right about needing to have him land in Hyde Park."

Sophie growled deeply. Jynx, the black cat, gave her a sidelong pleased look.

Eddie could only stammer and stare. "That's… that's…"

"That's a dragon. A real one. Come along now darling, we need to get out of here before anyone sees him. I think we'd have a tricky time explaining him. Quick now, follow Henderson and get up onto him."

As the cats leapt nimbly onto the dragon and Henderson went with them, Diovalo swung his giant head down close to Alice, and smiled at her. His deep voice rumbled like the skies above him. "It's good to see you, my friend. I wish that it was under better circumstances."

"As do I dear one." She grinned back at him. "Now let's get out of here before someone sees you."

Alice climbed onto the back of Diovalo's neck, just behind the great shield at the crown of his head, and before she knew it, Eddie had scampered up with her, and was holding tightly to her.

"Eddie, you should ride with Henderson and the cats. There's a hollow just under each of Diovalo's wings and you'll all fit into it nicely."

"No, grandma! No. I'm staying right here next to you!"

Alice saw that he wouldn't hear of anything else, and she relented. "Very well then. Dio, let's go!"

With a tremendous rush of air, they lifted off from the ground at an immediately dizzying height, and soared upward into the rainstorm and fog. Eddie screamed and held tighter to his grandmother.

She glanced back at him as he buried his face in her shoulder. "No! Eddie, open your eyes! Don't miss this! Even if you're afraid, open your eyes and let the fear pass through you! There's wonder on the other side of it! Don't miss it!"

Eddie peeked up and held fast to her.

Though her heart was pounding, and she had no idea if she could do it, Alice focused with everything in her and raised her hands up, moving them as if she were pushing the clouds aside. The storm parted, just a sliver, but it was enough for the end of day sun to come streaming through and spark a vibrant double rainbow.

"I… I think that will work! It's a natural arch! The first time we went, Chippa made an arch with trees for us to use as a portal. I don't know if this will do, but we can give it a go! Fly beneath it, Diovalo!"

Alice punched her fist into the air as adrenaline shot through her. There was never a rush in her life that felt the way riding on a fire dragon did.

With the cats and Henderson cowering and pressing as closely into the hollow under Diovalo's wing as they could, and Eddie screaming against Alice's shoulder, the great dragon ripped through the sky straight into the arch beneath the rainbow, and the clouds swept closed behind them.

Chapter Two

The Land of Dragons

Everything around Diovalo faded to black, and the din of the storm died away. Eddie leaned close to his grandmother's ear and whispered.

"Where are we?"

She drew in a deep breath and exhaled quietly as he tightened his arms a bit more around her. "I don't know."

The darkness disappeared as swiftly as it had come, and they found themselves gazing down at turquoise waves rolling into a white sandy beach. The beach was hedged on its far side by tropical jungle growth. The jungle spread over low foothills, and then graduated up into mountains, almost reaching the clouds.

Alice squealed with joy and delight.

Eddie gripped his grandmother as his eyes widened. "We're so far up!"

"Yes, we are!" She grinned. "Isn't it fantastic!"

A chuckle thundered deep in Diovalo's throat, and he brought them down to land on the wide beach, bathed in warm morning light.

"Get off!"

"You're crowding me!"

"Don't push!"

"Ouch! My tail!"

"Oh! My foot!"

"Bailey, you're suffocating me!"

"That's just more of me to love!"

"Everyone, let's get off!" Henderson climbed out of the hollow beneath Diovalo's wing, and was immediately followed by six cats which had suddenly grown much bigger; to the size of large horses, save for Oscar, who was the size of a pony.

"We're back! We're back in Corevé!" The giant kitten pounced around in the sand playfully.

All of the cat's fur coats had changed as well. Marlowe's fur had gone dark blue with silvery spots, making him look like a massive leopard. Bailey had turned pink with silver tips at the ends of all his hair. Sophie was awash in swirls of silver and lavender. Oscar looked like a gigantic tiger; all orange and red with stripes. Tao's fur could have been a summer sky; light blue with iridescent white that shifted and shimmered like misty clouds when she moved. Jynx remained black, though her coat took on a regal cobalt blue sheen in the light.

Alice giggled; she was so happy to be back in the extraordinary world of Corevé. Eddie scrambled down off of the dragon and gasped when his feet thumped into the soft sand.

"Where *are* we, and *what are those?*" He yelled, pulling at Alice to save her from the massive beasts before them.

Marlowe padded up to her and nuzzled her, purring so loud that it was a rumbling roar. She ran her hand up his nose and rubbed his ears.

"We are in the magical land of Corevé, and those are the cats. They look differently here." Alice gave her grandson an encouraging smile.

"We also speak here, too!" Oscar rushed to them and barely stopped short of Eddie, who cowered back from him.

Oscar tipped his head to one side. "Don't be afraid of us! It's just... us!"

Eddie shook his head. "I'm dreaming. This is a dream. A super... super realistic dream. That's all it is. There's no dragon. There are no... giant... colored... cats. No. This is just a really crazy dream!" He sounded as though he might convince himself of it if he continued to say it.

"I'm afraid it's real." Henderson sighed and changed his shoes into trainers. Alice laughed softly in surprise.

"I didn't know you owned anything like that!" She gave him a nod of approval. "They're quite nice!"

"I ruined my good shoes last time we were here. *Ruined.* I was unprepared." Henderson moaned, thin-lipped. "Not this time."

Alice turned Eddie toward the dragon, who had brought his head down low to face the group. "Eddie, this is my friend Diovalo, the dragon. Diovalo, this is my grandson, Eddie."

"What a true pleasure to meet you. Your grandmother is one of the most remarkable persons I know." Diovalo's eyes glittered like jewels in the morning sun, and his deep voice reverberated off of everything around them.

"It's... nice to meet you, Diovalo. Thank you for the ride. I'm afraid I'm... going to have to try better to wrap my mind around this." Eddie struggled, shuffling his feet.

"It's understandable that you might be surprised." Diovalo replied generously.

"My goodness! That was exciting wasn't it! I didn't know they had anything like this in the park! That's quite a fancy ride the city has put in. Must be for the tourists. I may get on and have another go!" Murray stumbled around Diovalo and patted him on the leg as he came to the group. Diovalo gave him a narrow look.

Alice's mouth fell open, as did Henderson's and Eddie's, as they all three stared at the old man.

"Huh. Looks like they've also done some landscaping since I was here last. It's nice. Glad the storm cleared up so fast. Terrible heavy rain that was, but it comes and goes. Lovely afternoon to be in Hyde Park!"

Alice took a few steps toward him and gave her head a shake, certain she couldn't believe what she was seeing.

"Murray! What on earth are you *doing* here? How did you *get* here?"

Murray shrugged and slid his hands into the front pockets of his sweater. "Well, I parked the car, and then followed you lot. You said we had to go to Hyde Park, so here we are! Though, I don't recall this much sand here before."

Eddie snickered and slipped his hand into the crook of Alice's arm. "You said *we* had to go to Hyde Park."

Alice exhaled sharply in disapproval.

Eddie gave her a wink. "You did."

"Well I meant all of *us*! Not *him*! He can't be here!" She huffed and pursed her mouth.

"Do you mean to tell me that he shouldn't be here?" Diovalo's eyes narrowed.

"That's exactly what I mean! How did he even end up on you?" Alice demanded with a scowl.

Murray was bent over, poking around in the sand. "Look! The landscapers have even put in seashells! How clever! Good attention to detail! So realistic."

"I thought he was with you. He was behind you, then he climbed up on my other side." Diovalo answered Alice evenly.

She huffed once more and clasped her hands before her, rolling her eyes sharply. "Well, it's much too late to do anything about it now!"

Alice sighed and pulled her hat down a little lower over her eyes. "Let's find some shade, and then Diovalo, you can tell me what's happening here."

Eddie tentatively reached up and ran his hand lightly over Marlowe's dark blue and silver spotted fur. "I can't believe how much you've all changed, and especially that..."

"That we can speak?" Marlowe gave him a pleased look. "It was strange for us too when it first happened. We all adapted fairly quickly. I suspect that you will as well."

Alice waved at them both as she headed for a stand of elegant trees; their barks swathed in rainbows of variant color, and their boughs draped with feathery fluff. Beneath them in the sand was a comfortable looking vibrantly colored fallen tree to sit on.

When she was settled with Henderson and Eddie on the log as well, and the cats sat around them in the sand, Diovalo lay before them, taking up the beach there and letting his tail swish through the waves.

"Shall we include your friend Murray?" Diovalo asked, glancing over at the old man who was wandering in the sand a short distance away.

"No." Alice answered swiftly. "I think he's shell hunting, and we should let him do it. He's a little hard of hearing, so he may not get everything we're saying, and that will only confuse him further. I think the less he knows, the better. Now, I'm glad to be back in Corevé, but why am I here? Why has your blood been glowing in the bottle on and off since I left?"

"Siang is in grave peril," Diovalo replied with a sigh, or at least, the dragons here are."

"What's Siang?" Eddie looked from his grandmother to the dragon.

"It is the land where dragons rule, within the world of Corevé." Diovalo answered him.

Eddie raked his fingers through his hair. "I'm still getting used to the idea that there *are* other worlds. Especially places with things like... dragons, and enormous house cats."

Alice chuckled. "Oh, there's a lot more than that here. You'll find out. Also, when the cats first came to Corevé, they were their usual selves, but an acquaintance of ours, Caraway, the Keeper of Light at the Light House, gave the cats some special catnip, and they've never been the same since. At least, here."

"I hope my mum and dad won't mind that I'm here." Eddie eyed the dragon doubtfully.

Alice cleared her throat and gave her grandson a serious sidelong gaze. "Might I suggest that they might only mind *if they find out*."

Eddie nodded, and the corner of his mouth rose conspiratorially. "That's a fair point. Well, what are we doing here anyway? Why did we come?"

Alice wrapped an arm about his shoulders. "We must heed the call of adventure; that whisper at the back of your mind, just behind your ear, that urges you to go."

"You are here because things have gone terribly wrong in Corevé since Alice left, though they were going wrong before she came the first time."

"I can't believe you've been here before, and you never told me." Eddie gave his head a shake as he eyed his grandmother.

"It's only been two days for us, so there hasn't really been much time, and you wouldn't have believed me anyway." She elbowed him with a kind wink.

Eddie's shoulders fell and he rolled his eyes a little. "Well, that's certainly true."

"What's been going wrong since I left?" Alice gazed at the dragon. "I thought everything calmed down after the Blue Fire Crystal was restored. Does it have to do with that sorceress you were telling me about? Because I have a suspicion about her. I don't think that the Illusionist at the Illusionary Palace was the real villain behind the theft of the Blue Fire Crystal. I think he was actually a front for someone else; possibly the sorceress."

"The elements calmed, yes. But you are right, the sorceress Baliste is causing trouble. She captured me twice, and the first time I managed to escape. The second time you rescued me."

"You should have seen the rescue!" Oscar piped up excitedly; his big eyes going wider. "It was amazing!"

"It was something else." Diovalo agreed. "It's why your grandmother and I have a lifeblood bond." The dragon explained to Eddie. Then he continued.

"The fire dragons have all been taken. My mother was among them, and she was killed. She was the queen of the dragons." Diovalo's gaze shifted down to the sand for a long moment.

"Oh, Diovalo." Alice sighed sadly, and rose from the log, going to him. She set her hand on his enormous snout and patted it. "I'm so sorry. What a terrible loss."

"It is a tremendous loss for us. There was no one like her; she was a warrior, powerful and strong. She was resilient and determined. You sometimes remind me of her. She changed the world of the dragons for the better, and her legacy will be legend always."

Eddie cleared his throat, studying Diovalo. "I'm sorry that your mother is gone. I can't imagine it." He set his hands on his knees and leaned forward. "So, does that mean you're the king?"

Diovalo was silent a long moment. "I am prince of the dragons. I have not assumed my mother's throne yet because all of the living dragons must be present for the coronation. They all vow an oath of allegiance to the ascendant of the throne. Coronations are rare. Dragons live a long, long time. I didn't expect to take her place for another few thousand years."

Eddie's mouth dropped open. "Few *thousand*?"

Alice went back to the log and her grandson, setting her hand on his arm. "Time passes differently here. Much faster than it does in our world. A thousand years here is much, much shorter in our world."

The beach rumbled and the waves roared, and Diovalo rose to stand on his hind legs, towering over them.

"We have company." He announced.

Three great dragons, each one a little different from the others, approached the group. They were dark brown and green, colored in shades of earth, and looking much like they were made of earth and stone. Had they been laying on soil, they might have been mistaken for rocky hills. One of them looked as though the ridges along his back and the bumps along his body were boulders. All of them had several legs with big, deep claws. Their snouts were long and thin, and their eyes wide and dark, made to see in places with very little to no light. Their tails were shaped as great spades.

Diovalo gave a nod of his head in greeting to them as they stopped before him and bowed low.

"Your highness." The biggest of them spoke. He was the size of a large train, perhaps three cars long. The others were only slightly smaller than him.

"Lord Malevor." Diovalo greeted him and his fellows evenly. "Liceverous. Gabbrod."

"You've returned. It's good to have you home." Lord Malevor turned to the group beneath the trees. "And you've brought friends."

"Prince Diovalo! So good to see you! We were worried you might have been taken!" Another voice rang out from the other side of Diovalo. Everyone turned to see four more dragons approaching them.

They swept out of the sea, and looked altogether different than the dragons already on the beach. They were half as long as the brown and green dragons, and colored in variants of white, silver, blue, turquoise, many shades of greens, pinks, yellow, some orange, lavenders, and violets. Their snouts were shorter, their bodies stood on six legs, and their claws were webbed. Their tails tapered into large fins. They bore great manes of fleshy streamers that seemed to float even in the air, and grew from their heads down their chests and onto their sides. Like the brown dragons, their eyes were also wide, but they shone like jewels of deep blues and greens. There was a lightness to them, and gracefulness to their steps and fluidity of movement.

All four of them bowed deeply to Diovalo.

"Lord Japheth, how good to see you." Diovalo smiled. "All of you." He nodded to the three slightly smaller dragons with Lord Japheth. "Keres, Callidus, and Galiphes."

Diovalo indicated the group on the beach at his feet. "These are my dear friends. Alice, Henderson, and Eddie, as well as Alice's cats; Marlowe, Sophie, Jynx, Bailey, Tao, and Oscar."

"What's a cat?" Keres leaned closer, eyeing them curiously.

"A dragon with fur." Diovalo chuckled. "Test them not."

Oscar stared wide-eyed at the tendrils wavering through the air off of Keres, and his tail twitched. Jynx licked the inside of her paw and spoke in a low tone.

"Don't even think about it. She could eat you in a single bite."

"But it's *moving*." Oscar murmured.

"*NO.*" Jynx cut her eyes at him. He sank down into the sand and rested his chin on his paws, looking at Diovalo's feet.

Diovalo spoke to the group again. "In Siang there are earth dragons which live underground. Lord Malevor, Liceverous, and Gabbrod are three of them, though there are many more. There are also sea dragons who live in the ocean here. Lord Japheth, Keres, Callidus, and Galiphes are sea dragons. They may only be out of the water a short time. I'm glad that you can see them."

Eddie stared at the mighty beasts around them; his mouth slightly agape. "What kind of dragon are you, Diovalo?"

The enormous ruby creature lowered his head some, closer to Eddie. "I am a fire dragon. You cannot go where I live, for you would not survive, but I will take you close, so you can see it."

"The fire dragons are the greatest of us." Lord Japheth gazed at Diovalo with great respect. "They live in and breathe fire, they can dig into the ground like the earth dragons, though not as deeply due to their sheer size, and they can swim beneath the waves for a while, though they don't do it often."

"We all have our own abilities and talents." Diovalo replied earnestly.

"Could this be the same warrior, Alice, who recovered the precious Blue Fire Crystal?" Lord Malevor studied her interestedly.

"One and the same." Diovalo spoke proudly. "Although now she has Inkling powers that she didn't have when she was here before. Ever more powerful, this mighty lady."

"What an honor to have you among us." Lord Malevor replied evenly. "Why are these friends here today?"

Alice spoke up so that everyone could hear her. "We're here to help find the missing dragons, I think."

"Indeed." Diovalo agreed, turning his attention back to her. "The fire dragons have disappeared. All of them have been taken."

"It's a mystery." Callidus chimed in. "No matter what they do to hide or escape, they are always captured."

"We've got to find the missing dragons." Diovalo grew impassioned, his eyes beginning to glow. "It is said among the mystics that Alice will be the one to find them and bring them home."

Alice furrowed her brow slightly. "Who are the mystics?"

Tao perked her ears up and listened more intently. "I'd like to know, as well please."

Lord Malevor answered in a deep voice. "They are the ones who see into the mists of the future. It's how the Blue Fire Crystal prophecy became known. The mystics foretold it."

"How many are there?" Tao padded a few steps forward, her eyes locked on the dragons.

Diovalo's voice took on a tender note. "I don't know, but I do know there's more than one. My mother was a mystic. They can develop in every race of creature here. She's the one who told me part of the what's happening now, though I think there may be more to it."

Alice smiled widely up at her dragon friend. "Well, I'm glad to be here to help you. I'll do all that I can to find your dragon friends and bring them home."

"As long as it's not too dangerous." Henderson held up his hand.

"Even if it's dangerous." Alice added. Henderson groaned.

Diovalo neared her, so close that his voice made the sand tremble at her feet. "The one to restore the Blue Fire Crystal will also be the one to save the dragons from themselves. That's what my mother told me. I don't know what it means, but I do know that it's you, Alice, and with the fire dragons all taken, we desperately need your help."

"I am here to serve you, your majesty." She beamed at him proudly.

Lord Japheth turned to Diovalo. "Our prince is the last in a sacred family lineage, from the first dragons in the land His offspring will rule one day, and all the dragons of Siang will live under his rule."

Diovalo looked toward the mountains reaching to the clouds. "First we must rescue our lost ones. That is the only priority right now."

"And so we shall." Lord Japheth nodded.

Eddie cleared his throat. "It's my first time visiting this world. I wonder if you could tell me more about it."

Alice set her hand gently on his shoulder. "I'll be glad to do that."

Diovalo shared a look with both dragon lords. "I would speak with you both on our own." They followed him down the beach, leaving Galiphes, Callidus, Keres, Liceverous, and Gabbrod there with the group.

Keres lowered herself to the sand and inched forward, twisting her head from side to side, making her tendrils dance wildly.

Oscar's whole body twitched. Keres laughed. "What is it that makes you so tense, cat?"

"I need to catch the flying mane!" Oscar's voice was high-pitched and thin. It was taking everything in him to hold himself back.

"Then come and get it!" Keres roared with laughter.

Oscar could not resist, and he leapt forward, pouncing on Keres, but the sea dragon twisted out of the way just in time, and rolled in the sand. Oscar chased her, and the two had a raucous time playing with each other.

Jynx watched closely, but there was a hidden smile at the edge of her mouth.

Alice got comfortable and gave a loving smile to her grandson. "Corevé is a magical world. Things that we can scarcely imagine thrive here. I wish I could show you everything I've already seen, but I do know that what I've seen wasn't even a fraction of it. There are many kinds of landscapes... beaches obviously, and mountains. Valleys, plains, deserts, and oceans. There are kingdoms within the world, like Siang, the dragon kingdom. There's also the cloud kingdom above us. You see all those clouds up there? If you look closely, you'll noticed that many of them have specific shapes, and they move; not just as our clouds do, drifting across the sky, but they actually move with each other."

"I love the cloud kingdom." Bailey reminisced pleasantly. "Remember when we watched them playing leap frog?"

"I do remember. It was sweet." Sophie smiled.

Alice turned to Callidus then. "Do you think anyone in the cloud kingdom might know what's been happening to the fire dragons? How they're being taken or where? They might be of some great help to us!"

Callidus shook her sea-ribboned mane. "No, they never get involved in land or sea matters."

Alice sighed. "We'll find them. There's always a way."

"That's true!" Galiphes agreed wholeheartedly. "I say the same thing. It's like water... water always finds a way; over, under, or through."

Eddie turned to Liceverous, laying on the beach nearby. "What about the earth dragons? Do you live underground all the time?"

Liceverous smiled. "We live in the earth most often in deep tunnels where not even light can follow, or sometimes right in plain sight, when we're able to blend into the environment around us. Hiding in plain sight is one of our hunting tactics."

"What do you hunt?" Eddie's eyes were wide with fascination.

"Birds and mammals, mostly."

"It's fish for us!" A small voice called out, and everyone turned to see a tiny blue dragon with fluttery wings hovering near Callidus.

"Oh my, you're so *cute!*" Sophie squealed.

The baby dragon was no bigger than a large dog, and much smaller than all the cats.

"I'm Piper!" She announced, drawing nearer to them. "Who are you?"

The group introduced themselves, and Eddie left the log and went to the little dragon, who settled in the sand.

"What kind of dragon are you? You're a little different looking than the sea dragons."

Piper beamed. "I'm special! I'm half and half! My dad was a sea dragon, and my mom is a fire dragon!"

"Well that is special!" Alice grinned.

"I can blow flames *and* swim in the ocean! I'm a very good swimmer, but I'm learning to be a good flyer, and my flames are the best! Want to see?" Piper drew in a great breath and blew out a burst of fire, nearly singing Sophie and Bailey.

"Oh no! Let's be careful! Cats aren't fireproof!" Sophie tutted worriedly, backing off a bit.

"You are cats? I've never seen a cat before. I like you. I think you're so pretty!" Piper gushed excitedly.

Sophie flipped her head slightly, shaking her long hair. "Why thank you, I can't help but agree with you!"

"Ate the whole humble pie today, did you?" Jynx intoned coolly, giving Sophie a half-sidelong glance.

"Oh! I want pie! Is there pie?" Bailey sniffed hopefully.

"Nobody likes you Jynx." Sophie shot back darkly.

"You're right. They love me. There's a whole month every year dedicated to celebrating me before Halloween. You're just a grooming expense." Jynx strolled off further down the beach to keep a closer eye on Oscar and Keres who were still frolicking and having a great time.

"I miss Montgomery." Sophie sighed sadly.

Eddie had been told that Montgomery, the oldest cat in the family, had died that week, and he didn't want to linger on it.

"If your mum is a fire dragon, is she around here? Is she hidden and safe?" Eddie sank down in the sand with Piper.

Galiphes shook his head. "No, she was captured, and she is no longer alive. Both of Piper's parents are gone. She is an orphan. Callidus, Keres, and I look after her."

Piper drew closer to Eddie. "My father is gone. He was killed by the sorceress, but I don't think my mom is dead! I know she's still alive. I know it! I just have to find her!"

"I have to agree with Galiphes, young Piper." Liceverous spoke sorrowfully. "Your mother can't still be alive. She was attacked and defeated. She couldn't have made it."

Piper lifted her chin resolutely. "Well, I still believe. I'm not going to give up on her. I am not alone!"

Callidus gave her a pat on the head. "You're not alone, little one. We're with you. We're always going to be with you."

Piper gave the bigger sea dragon a smile. "Thanks Callidus, but she really is alive, and I'm going to find her!"

Eddie gave her a pat. "I'll try to help you!"

Piper beamed at him. "Oh thank you! I'm so happy to have a new friend!"

"Well, if we plan on doing much of anything in Corevé, especially rescuing dragons, I know one thing for certain. We're going to need some help! I think I'd better go to Mari Village." Alice stood up from the log and took a few steps.

Diovalo was just coming back to the group, as the earth dragons left the beach, and he heard her. "I agree. I think it would be a great help to have an Inkling with us, or several if possible. I'll fly you there."

Alice shook her head. "No, thank you Diovalo. You'd be such an easy target up in the sky. I'm sure anyone could see you for miles around. I don't think that's the safest idea. What if you're captured? We can't have that."

"We could take you. We'd be glad to help." Lord Japheth offered, shaking out his fringy, floating, wild mane. "It's time we were getting back into the water anyway. We can't stay out for too long."

"Well that would be quite helpful! Thank you so much!" Alice clapped her hands together happily.

"I'm ready to go." Henderson stood up and went to her side, and Marlowe was a step ahead of him. Eddie was right beside them as well.

Alice shook her head. "No, no, Henderson. I don't want Eddie going. I'd like you to stay here, please, and watch over him. You could do me no greater service."

"Madame, it's a risky idea." He pressed.

Alice's warm brown eyes twinkled. "Those are the best kind!"

Henderson's mouth opened, and it was clear that he wanted to argue the point with her, but he couldn't. Instead, he clamped his jaw shut and looked away, jamming his hands down into his pockets.

Eddie lost all the wind in him, and he launched himself at Alice. "No! You can't leave me here! You can't go alone! I need to go with you!"

"I'm not sure it's safe, darling. I'd rather have you here, where I know you'll be looked after." Alice hugged him, and he wanted to protest further, but she shook her head. Panic painted Eddie's face.

"I'll go with her." Marlowe announced.

Oscar came tumbling back into the group just in time to hear what was happening.

"I'm not going. I have no interest in getting wet." Sophie announced importantly, preening herself. "I've just had my hair done."

"I'm not going either." Jynx added.

"Oh! I want to go! I want to ride a sea dragon!" Oscar gasped; his green eyes wide with the thrill.

"You're not going." Jynx sat on Oscar's tail and he grumbled. She looked straight at him. "Sea dragons swim in the sea. I don't want you in the sea. You're not going."

Alice gave an adoring smile to all of her cats. "I don't think any of you should go."

"You're not going without me." Marlowe stated flatly. "I get wet when we walk in the rain, and I dry off. If I happen to get wet in the sea, I'll dry off."

"Oh, you're definitely going to get wet." Callidus assured him with a spirited laugh.

Alice tapped thoughtfully at her chin. "We're just going to have to find another way then. Let me think about this." She paced a few times, and all eyes stayed on her. Finally she stopped and held her finger up in the air.

"I've got it! Remember when we were in the underground river, and Chippa had to make an air bubble in the water so we could get out safely?"

Sophie gasped in horror. "Safely? We shot out of the side of a mountain and crashed into a raging river, and I almost *died*!"

"Yeah, but I saved you!" Oscar reminded her with a gentle nudge and a laugh. Sophie groaned and looked away.

"That you did, little one."

Alice waved her hand to quiet the cats. "What I mean is, Chippa made an air bubble in the water so that we could all breathe in it when we were surrounded by the river. He's an Inkling. Inklings can manipulate the elements and control them to an extent. The chief of the Inklings bestowed that power on me. I'm still learning to use it, but maybe I could do the same and make an air bubble for Marlowe, then he could go without getting wet!"

Everyone shared a curious look.

"I'm willing to try it, though going to the vet sounds more fun." Marlowe groaned.

"I don't like the vet." Bailey whined. "He always says I'm fat!"

"You are fat!" Sophie snapped back.

"I'm not fat, I'm fabulous!" Bailey strutted ahead of her, flipping his pink tail in her whiskers.

The group went to the water's edge, and the sea dragons entered the waves with Alice riding on Lord Japheth's back, and Marlowe precariously perched on Keres.

"Okay. I'm ready to try!" Alice concentrated on the water and the air, trying to use her hands to mold them into the shape she wished them to be in, similarly to what she had seen Chippa do.

The group stared, awestruck, as a wall of water rose around them, wavering wildly. Alice bit her lower lip and tried harder.

"You can do it, grandma!" Eddie called out to her from the shore, ten feet away. "Just please be very careful!"

The wall of water began to arc at the top, and then folded down around them, until it reached the waves on the other side of Alice.

"I did it! Did you see that! I did it!" Alice cried in utter delight.

Suddenly the shell of water around them crashed down, drenching Marlowe while Alice remained dry.

"OH!" Marlowe hissed and shook his paws and body furiously. "I'm soaked!"

"Oh no! Marlowe, I'm so sorry! I thought it would work!" Alice's hand flew to her mouth as her eyes went wide.

"How are you still dry?" Marlowe turned to look at her with a frown.

"I don't know. Perhaps it just worked on me. I couldn't say." Alice shrugged. "Perhaps you'd better stay here with everyone. I'll be all right, and I'll be back with Chippa and the others as soon as I can."

Marlowe grumbled. "No, I'm still going. Even if I don't like it. I'll dry. Eventually."

Marlowe steadied himself on Keres' back with his ears flat against his head and his tail wrapped tightly around him.

"Sorry old sport." Henderson gave him a wave. "I wish we were all going. Best of luck."

"Good luck grandma! Please be careful! Marlowe take good care of her!" Eddie begged worriedly.

Marlowe only closed his eyes and groaned deeply. "That I can do."

"Well, it looks like I can keep myself dry." Alice gave it another try, and managed to get at least an air shield up in front of her, if not an entire bubble.

"We'll swim on the surface of the water, so that will help keep you both somewhat dry." Lord Japheth assured Diovalo and the rest of the group. "You'll be fine."

The mighty sea dragon gave Alice a look over his shoulder and winked. "You might want to hold on to my mane."

Marlowe glared, digging his claws into the edges of Keres' thick scales as Alice waved to her family and friends, and then closed her hands fast on Lord Japheth's tendrils.

The sea dragons dove into the waves, racing one another wildly as they headed southward, skimming over the water and scattering enormous sprays of it everywhere.

"Waaaaahoooooo!" Alice shouted as loud as she could, grinning ecstatically. The dragons around her laughed and Lord Japheth sped up, spurring the other dragons on to do the same. Each of them competed playfully and almost in synchronicity at their race, taking the lead and reveling in it, and then handing the lead off to one of their fellows to share in the fun.

Marlowe loathed it, but before Alice was ready for the ride to be over, it was, though the journey had been a long one. It was nearing midday when they reached the shores at Mari Village.

All of the dragons walked out of the water, and Alice alighted onto the ground dry and as safe as she had ever been. Marlowe leapt to the grass and shook every part of himself.

"Thank you, Lord Japheth! All of you! It was such a fun ride!" She giggled, giddy with the thrill of it all.

"It was our honor." Lord Japheth answered. He flung his mane about, sending sprays of seawater in every direction. Marlowe grumbled as he was spattered with water again.

"Indeed!" Callidus added, and the others agreed.

"I had a great time!" Keres shook her elongated, almost serpentine body out. "We haven't gone for a long swim in a while!"

"So this is Mari Village?" Galiphes rose up on his hind legs to get a better look.

"It is! Come along." Alice waved her hand at them and the group headed over the small knoll from the beach on the south side of the village.

Alice beamed with delight when the little community came into view. The homes were constructed of clay in burnt orange, light brown, and crème colors. They were circular, with no sharp edges, reaching only three to four feet in height, and featured arched wooden doors. The homes were built along meandering paths that all eventually led to a courtyard at the center of the village.

Mari was the name of the tribe of Inklings that lived in the village. Alice had been so surprised by Chippa Mari when she'd met him. She'd never heard of an Inkling before; a magical creature with a silky soft fur coat and a big feathered tail that, when fanned out and drawn over and around the creature like a bubble, could camouflage them so well that they practically became invisible. She thought they looked like the cutest version of a cross between a puppy and a teddy bear, walking upright, having rounded bellies, big eyes, and pointed ears that flopped forward.

They were the caretakes of the four element crystals which served to protect and balance the elements in the world of Corevé. Inklings had magical powers that correlated to the elements, as part of their role in protecting them. They could control and manipulate the elements when needed; something they only ever did for the protection and betterment of their world.

The village was silent, and empty. Alice remembered that Inklings were mostly nocturnal, not usually rising until late afternoon. She went to the first small hut near them and tapped at the door.

"Hello? Is anyone home?" She called out.

A moment later, the door opened, and a young lady Inkling started in surprise when she saw Alice standing before her. Most of the Inklings only stood at two to two and a half feet tall; Alice towered over them.

"Messus Peffle!" She greeted Alice excitedly, coming out of the hut to embrace her knees. Alice patted her back.

"Hello there! It's Channa, right? Channa Mari?"

"Yes! Yes!" Channa bubbled.

It was then that the Inkling noticed the sea dragons, with their wild, billowing manes and their floating tendrils who stood three times Alice's height.

Panic flushed through her, but Alice held a hand to her shoulder to calm her. "It's all right. They're with me. Fun and friendly as can be!"

English was not the first language in Mari Village, and Alice had always been impressed that any of them could speak it, though they spoke with a bit of an accent. None of them could manage to say her name correctly, but they all tried. She'd finally given up with Chippa and allowed him to call her Mrs. P. It had been easiest for him.

"Who 'es these friends of yours?" Channa peered behind Alice in amazement.

"They are sea dragons, and they were kind enough to bring me here. I'd love to chat with you, but I'm afraid we're in a bit of a rush. Is Chippa about?"

Channa nodded, though she was enormously distracted by the much larger guests. Placing her soft paw, which looked more like a racoon hand, against her mouth, she trilled an extremely loud whistle.

A minute or two later, nearly every door in the village opened, and Inklings emerged, yawning and stretching, wondering what was going on until they finally took notice of the visitors. Then the entire population of Inklings in the village hurried to the center courtyard and met at the water well.

Bayless Grand Mari, the chief of the tribe, came lumbering to the gathering. It was he who had given Alice her new powers.

His furry old face broke into a great smile. "Well! We has visitors! Hello Messus Pivvle! What 'es you doing back 'en Corevé?"

Alice waved at all the Inklings who were crowding together. "Hello, Bayless Grand Mari. It's so nice to see you all! Actually, the reason I've come back is something that I need to discuss with you, and with Chippa. Is he here?"

Just then a shout came up from the tangled old woods that grew to the west of the village. Everyone looked, and Alice clapped her hands together joyfully.

Chippa Mari was just emerging from the forest with Oppa Mari, who was the village healer. He was apprenticed to her; something he had always wanted and had more than earned when he'd helped Alice save Corevé the last time she was there.

Chippa ran to her, and she picked him up when he reached her, hugging him tightly before she set him back down.

"My goodness! You've grown!" She complimented him.

Chippa had indeed grown a couple of inches taller, and she could see that he had come into his adult years. It was strange to her, because in her time, she had only been away in London for two days. In Corevé time, it had been a great deal longer, and she knew that there was much she'd need to catch up on with Chippa.

"Mrs. P!" He exclaimed excitedly. "You are back in Corevé! What is bringing you back?"

She turned to gesture at the four dragons behind her. "Dragons, actually. The fire dragons have all gone missing, and I came to help Diovalo rescue them! These sea dragons brought me here to you. I came to ask for your help! All of you! Any of you who can come with us. We need to find the missing dragons and save them! Can you help us please?"

Chippa nodded immediately. "I doesn't know if I can do it on my own, but I will try to help you. You helped us and saved our world. I can return the flavor."

Alice chuckled. "Favor."

Chippa smiled bashfully. "Yes, favor."

"Thank you, Chippa, that's wonderful!"

Bayless Grand Mari frowned and stroked his beard. "I doesn't know 'ef we can send anyone to help you right now, besides Chippa. We 'es needing our healer and our warriors to stay here and protect the village and the tribe."

Oppa harrumphed and set a paw firmly on her hip. "Do we need all of them?"

Bayless Grand Mari nodded. "Yes, all of them."

Oppa Mari sighed and rolled her eyes. As the village healer, she was equal to the chief in authority, though she exceeded him in magical powers.

"Very well. For now, I will stay." She looked as though she'd rather go with Chippa and Alice.

Alice gave Chippa a wink and a smile. "Your English, and Oppa's, is much better! Have you been working on it?"

It had been a little more difficult to understand him the first time she'd met him.

Chippa nodded enthusiastically. "Yes! I learned more English from you and the cats and I have been teaching Oppa, and we are practisaying!"

"Practicing." Alice chuckled. "You're doing very well. Keep it up."

"Thank you! Where are the cats?" Chippa looked around hopefully and then hurried to Marlowe to hug his leg. Marlowe smiled down at him.

"Hello, Chippa. It's very good to see you."

"Where are the others?" The Inkling looked about.

"They are in Siang with Henderson, my grandson Eddie, and Diovalo. We must go back to Siang right away. I'm afraid we'll have to leave soon, it's a long ride on the sea dragons through the ocean."

Chippa beamed. "We doesn't have to go back on the sea! I learned how to make a portal to travel within Corevé!"

Chippa had learned to make a portal to get to London to find her by sneaking around and watching Oppa Mari when he was too young to apprentice. He'd figured out the interworld portal, but hadn't quite worked out how to do an in-world portal. Alice grew excited for him.

"Oh that's wonderful! Goodness, you've grown and learned so much, just in the short time we've been apart! I'm so very proud of you!"

Chippa grinned as he glanced bashfully at the ground for a moment. "Thank you! I am working hard at it!"

"You're doing quite well!" Alice eyed the rest of the Inklings. "We should go now. Is there no one else who might come with us?"

Channa almost raised her hand, but then after a stern look from Bayless Grand Mari, she lowered it. Oppa grumbled under her breath.

"It's time to go!" Chippa stepped away from the crowd and traced his paw in the air, creating a shimmer of translucent light. He pushed at it, spreading his paws out in each direction, until it was big enough for the sea dragons to get through as well.

"Okay, we go!" Chippa was quite proud of himself as he hustled through the shimmering outline of an arch. With a wave at the Inkling tribe, Alice followed, and they called out a farewell to her. The dragons went through last, bidding the group goodbye with big smiles on their faces.

A split second later they stepped out onto the white sands of the beach at Siang. Chippa fluffed his tail out and checked around for any dangers he might need to hide from.

Diovalo was waiting on the beach with Henderson, Eddie, and the cats. Eddie rushed to Alice, his eyes roving over her from head to toe as he took her hands in his.

"How are you? Were you safe? Did anything happen?" He bombarded her with questions.

"I'm just fine. In fact, it was one of the most fun things I've ever done! Riding on sea dragons is spectacular!" Alice rubbed Marlowe's ears and he closed his eyes and purred loudly, making the rainbow trees tremble.

"I disagree." Marlowe mumbled through his purrs.

"Chippa!" Oscar loped over to them happily.

"Hello cats!" Chippa patted Oscar's leg, and Tao nuzzled the Inkling.

Eddie stared, fascinated with Chippa. "I've heard so much about you! You're amazing! I'm Eddie."

"I'm Chippa."

Eddie tried hard not be obvious as he looked Chippa over. "Your... what are those, antennae? Those are so unusual!"

Chippa reached up and delicately touched the fringe hanging a few inches above his eyes. "Eyebrows."

"They're really neat!"

Chippa smiled. "Thank you!"

"Well look at that! We've found a new little friend! Here boy! Come here! Who's a good boy?" Murray's voice broke through their group. Everyone turned to see Murray plodding through the sand, his pockets stuffed with seashells. When he was about six feet from Chippa, he bent over and patted his knees.

"Here boy! Come on! Come here!" He whistled.

Chippa frowned slightly and turned his eyes up to Alice. "Who is this?"

She cleared her throat.

"Chippa, this is Murray. He's my neighbor in London. He came along on accident."

"What does he think I am?" Chippa was still frowning.

"Um… it looks like he thinks you're a dog." Eddie answered carefully, trying to hide the snicker at the corner of his mouth.

"What's a dog?" Chippa asked, not certain he really wanted to know.

"A foul creature, and an annoyance of the highest order." Sophie grumbled darkly. "You're about the same size as one, though you look nothing like them."

Alice laughed. "Oh now, Sophie, they are aren't so bad. Most people really like dogs. They're said to be man's best friend."

"They only say that because everyone hasn't met me yet." Sophie flipped her tail irritably.

"This must be one of those new hybrid dogs! Is there a dog show on in the park this weekend?" Murray furrowed a bushy, gray brow.

"He's old and hard of hearing." Alice patted Chippa. "He thinks he's still in London. It's probably best to let him think you're a dog."

"Fred! Freddie!" Murray waved at Alice's grandson. "Have a look at this funny dog!"

Eddie only laughed. Murray stood back up and peered around the beach. "You know, just a little while ago there were people here in the most beautiful costumes! Great big costumes. Looked like Chinese sea dragons or something. The things they come up with for the tourists! I was so impressed that I'm almost of a mind to get my own photo taken with one! Ha! Imagine." He chuckled and wandered off once more.

Eddie slipped his hand into the crook of his grandmother's arm.

"I think this is going to be quite an adventure!" Alice chuckled as she shook her head. "Let's make a camp here tonight, and we can figure out what we're going to do. There's a lot to talk about."

CHAPTER THREE

AND ALICE MAKES THREE

The claws on Baliste's feet scraped the flagstone floor of the great hall as she strode into it. "Someone is coming. Open the door." She ordered sharply.

Two goblins ran to do her bidding, and she sat upon the bench that served as her throne, her long, tapered tail hovering behind her, twitching back and forth.

The same two creatures as before walked into the room. She narrowed her eyes at them, barring her jagged teeth.

"I see that you have not brought me the dragon prince! Why is Diovalo not with you?" Baliste hissed furiously.

"He has returned, my queen." One of them answered humbly. "But there has been no opportunity to take him yet; he has not been alone."

"I don't want excuses! I want that dragon!" She roared, standing up and swinging her tail wildly behind her. "I want the greatest of the fire dragons! Now!"

"As you wish, my queen. We are here to serve only you."

She stepped down from her bench and stalked toward them, looking up at the one who spoke. "And you shall be rewarded, if you do, but fail me, and you cannot begin to imagine the miserable death that awaits you!"

"Yes, my queen. We will bring him to you right away. There is more news."

"Well? What is it?" Baliste glared.

"The prophesied one... Alice... she has returned. She is in Siang with Diovalo, and... there is more. I have discovered that the Inklings have shared their magic with her. She is as powerful as they are."

In a dark corner of the great hall, watching silently from behind a pillar, Mendax raised a brow and frowned.

"Then bring her to me as well. Perhaps she may be of some use to me." Baliste began to pace, thinking through myriad thoughts.

"But, my queen, we cannot overpower her! Not if she has the Inkling magic!" The creature insisted, growing frustrated.

Baliste spun and faced him. "Find a way, Wurm! I want Diovalo, and I want Alice! Get them and bring them both here!"

"Right away, my queen." The creatures both bowed, scraping the floor, and then left.

Mendax vanished.

Lowering her gaze to the squad of goblins near her, Baliste's voice cut like a razor's edge.

"I'm not leaving everything to chance on those two fools. Send the Quiri birds out to find Diovalo. They got him once. Perhaps they'll succeed again."

"Yes, mistress." They bowed low and scurried off.

Baliste stormed into the room adjacent to the great hall, and closed the door behind her. The three women inside it turned to look at her.

"Alice!" She began, drifting slowly along the length of the room as she stared at each of them. "I have not yet told you this, but I made you... all three of you, when I created the Illusionary Palace. The original Alice went into the Illusionary Palace to find the Blue Fire Crystal, and when she stepped into the cursed circle of mirrors, she was caught. The moment she did it, the mirrors reflected her back to herself at different ages. You were each three of those reflections; you reflected Alice at various ages throughout her life. One of you is Alice in her thirties, one of you is Alice in her fifties, and you are Alice in her sixties. You are exact replicas of the original Alice, except that you were merely reflections. When Alice destroyed the mirrors and the palace, Mendax saved you. There were more versions of you; more ages that Alice had seen reflected back at her, but unfortunately only you three survived because Mendax brought you to life. You are human now. You are no longer reflections."

The Alices eyed each other curiously and looked back at Baliste, who softened her voice somewhat.

"I want to know everything about you. I don't think you told me everything the last time I asked you, but that's fair, because there's something that I didn't tell you. You are all three part of a prophecy, and in it, you are meant to help me. You each have a great purpose ahead of you, and you will fulfill it by serving me in my mission."

The Alices shared a look, and nodded.

"Thank you for creating us and having Mendax bring us here. We will help you." Thirty-year-old Alice replied.

"Good. You can begin by telling me what powers the Inklings granted you. What can you do? How can you use them?" Baliste drew closer to them.

All three of them shared confused glances. Alice in her fifties spoke up.

"What's an Inkling? I've never heard of one, and I certainly don't have any powers."

"Nor I." Answered the other two, nearly in unison.

Baliste growled sharply and turned away from them with a glare.

"Why would they tell me you had Inkling powers?" She wondered, thinking back to what her servants had told her. "Perhaps they were lying to me."

She narrowed her eyes and hissed softly.

* * *

A campfire, courtesy of Piper, who was only too happy to make it, burned brightly against the fading light of the early evening.

Chippa, with just a small bit of Alice's magical help, created a bed for each of the humans from giant leaves, forming them while the leaves were still on the vine, so that the beds hovered three and a half feet from the ground and were sturdy enough to hold the weight of the humans. Around the beds, Chippa had also created tents from the same massive leaves, shaping them so that there would be cover if it rained.

The cats would be sleeping outside; something they never did in London, and quite enjoyed in Corevé.

Murray had been surprised to see tents and leaf cots up in what he still believed was Hyde Park, but he'd assumed that they were some sort of art installation, and Alice went with it, telling him they were interactive, and he should try one out and rest for a bit. He had fallen asleep as soon as his head touched the leaf.

Eddie had gone off for his first ride on a horse-sized cat; something Jynx was glad to do for him. Piper and the other cats went along for the walk and to do some exploring. Henderson was making tea over the fire, while Alice and Chippa sat to talk. She took Chippa's paw in her hand and enjoyed the softness of it.

"It's so good to see you my friend." She gave his paw a pat.

"It's good for me, too!" Chippa answered happily. "I miss you and the cats."

"Well, we're all together again. I do wish I could take a sort of holiday through Corevé and really see it all. It's so beautiful, and it's only been when there's trouble that I've been here. This place... Siang... it's so beautiful. I've never seen anything like it! Flowers on everything, and vines with... what are those? Fireflies? She peered at some of the flowers on the vine which had begun to glow. As the glowing grew brighter, the petals opened.

"It looks like Christmas." She laughed and shook her head. "I do need to talk with you, Chippa. There's something strange that I've noticed since I got back this time, and I don't know what's causing it."

Chippa lifted his fluffy brows curiously. "What is it?"

"From the moment I got back, I've been feeling some kind of... force. Some kind of power. It's almost electric, and it's everywhere! It's almost like it moves through the air and everything that exists here, as though everything was transparent or had no shape or form." She puzzled it over in her mind.

Chippa nodded. "That's magic. It is in everything here; in the air, in the ground, in the leaves and trees, in the light, in the clouds and water. It does move through everything, has no barriers. Just always keeps moving."

"It's so powerful! I never felt it when I was here before." Alice remarked, looking about in wonder. "It feels so strong that I think if I looked hard enough, I might be able to see it!"

"You didn't feel it last time because you wasn't in the way of magic. Now you has magic, so you can feel it." Chippa replied happily. "This is what we moves when we makes the portals. We use the magic that's all around, and shape it. We show it what to do."

Alice chuckled. "You've really learned so much. Oh Chippa, I'm so proud of you!"

"Does the magic bother you?" Chippa worried for her.

"No, not at all. It feels... it feels like it fills me so much that it overflows, it's so much bigger than me. I'm a part of it, and it's part of me, and yet it's so enormous that it makes my soul take flight. It feels like a flock of birds exploding out of me and soaring into the clouds, carrying me with it. If that makes any sense." She laughed at her own romantic telling of it.

Chippa smiled wide. "That's my feels too. Just like that."

The sand on the beach began to swirl upward into a cone several feet high, widening at the top, as a strong breeze whipped around it.

"Oh no..." Chippa groaned.

"What is it?" Alice frowned, and then realization struck her. "Oh no."

Marlowe, followed by all the other cats, Piper, and Eddie who was holding fast to Jynx, came rushing back.

Henderson left the fire, and went to Alice's side. Diovalo stood on his hind legs, towering over them all.

Jynx knelt down and Eddie scrambled off and rushed to his grandmother, taking her hand in his. "What is that thing?"

"It's not good!" Chippa snapped grumpily as his whole face contorted into disgust.

The strong breeze slowed, and the sand settled back down. Where the center of the cone had been, stood Mendax, with his brightly colored sash tied about his round belly, his turban set atop his head, and his sheer golden robes flowing out around him. Behind him, were two women. Alice gasped, clamping her hand to her mouth.

"Grandma, who is that? Who is the sandman? Who are those women?" Eddie gushed in a whisper.

"Madame..." Henderson murmured in concern.

"Hello, Alice." Mendax stepped from the place where he hovered in the air, down onto the ground. As he did so, the two women behind him did the same. They stared hard at Alice, just as she did them.

"May I introduce you to... yourself." He indicated the two women with him. One of them was young, with wavy brunette hair tied back in a ribbon at her neck, flawless skin, big dark eyes, full lips, and high cheekbones. The other was twice as old, also with brunette hair cut to her shoulders, and her face resembled that of the younger woman, though it was slightly fuller and there were fine lines around her eyes and the corners of her mouth.

"Mendax!" Alice shot out with a thin voice. The last time she had seen him, he had taken her, the cats, Chippa, and Henderson for a wild ride across a massive desert in his sand cyclone, and then dumped them on top of a massive rock cliff plateau.

"Who... who are these ladies? What are you up to?" Alice demanded, her heart pounding.

Chippa growled. "He's up to no good!"

"Oh now, I wouldn't say that." Mendax drawled coolly. "I have brought you a gift. These two ladies, are you, Alice."

"You'd better start explaining while you still can, Mendax!" Alice warned him heatedly.

Diovalo swept his head down close to the group. "*Now.*" His voice shook the ground, trees, and everyone gathered there.

Mendax straightened his turban, which had been shaken askew. "Fine, fine. I am!" He huffed in exasperation.

"I've brought you these two ladies from Illusionary Palace. You recall that you stepped into a circle of mirrors, yes Alice?"

Alice remembered it so clearly. It had only just happened earlier that week for her. She had been in a dark room with her family, and then suddenly they were gone; Henderson, the cats, and even Chippa. She'd stood alone in a circle of mirrors, and in each mirror she had seen a younger version of herself at different ages; Alice in her twenties, her thirties, forties, fifties, and sixties. There were some other ages in between them as well, but versions of her in those decades of her life had appeared in the mirrors and each one had seemed alive. They had beckoned to her, calling her to touch the mirrors, and go back to one of those times of her life so that she could feel needed again. It would have been an escape from her reality; an illusion, and she hadn't fallen for it.

"I do remember it. As I recall, I broke all of those mirrors." Alice pressed her lips together impatiently.

Mendax nodded. "Indeed you did. You broke the mirrors, and when you did, I was there to pick up the pieces, such as they were. I rescued two of the Alices; these two, and I brought them to life. I managed to retrieve them from the Illusionary Palace just before it was destroyed."

Alice's brow furrowed sharply. "Now wait a moment! How did you even know about the room with the mirrors, or the Alices, or the destruction of Illusionary Palace? You dropped us off on the cliff and left! You were gone! How could you have known any of that?"

Mendax dismissed her questions with a wave of his hand. "Let's focus on the present. We're not there. We're here. All of us. Now I-"

He was going to continue, but Alice stopped him short. "You little fink! You were in the palace, weren't you! You had to have been, you wouldn't have known otherwise! What were you doing there?"

"Perhaps I might have been," he shrugged, "and what a lucky thing that was, because I managed to save just these two versions of you, and bring them to life."

"He was there because he's a lying, slickery little fish!" Chippa snapped at Mendax.

"Slippery." Bailey corrected.

"That too!" Chippa added hotly.

"Well, no matter how it happened, the ladies were brought to life. They are as real as you are, Alice, and I've brought them here to help you."

"Help us with what?" Alice narrowed her eyes into razor thin slits. "What is it that you think we're doing here?"

Mendax gave her a knowing look. "You're not on holiday, Alice. I know you're here to help Diovalo rescue the dragons. I thought I'd give you a hand and let these younger Alices help you."

"You doesn't help anyone if there's not something in it for you!" Chippa growled.

"Oh now, is that fair? I ask you. Didn't I help you all to get to the Illusionary Palace?" Mendax reminded Alice of a salesman.

"Only because the world was collapsing and you wanted to save your desert, and you still haven't told us what you were doing at the palace!" Alice was strongly considering poking Mendax with one of her knitting needles, thinking that perhaps that might get him to talk.

"I was helping you then, and I'm helping you now with these younger versions of you. Everything that both of them knows and has experienced is everything that Alice had known and experienced up to those ages. This is a necessary gift. Make good use of it. Go and look for the dragons on an island off to the northwest from here. The dragons are captive there." He rose in the air a few feet and sand began to swirl around him again.

"Oh, and Diovalo, if you want to remain safe, stay in the skies." With a flick of his hand, the sand cyclone twisted wildly around him, and then disappeared, taking Mendax with it.

Chippa shook his head. "I doesn't trust Mendax. You'd better stay on the ground."

Diovalo grimaced. "I agree."

There was an awkward silence for a moment as the two new Alices stood looking around them at the gathering.

Henderson spoke first. "Tea, anyone?"

A chorus of yes's answered him. "Right. I've got some ready, thankfully."

"I'll help you." Eddie offered, staring at the two women who were younger versions of his grandmother. The older of the two gaped at him.

"Edward? Is that you? What on earth are you doing here? Shouldn't you be back at the house? Or at the academy?"

Alice drew in a long breath and held her hands together. With careful steps, she approached the two ladies. Marlowe remained right at her shoulder.

"If you don't mind my asking, how old are you?"

The younger of the two answered first. "I'm twenty-five."

"I'm thirty-f..." the older one began and then blushed. "I'm forty-two."

The corner of Alice's mouth turned up slightly. "Oh yes... I used to fib about my age, for at least as long as I could get away with it. Time catches up with us though, and someday you won't even believe yourself. Well... uh... Alice. This isn't Edward. This is his son, Edward junior. We call him Eddie."

Alice motioned for her grandson to come to her, and he did. Forty-two-year-old Alice stared and shook her head in disbelief. "You look so much like your father. It's uncanny."

Eddie smiled widely. "People do say that often. It's nice to meet you… uh… Alice." He trailed off uncertainly.

She shook his hand and gave him a warm smile.

The youngest Alice tapped her chin thoughtfully. "It's going to be much too confusing having three Alice's here all at the same time. We should come up with nicknames so it's easier. Do you know I've always liked going by the name Ali. I think I'll use that one. People used to-"

"Used to call me that at school." Alice finished for her, staring in wonder. "This is absolutely bizarre."

"Well, it's strange for us too." Forty-two-year-old Alice agreed. "What shall I go by?"

"What if you went by the name that George always called me… uh… us." Alice offered.

The middle-aged Alice grinned; she couldn't help it. "Cherie. It means darling in French. Ma cherie, he would say. I like that. I'll go with it. You may call me Cherie." She nodded resolutely.

"Well, that's settled then. Ali, Cherie, welcome to our group. I suppose I should introduce you to everyone while tea is being set up for us." Alice took the ladies around to meet the rest of the family and then sit to tea.

"Can you tell me what happened at Illusionary Palace?" Alice gazed at them both, wondering how it could be possible that she was talking with real versions of herself from earlier in her life.

"Well, I don't remember any room with mirrors, or even the palace that Mendax was talking about. All I remember is a great flash of light, and then I was alone in my room at Mendax's palace in the Aridan desert." Ali sighed. "I mean, I had my whole life up until that flash, and then I was here, but my life somehow feels like a dream that happened a long time ago."

"I think we don't remember the mirrors or the palace because we weren't alive yet." Cherie considered. "It's the same for me; I was living my life and then bang, a flash of light, and I was in my room at Mendax's palace. I know what you mean about everything before this feeling like a dream. It feels like I've been here a long time, but I don't know how long. I just didn't know there were any other Alices. I thought I was the only one, until he brought us both here."

"That's me, as well. I only knew my life in England, and then I was here, and then there were more versions of me in you two." Ali shrugged. "It's the strangest thing."

Cherie agreed with an ironic laugh. "Do you know, I've always wished that there were more of me because I have so much to do. George is gone so much with the military, and I have Edward at home when he's not at the academy. I'm on so many boards and involved in organizations and groups. I run such a big home; we live in the country, you know." She blinked. "Oh, Alice, I guess you do know."

Alice chuckled. Ali watched and listened enraptured.

"There's just always so much to do and so little time, and I don't know how many times since Edward was born that I've wished for more versions of myself so I could get it all done and still have some time to relax. Now here I am, with two more versions of myself, and it's *so strange*! I don't quite know what to think of it! What do you both think?"

Alice shrugged. "I don't know enough about it yet to answer that. I'm not even sure where you two came from. You're not from my world, but all of your memories and experiences are. That's... that's a tough one to wrap my mind around. What about you, Ali? What do you think?"

Ali shook her head slowly, gazing at the other two. "It looks as if I've taken good care of myself in coming years, at least, so that's good."

Cherie and Alice laughed.

"I do work out regularly." Cherie stated proudly. "I swim often and go for long walks. I am careful about eating healthy. I want a long, healthful life, and I can see by looking at our Alice that I've done that. Definitely worth it."

Alice chuckled. "Oh, there's still a little extra weight; there's no escaping it. That comes naturally. You can see how busy we are in our middle years; just listening to Cherie talk has almost worn me out, but even with all that extra running about and exercise, the body changes as we get older. It's the natural course of things, but I am still strong and fit."

"I'm glad we're all in good shape, because no matter what happens, it's clear that this is going to be one wild adventure." Cherie waved her hand emphatically.

"It is indeed!" Alice laughed.

"What is it like being part of a prophecy?" Ali seemed to want to know everything about Alice.

Alice considered the query a long moment before she answered. "It's extraordinary, especially at my age. You'd think they'd have had someone younger, maybe like you, Ali, to meet their prophetic requirements, but there I was, right in the middle of it, needed desperately, and able to meet the challenge. In all honesty, I loved it. Adventure is the fire that ignites my soul."

Henderson sat beside Alice and gazed at the younger versions of her. "I'm so curious to know what you were like before I came. Now I'll get to see it! This is truly fascinating."

"I was precocious, determined, headstrong, stubborn, quite concerned with my looks, and… at twenty-five, I was a cartologist, among other things."

Sophie sat close to Ali and purred softly. "I knew I'd like you. You're just like me!"

Ali gaped at the collar around Sophie's neck. "My goodness! Are those all diamonds? Are they real? They're enormous!"

Henderson nodded. "The cat and the diamonds are much smaller in London, but when we come here, everything gets bigger. They'll both revert to normal when we go back."

"What about you, Cherie?" Tao asked with a kindly tone.

Cherie smiled. "Well, I'm a wife and mother. George is a wonderful husband, and our son Edward has just turned ten. I can't believe he's gotten so big. Goodness, Eddie looks just like him. It's astonishing. I am busy with my marriage and my child, with making costumes and going to meetings, and with running a household. I don't ever really take any time for myself; I'm too busy."

"I'd like to hear from Alice." Ali brightened. "What are we like at your age? Do you mind if I ask… what *is* your age, anyway?"

Alice chuckled and shook her head. "No, I don't mind. I used to mind," she glanced at Cherie, "but now, it's more like a mark of success. When we are children we are so proud of each year that we get older we usually share our age in fractions; I'm ten and a half, I'm twelve and three quarters... remember that? Why do we stop being proud of our ages that way? I'm seventy-three, now. I have a home in London where I live with all the cats and Henderson. I see Edward and his wife Annabel when they are free, and I spend time with Eddie when he's not busy. It's fairly quiet in my life now, though I did just join a local group so I could start teaching classes and helping out around the community."

Henderson held up his hand. "If I may. I've lived with Alice for more than a decade now, and I will stay with her all the rest of her life to look after her. It's my honor to do so. I can tell you that she is wise, patient, kind, sometimes shockingly unfiltered, most often relaxed, balanced somewhere between no-nonsense and a lot of fun. She has a cool intellect, she is quite good at slow burns and subtle shade when people annoy her, and she will use any manner of clever means to get her way when she wants it."

Everyone laughed.

Ali's eyes glittered with fascination. "I want to know more. I always think if I knew more and understood the world better, it would be easier living in it. What have you learned at seventy-three?"

Alice sipped her tea and grew thoughtful. "At this age the most important thing is to feel needed and to be of use to others. I want to be valued, and I've found out the hard way that many old people aren't valued, which is ridiculous, because there's a lot I've learned along the way that could be useful to others. First and foremost, be true to yourself; every part of yourself, before you commit to anyone else. Also, life is the masterpiece we create, and we do not see it until the very end.

"Every one of our days is a canvas; blank and waiting for our choices and actions to color it, to give it depth, volume, meaning, and definition. We define ourselves with every part of the canvas we create, and at the very end, we see it all; all the colors and the light, and all the dark as well. Nothing is hidden from us, and we have to face every bit of it; good, bad, and in between. We can't take any of it back. We've got one chance to do it all as best we can. We make memories as we go, and at the end we look at our collection of memories to see what we've done and decide if it was all worth it.

"Time is the tide that pulls us over and over again, all of our lives, away from where we've been to where we must go. Our words and choices define us, so we must choose carefully; every word from us has an impact, whether great or small.

"Knowing that, you could ask yourself, how far will you go to do the right thing, no matter what comes, no matter the loss or the time spent, or the sacrifice? No matter the fear and doubt we must face, as time runs out, how far will you go? Is going the distance recklessness or determination? Is it a noble aim and one that cannot be laid down? Commit to the end, no matter the cost. Every step we take directs the path of our lives from beginning to end, and every single one counts. Every step takes us to the next place, hungry for more; for answers, for explanations, for resolve, for everything we do not already have, and at some point we may see that we've lost more than we could ever gain. Is there freedom in that? We carry every step, every breath, every thought and act with us, always, tucking them into our life-suitcase, and each one becomes a part of us, never to fade. They define us, all those parts, as a whole. They're all we've really got at the end. Not that I'm at the end, mind you.

"Now, that's a lot to think about, but really what it boils down to is that everything counts, so make it count. That's what it's like being this age. I look back and I can see how each choice I made and thing I did brought me to where I am now. Think carefully before you act, or react, because you have to live with it always. I'm still learning that one. Just ask Eddie."

Alice laughed softly before her closing thought. "I haven't got it all figured out yet. Life is a work in progress."

Ali, Cherie, and Alice talked a while; long past the tea being gone, and finally the two younger ladies went to bed in tents that Chippa created for them.

Alice sat on a log looking out at the ocean, and Tao sat with her, watching the waves roll in endlessly.

"Are you all right?" Tao asked in her smooth, calm voice.

"How so?" Alice wondered aloud, looking up at her Siamese cat.

"What is it like for your self-identity to see more than one version of yourself?"

Alice was thoughtful for a while. "It's really strange. I'm a bit torn. I like to think of myself as a singular person, and though these other versions of me do exist in my mind and memories, and they are me, in *this* place and time they are outside of me and have their own versions of self and identity. I feel… splintered."

Tao nuzzled her shoulder, and she shrugged. "It's okay, and simultaneously unsettling. I'll have to get used to it."

There was quiet between them for a long moment, and then Tao spoke again. "Your own heart and mind remain strong inside of you, and that's who you are. The others are themselves, and only a part of you. The real you is a whole amalgamation of your entire life experience; it's all the single parts put together into one, and the whole version of you at your present age and point in life is much more extensive than the other versions of you. They are entities still being formed, and so are you, but your sphere of existence is much greater, and it is your own."

Alice considered it. "You have a very good point."

Tao's gentle voice continued. "If you begin to feel yourself lost, look inside deeply, and you will find your true self."

The hush of the waves crashing against the sandy shore filled all the space between them, and between Alice's thoughts. "Thank you, Tao. How did you ever come to be so wise?"

"I listen, I meditate, and I connect to everything around me, always."

The cat purred softly, and Alice rubbed the spot behind her ear.

When morning came, everyone gathered around the fire for breakfast, which Cherie had been up making since sunrise.

Ali had gotten up early as well, and was bursting with energy as she buzzed around the campfire, handing out scrolls of paper made from dried leaves.

"I've been up working with Diovalo and Chippa this morning... where is Chippa?" She interrupted herself.

Alice smiled. "He's sleeping in my tent. He's mostly nocturnal."

Ali frowned slightly and then brightened once more. "Strange. Anyway, I was working with them this morning to get a lay of the land. They helped me design some maps, so that we can all have a resource to find our way. I've made one for each of you."

"I'd like some more breakfast please!" Bailey nudged Cherie.

She blinked, wide-eyed. "Fourths? Are you sure you're still hungry?"

"He'll eat until you stop feeding him." Henderson advised.

"Now, now! Let's be fair. There's a lot more of me to feed in Corevé." Bailey flashed his pink tail with silver tipped hair at Henderson, and the butler chuckled.

"That is true."

"Has anyone seen my teeth?" Murray bellowed, coming out of his tent. Cherie handed them to him wrapped in a leaf.

"Oh, thank you miss. Do you work here?" He asked congenially as he pushed his teeth into his mouth.

"I do now." Cherie chuckled quietly.

Everyone opened their maps and Alice knit her brow, trying to focus on it. "Oh dear."

"What is it, Madame?" Henderson asked, eyeing her in concern.

"I've forgotten my reading glasses. I can't see anything on this." She handed the map to him. "Here, you can read it and tell me if we need to change direction."

"Very well, Madame." Henderson smiled and set her map with his. "Also, here are your morning pills." He handed her a small plastic cup full of them.

She gazed at them with a sigh. "Well, if I get lost you won't need a map to find me, you can just listen for me; I'll be the one rattling when I walk."

When Ali had finished telling the group about her maps, and Cherie had made certain that everyone had eaten, saving her own breakfast for last, Alice spoke.

"This morning we'll embark on our mission to rescue the dragons. I want everyone to stay together and be safe."

"How far is this island?" Cherie wondered aloud what most of the group was already thinking.

"We should reach it by midday." Ali answered, checking her map.

Alice continued. "Thankfully, Diovalo has enlisted the help of the sea dragons, and they are more than ready for this rescue. Unfortunately, the earth dragons won't be joining us because there's no way for them to get to the island; they neither swim nor fly. Speaking of which, some of us will be flying on Diovalo, and some of us will be riding the sea dragons."

Ali's hand shot straight up in the air. "I have dibs on a sea dragon!"

Alice nodded. "That's fine. As for the cats, you'll all be riding on Diovalo."

"Oh, grandma, may I ride a sea dragon too, please?" Eddie clasped his hands in fervent prayer.

Alice bit at her lower lip. "Only if I ride with you. I'm sorry, Diovalo." She smiled up at him and the mighty dragon laughed.

"I'm not jealous, but thank you."

"I think we'd better put Murray with Henderson and the cats on you." Alice replied.

Marlowe grumbled. "I don't like this idea."

"Well, Eddie's not riding alone, and you didn't enjoy riding on a sea dragon, so you'll be near me, just not next to me." Alice offered comfortingly.

"I still don't like it." Marlowe scowled.

"Oh, I'd like to ride Diovalo, please!" Cherie chimed in. "I've never ridden a dragon before!"

Alice laughed. She had ridden a dragon a few times, but just not at Cherie's age. The irony tickled her.

With everyone organized, they headed to the beach where the sea dragons were waiting for them. Murray cried out with delight and pointed at the sea.

"Ah! The Serpentine! I love this part of Hyde Park! If we can find the boathouse, they rent rowing and pedal boats!"

Alice rolled her eyes. Eddie saw it and stepped closer to the old man. "Ah, Murray? The Serpentine is a lake in the park. This is an ocean."

Murray shook his head. "Oh, I don't think the Serpentine goes all the way to the ocean. I'm certain it's just here in the park."

Eddie looked to Alice for help, and she just waved her hand at him. "Don't worry about it. He won't know the difference. I'm sure he'll have lots of fun."

Piper fluttered about excitedly. "I get to see my mom today! I do! I can't wait! I'm going to show her all the things I can do now!"

Lord Japheth sighed and nudged the baby dragon with his nose. "Piper, your mother is gone. You need to accept that."

"I believe otherwise." Piper announced stubbornly, zooming around Oscar's head. Oscar twitched, wanting to bat at Piper, but Jynx gave him a cool eye.

"Don't go after the dragons. Any of them."

"What are we going to do if the dragon kidnappers are there?" Oscar worried. "Will we fight them?"

"We will fight anyone who tries to keep the fire dragons from us!" Diovalo called out fiercely as he spread his wings.

"I'll bite them! That will be the end of them!" Piper's small roar sounded out boldly.

"I don't think a bite from a baby dragon is going to end anyone." Sophie gave a sidelong look to the little blue and white creature.

"If it's my bite it will!" Piper sang out happily.

"Piper does have a lethal bite." Callidus corrected the cat. "It's one of the rare and unusual things about her; one of the things that makes her stand out; makes her special. One skin-breaking nip from her and it's all over for the sorry sod she bit." Callidus chuckled. "Luckily, she's a really happy little thing."

"My mom told me I can never bite anyone unless I'm saving someone else's life." Piper grew serious for a moment.

"It's a good rule. Let's follow it." Jynx took a few steps away from Piper.

"So, I think I'm just going to stay here and wait for all of you." Sophie gave everyone a pleasant smile. "You have fun, and I'll… watch the camp. Good luck with the rescue."

"You're going." Marlowe replied sternly without even looking at her. "We may need you if it comes to a fight."

"No! I can't go! Look at this, I've just had my pawdicure! My claws will be ruined!" She held her paw out to show everyone just how pretty it was, and how nothing so lovely should be spoiled by a battle. "Besides, it's not up to you, Marlowe!"

She gave him a nasty frown and Henderson cleared his throat. "You're going, Sophie. Get on the dragon."

With a deep whine, she turned her back and flipped her tail straight up in the air, showing Henderson exactly what she thought of that, but she was the last cat to get on Diovalo.

Piper dove into the water with the other sea dragons, and it was time to leave.

Everyone was ready, and with a mighty roar, Diovalo took to the sky, though he flew low over the waves, so that he wouldn't be such an easy target, as Alice had said.

The sea dragons skimmed the surface with their riders; Ali, Alice, and Eddie, who were having a grand time.

Several more sea dragons joined them, so that there were at least two dozen that Alice could count, riding along behind them. She loved seeing them race and play, never putting one before the others, and instead making sure everyone always had fun. It wasn't ever a competition with them; only games and good times.

It was a long ride, and Ali was only slightly off about the travel time; it was just after midday when they reached the small island. It was little more than a few mounds of hills and a rocky coastline around most of it, apart from one big sandy beach.

Diovalo landed, and everyone got off of him. Sophie headed for a low-lying area and threw up. Jynx chuckled as she glanced over her shoulder at her.

"Oh come on, princess. You still haven't gotten used to that? It's fun! You're a big girl now. Learn to live a little!"

"Where are the dragons?" Diovalo growled angrily.

Alice stepped off of Lord Japheth and helped Eddie down as well. The beach was swarmed with an influx of sea dragons who were ready to rescue their fellows.

"Is there nothing?" Alice called out to him. He took to the sky again on his own and circled around the island twice before landing.

"There is nothing on this island but grass." Diovalo roared furiously.

"My mom is not here!" Piper cried sadly, fluttering her wings as she hovered near Eddie.

Eddie sighed and gave her back a pat. "I'm so sorry my friend. I thought for sure we could find her here. We're going to keep looking. I won't stop helping you until we find her!"

"Thank you Eddie!" Piper nuzzled his shoulder before settling on the grass. "I just wish I knew where she was."

Alice went to them and gazed at the baby dragon. "I'm so sorry darling."

"Are we on the right island?" Cherie unrolled her map.

Ali knit her brow. "Yes. It's the only island out here."

"So, where are the dragons?" Eddie wondered, scratching his head. He took his grandmother's hand in his and she gave him a small smile.

"That's what we need to find out." Lord Japheth spoke gravely.

"I don't understand what this means. We came to rescue dragons and there are no dragons here." Oscar sniffed the air, but there was nothing.

"It means that Mendax lied to us!" Chippa fumed, stomping through the grass.

"When I get my claws on him…" Diovalo snapped.

"Have we stopped for fish and chips? I think there's a good place just over that hill. Nice mushy peas too!" Murray beamed with delight. "I could do with lunch!"

"We'll have lunch back at the camp." Cherie promised Murray, leading him back to where the others were.

"I'd give my new hip if I could get my hands on that diabolical little trickster." Alice grumbled. "Well, if there's nothing here, perhaps we ought to be getting back to camp. We need to come up with a new plan of attack."

Piper rose in the air and a gleam shone in her eye. "Next time, we'll be the ones tricking Mendax!"

"Now there's a good idea!" Ali agreed with a wink.

They left the island to return to their camp, and as they drew near to it, the sea dragons all shared a laugh and a wink with each other.

"Alice! Ali! Eddie! Hold your breath, we have a surprise for you!" Keres called out. The trio did as they were told, and suddenly they were plunged beneath the waves.

The dragons flew swiftly through the water, gliding gracefully over a great dragon city below them. Coral arches and structures, as well as caves and castles made up a vast area of the sea bed. Mermaids swam past, blowing bubbles at them with a grin. Everything that they saw was ablaze with color, in unusual shapes and designs.

All too soon, the sea dragons resurfaced, and the humans all gasped for air, laughing and crying out with excitement.

"That was amazing!" Ali shouted, driving her fist into the air.

"I want to go back and see it all!" Eddie pleaded, quivering with the thrill.

"Perhaps when the dragons are all home and safe, we can visit the sea dragon city." Alice smiled widely.

"Did you see the mermaids? There are mermaids down there!" Eddie went on.

"Those are saltwater mermaids." Alice told him. "I've haven't seen them before, but I have heard a freshwater mermaid sing, and that was something very special."

Oscar was peering out from the hollow under Diovalo's wing, and he saw the sea dragons go underwater and then come back up. He could see that there was something very bright and colorful beneath the waves, and he desperately wanted a better look.

He leaned out just a little further, and slipped. Oscar plummeted to the ocean below Diovalo, and both he and Jynx screamed.

Alice looked up and cried out as well, reaching her hand out to him, though it would do no good at all.

"OSCAR!"

Faster than a streak of lightning, Galiphes zipped through the waves and the moment Oscar hit the surface, the sea dragon pulled him out and placed him on his back.

Oscar coughed up some water and laid his head down, resting as Galiphes slowed quite a bit and swam smoothly over the surface. Jynx watched in a panic from above, though she wouldn't get too close to the edge of the hollow they were nestled in.

The moment the dragons all came ashore and Dio landed on the beach, Jynx raced to Oscar, and Chippa wasn't far behind her. Alice and Henderson were there as fast as they could be, followed by the others.

"Is he alright? Oscar, are you breathing?" Jynx worriedly sniffed him and licked his face.

Oscar opened his eyes. "I was in the ocean! I'm sorry Jynx, I didn't mean to get so close to the edge."

"Are you okay?" Alice ran a hand over his forehead.

"My ribs hurt." Oscar moaned.

"I can help him." Chippa moved around the cat and began to brush his paws over Oscar's body. "Don't move." Chippa instructed. Oscar listened and obeyed.

In a few minutes, Oscar opened his eyes wide and drew in a deep breath.

"I can breathe! I can breathe and it doesn't hurt!" Oscar was relieved, but perhaps not as much as Jynx, Alice, and Henderson.

"He's fixed." Chippa announced happily. Alice hugged the Inkling tightly.

"Oh thank you so much! You've learned how to heal as well! That's wonderful!" Alice rubbed Chippa's ears and reached into her coat pocket, pulling out a handful of ginger chews.

"Here you are my dear, all for you."

Chippa's eyes grew wide and he began to chirp from deep in his throat. "Oh… ginger… I missed this!" He took them from her and immediately popped one in his mouth, savoring it happily.

"I told you not to get too close to the edge, you always get too close, and this time you almost… you almost…" Jynx was despondent.

Alice placed a hand on the black cat's back and stroked it. "I think our little one has had enough punishment and guilt for his fall. It was an accident, and I'd be willing to bet that he's learned from it. Let's just be glad that he's okay now."

"I am." Jynx acquiesced. "I am." She sighed heavily and then rubbed her head against Oscar's. "But you're still grounded for the entire trip here."

"Awwwe. Dang it." Oscar pouted.

"Why don't I get started on dinner. It'll be dark soon. That journey burned up most of our day." Cherie headed for the makeshift kitchen she'd created at the camp. The sea dragons bid them farewell, and Alice faced Diovalo to talk with him.

"We've got a serious problem." She stated darkly.

"Yes, we does. Mendax." Chippa snapped bitterly.

"To be honest, I can't tell whether he's helping us or not. I mean, he brought Ali and Cherie to us, and they're wonderful, but then he sent us on a wild goose chase to an empty island. Why would he do that?" Alice pondered with a frown.

"A wild dragon chase!" Chippa waved one paw in the air haphazardly. "I doesn't trust him. I never trusted him!"

Diovalo glowered. "We're going to have to figure out our next move without any help from that lying wretch, Mendax. Those dragons need to be rescued. That is our first priority."

"It is indeed." Alice agreed. "We *will* find them. The question is how."

Chapter Four

A Twist in the Tail

Cherie served dinner to everyone and then sent them all off to bed to rest after such a dramatic day. Everyone was tired, and it wasn't long before Alice had fallen asleep.

Not long into her rest, she was awakened by little tickles of cold on her skin. Opening her eyes wide, she flipped on her flashlight and saw that it was snowing inside her leaf tent.

"What in the world?" She murmured, holding her hand out. Flakes fell into her palm and began to build there, and she saw a thin blanket of snow across her, the leaf bed, and the ground.

"Now what is causing this!" Alice pushed herself from the bed and left her tent, only to stop in surprise. Eddie was sitting on a log out in front of her tent, and Marlowe was a few feet away, watching over him.

"Eddie! Whatever are you doing up so late? You should be dreaming by now. Can't you sleep?" Alice went to him and wrapped an arm around him.

Eddie was quiet, and the only sounds lacing the night were the sparks from the campfire, and the raucous rattle of Murray's snoring from a few tents over.

"No, grandma. I can't sleep." Eddie answered softly, reaching for her hand, taking it in his. "Are you all right? Why are you up?"

A chuckle escaped Alice as she rolled her eyes. "Oh, it's a bit cold in my tent for some reason, but let's not worry about that now. I'll get it sorted soon enough. Talk with me."

She sat with Eddie and kept hold of him. Together they looked at the differences between their hands; the size, the colors, the skin old and young, and a sob escaped Eddie.

"All right now, I think it's time you told me what's going on. You came for dinner with your parents and then insisted on staying with me, which I was thrilled for of course, except that now you're here and I'm not sure that's the best for you."

She looked him right in his dark eyes; mirrors of her own, both of them reflecting the flames crackling nearby. "You've been hovering closer than usual, you're not sleeping, you're sitting out here in front of my tent, and I know very well that you're worried by something. What's on your mind my dearest? I'm here for you. You can always talk with me about anything."

She stroked his hair with her free hand, and he leaned into it. His wet cheeks shone in the firelight.

"One of my friends at school, he… he lost his grandma this week. She passed away. It hit me really hard when I realized that I could lose you at any time. You mean so much to me, and I don't see you that often because we're all so busy. I can't imagine losing you! What am I going to do without you? You can't go!"

Eddie began to cry in earnest then and he wrapped his arms tightly around her. Alice bit her lip hard, and her chin quivered. She didn't know how she was going to find her voice. Closing her eyes, she rested her face against his head, and his shoulders began to shake. Her eyes stung with tears and she swallowed hard.

"Eddie," she choked out a whisper, "no one and nothing lasts forever, though we often wish that it would. We only have a short time together, and we must be glad for that. Every hello we ever say is always going to end in goodbye."

"It's going to sound awful," he sniffed, "but I know that you're part of the prophecy here, so I hope the prophecy is never fulfilled because as long as it isn't, I know you'll live. It can't end without you. If it remains unfulfilled, then I can always keep you!"

Alice's heart nearly broke. He'd been trying to find a way to make sure she didn't leave him. She drew in a long, slow breath and took Eddie's hand again, giving it a gentle squeeze.

"Sometimes our experiences can be so difficult that we feel we will never make it through; we face a battle we think we can never win. It becomes overwhelming, as if the things we can't control are more than we can bear, but the truth is, our most formidable challenges are the very things that really show us just who we are and what we're made of. They test our true colors and force us to discover and develop our strengths. The trick is to take those trials one step at a time, keeping our focus on each little moment as we get through them, and then each one of those moments becomes a success. We go on bit by bit, and before we know it, we've reached the other side, and gotten past the impossible. It's the most difficult things we go through which make us the strongest."

"But if you're gone, I will lose you forever! There's no other side to that!" Eddie insisted tearfully.

Alice swallowed the lump in her throat. "Just because you can't see me in this form doesn't mean I'm not on the other side of the grief with you. Eddie, look up at the stars. Go on."

Eddie turned his head and blinked through his tears, looking at the night sky bedazzled with starlight.

"There are so many. I've never seen so many." He whispered.

"They're always there, whether or not you can see them. You know, those stars all shine in the daytime too; we just can't see them because of the sun, but they're always there. Someday I will have to go, but just like those stars, even when you can't see me, you know I'll be there. Anytime you wish you were with me, you just look up at the sky, day or night. Look at the stars and know that we are connected by them. I will always love you, and I will always be there with you. You have a forever home in my heart, my dearest, remember that. I will never be more than a star away."

"I love you, grandma." Eddie wept quietly into her shoulder as he hugged her tightly.

"I love you, too. Promise me you'll remember what I said."

"I promise."

"Good boy." She murmured, closing her eyes and breathing in the scent of him.

A rustle in the trees nearby caught their attention, and they turned swiftly to see what it was. Chippa waddled toward them with a smile on his face and his paws rubbing his full belly.

"What… what is he doing?" Eddie sat up and stared.

"Inklings are mostly nocturnal. He probably went out for something to eat and is just coming back. They're usually awake from late afternoon through early morning, and then they sleep the rest of the time."

"Why are you not sleeping?" Chippa worried, going to them. "Is things okay?"

Alice smiled at him. "Yes, and no. Chippa, I'm out here because it's snowing in my tent."

Eddie swiveled in his seat and stared at his grandmother. "It's what?"

"Snowing. It's snowing in my tent. I was asleep, and it woke me up."

Eddie left the log and hurried the few steps back to the leaf tent. He peered in and laughed, going in all the way. Alice was relieved to see that it had cheered him up some.

"Was you dreaming?" Chippa asked, going to the tent as well.

"I was." Alice pondered it.

"You hasn't mastered your powers yet. You keep working on it. You will understand it." Chippa moved his paws through the air in the tent and the snow disappeared. The chill was replaced with comfortable warmth.

"Oh, thank you, Chippa! How nice." She gave the Inkling a pat and then hugged Eddie and pointed to his tent, not too far from hers. "All right young man, it's much too late for you to be up. Time for bed."

"Goodnight, grandma. I love you." Eddie kissed her cheek and gave her another tight hug.

"Goodnight, dearest. I'll see you in the morning." She watched him go and waved back at him when he slipped into his tent.

Alice nestled into her leaf bed again and fell asleep in no time. She was in such deep slumber that it took a moment for her to realize her dream hadn't gone horribly wrong. The terrified crying she heard in her dream was not a dream at all. Someone was wailing in horror, not far away.

Shooting up from the bed, she dashed outside. Brilliant moonlight bathed the beach and the foothills beside it in a near-daylight glow. Alice could see everything with perfect clarity.

She could see two great earth dragons poised before a gaping hole in the earth. Lord Malevor, and Liceverous. Eddie was clutched tightly in Lord Malevor's claws, and he was struggling to get free, calling out desperately for help.

"EDDIE!" Alice shrieked, running toward the earth dragons.

"GRANDMA!" He screamed out to her.

Their cries were drowned out by a thunderous roar of outrage. Diovalo appeared almost out of thin air, reaching the earth dragons before Alice got there.

"Lord Malevor! You put that boy down *NOW!*" Diovalo raged as fire blazed around the edges of mouth and through his enormous teeth. "What do you think you're doing?" He demanded.

Liceverous shot into the hole in the ground, and peered back out from behind Lord Malevor.

"I am ensuring my success!" Lord Malevor answered, hissing loudly and cruelly. "You do not deserve the throne of the dragons! It should be MINE!"

Diovalo lunged at Lord Malevor, but the earth dragon held his claw high and closed it tighter around Eddie, making the boy cry out in fear and pain. Diovalo stopped short, heaving plumes of scarlet and dark orange flames with his every rapid breath.

"Ah now, you mustn't get too close, or this little morsel will be no more than a midnight snack for me." Lord Malevor laughed wickedly, and it sounded like gravel being raked across metal.

"I am going to take the throne, Prince Diovalo, with the help of a great power and her army!"

"You will *never* have the throne, and you will release that boy now or it will be the last thing you ever do!" Diovalo roared again at Lord Malevor, whipping his gigantic tail fiercely behind him.

"Do you think you can stop me? How could you stop me when your mother couldn't? That's right, mighty prince, I am the one who took your mother to Baliste as a prisoner! She refused to serve Baliste, so Baliste killed her! It was a horrible death! Just as yours will be. You've already lost all the other fire dragons; I stole them away to Baliste as well. You had better take me seriously if you don't wish to lose another family member!" Lord Malevor shook his claw, and Eddie with it.

Eddie screamed again, and Alice tried to get closer. She had no idea what she could do, but she'd never been so afraid in her whole life. She was so focused on her grandson that she hadn't even noticed that every one of the cats, as well as Chippa, Henderson, Ali, and Cherie were all encircled around the great hole in the earth, and all of them had their eyes locked on Eddie.

"Malevor, why are you doing this? Why does Baliste want the fire dragons?" Diovalo snarled. "Why are you forsaking your own for that evil witch?"

Lord Malevor flashed his teeth. "It is not for you to know what she is doing! I am serving her because in turn she will serve me, and I will be king of the dragons! I will rule, as I always should have!"

"You will fail and die!" Diovalo warned him ferociously. "If you want the throne, then come for it right now! I'm here! Put the boy down and fight me! If you win, the throne will be yours!"

The earth dragon was big at the size of three train cars, but he was nothing compared to Diovalo, whose body could fill a stadium.

"I'm not going to fight you for it! It's going to be given to me as a reward!"

"Coward! Fight me now!" Diovalo persisted.

Lord Malevor only laughed hollowly. "You will be the coward when you face Baliste! You don't know what you're up against!"

"Chippa! Chippa do something!" Alice pleaded desperately. "I've been trying, but nothing is working!"

Alice had already attempted to bring a tree down on the dragon's head from further up the hillside, and she had also tried to raise the dirt around the dragon and blind him with it. Nothing she did with her powers would work.

Chippa scurried from one point to another, looking for some way to stop the dragon. "He will hurt Eddie!" Chippa called back to her quietly. "I must find a way!"

"You're not taking my friend!" Piper yelled, and rushed at Lord Malevor with her mouth wide open, and her sharp white teeth glistening. Lord Malevor saw her and thrust Eddie in his claw between them.

"Piper! Help me!" Eddie begged desperately, wriggling all that he could in the earth dragon's grasp.

"Come any closer and I will crush him!" Lord Malevor railed bitterly. "Do not test me again!"

"Piper no!" Alice cried, jabbing her open hand out toward them as her other hand clutched at her pounding heart. Piper swung wildly to get out of the way and avoid hitting Eddie. She fell back and hovered near the ground roaring her small roar at the massive beast before them.

"I will do anything! Give you anything if you just let him go!" Alice yelled at Lord Malevor.

The earth dragon laughed. Diovalo roared at him again. Lord Malevor eyed Diovalo hungrily. "If you want this boy, come and get him."

With that, he turned and disappeared into the gaping maw of earth, leaving nothing but emptiness behind him. Alice ran after them, but reality struck her, and she knew that she could not keep up with the dragon, or find him in the pitch darkness of their lair in the earth.

Diovalo's voice shook the hills and mountains beyond them. "TRAITOR! YOU WILL DIE!" He rushed at the hole, but Alice screamed for him.

"DIOVALO NOOOOO! STOP!"

It would have been too late if Marlowe and the other cats hadn't blocked him. Diovalo nearly crushed them with his claws as he leapt for the entrance, but he managed to stop short just in time.

"Diovalo, you can't follow him!" Alice shouted, waving her hands. "It's a trap! It's obviously a trap. He has no interest in Eddie, he's using him as bait to get *you*! It's too dark to see down in that hole anyway."

Diovalo stopped, and Alice's words held him back. "You are right. I hate it, but I can hear truth in your words. You are right. Mendax was right too, when he told me if I wanted to remain safe I'd better stay in the sky. How did he know?"

Alice hit her knees and sobbed into her trembling hands, barely able to breathe. "He's gone! He's gone... I never should have brought him... oh what have I done? My poor Eddie! I can't lose him! I don't even know if he's alive!"

She grew quiet for a long minute as the others encircled her. Her entire body shook, and strong arms closed around her as Henderson helped her to her feet.

When Alice raised her head again, fire blazed in her eyes. "I am going to get my grandson back no matter what it takes."

Henderson and Ali stayed close to Alice as they trudged back to their camp. When they passed Eddie's tent, they saw that it was thrashed to pieces on the ground.

Fury burned through Alice. "He must have been so terrified! He must still be, there in the dark with those two horrible worms, so lost and alone! How are we ever going to find him? How are we ever going to see anything down there in the d-"

Alice stopped short suddenly as realization washed over her.

"Caraway." She murmured, looking up.

"What?" Ali asked in confusion as Cherie made a cushioned seat on a nearby log and Alice sat on it. Marlowe stayed right beside her, and the other cats got as close as they could. Piper perched on Bailey's shoulders.

Henderson brightened. "Caraway! That's brilliant!"

"What's Caraway?" Ali pressed again.

"Not what; who."

"Who is Caraway?" Cherie asked as she brought a warm cup of tea.

Chippa climbed up on the log and sat beside Alice. "He's the keeper of the light. He would be a big help in a dark hole."

Alice spoke in a low voice. "Malevor said he's taking the throne with the help of a great power *and her army.* He meant the sorceress Baliste. This is more than just rescuing dragons. Malevor is going to try to take your throne from you, and he's got an army to help him. We are about to go into a battle. We're going to need more help if we ever hope to get Eddie back and win this fight."

Everyone around Alice shared dark looks. They knew that she was right.

"What kind of backup are we talking about?" Marlowe asked evenly.

"Think about the opponent we'll be facing. The sorceress and the earth dragons, and whatever else she's got fighting for her on her side. We're going to need numbers and power." Alice replied with razor sharp clarity.

"Fairies!" Ali shot up from her seat on an adjacent log. "You told me about the fairies that helped you last time! You said there were warriors among them. What if they helped? They have power, don't they?"

Chippa nodded and scratched his chin thoughtfully. "Yes. They has lots of power, and lots of numbers. They could help."

"I'll go get the fairies. Chippa, just show me where they are on the map and I'll go get them." Ali clenched her hands in determination.

Sophie's eyes went wide. "Montgomery is with the fairies! I'll go with you!"

"Oh, I want to go see the fairies again! I'll go! Besides, you guys might need me!" Oscar added quickly; his tail poked out in anticipation.

Jynx shook her head. "You're not going without me."

"Then come with us, Jynx!" Oscar pleaded.

Jynx lowered her eyes some and nodded. "All right. We'll go."

"Oh! I'll go with you too!" Piper rose in the air a few feet, flapping her wings swiftly. "I've always wanted to see the fairies! My mom told me all about them! Now I can meet them and then tell my mom all about it when I find her!"

Diovalo sighed. "Piper, they say your mother is gone. Perhaps you should..." He trailed off, not having the heart to say it again.

Cherie spoke out with a helpful, encouraging tone. "I'll set up a base camp here at the beach. Alice, it sounds like you're going to get Caraway, is that right? And Ali is heading off to get fairies, yes?"

Ali nodded. "I am. I'm going to come back with as many fairies as I can."

Alice took the tea Cherie offered her. "Yes, I'm going to go get Caraway. He can light the tunnels for us, if I'm not much mistaken, and I will move heaven and earth to find my grandson."

Cherie gave a nod. "That works. I'll stay here and manage the camp. We'll be ready to go as soon as everyone gets back."

Henderson gave her a smile. "Thank you, that is a help."

"I'll start with something to eat. I'm sure you'll all be leaving as soon as possible, and you shouldn't go on an empty stomach." Cherie hurried off to start cooking.

Alice continued her planning as she finished off the tea she'd been given.

"Marlowe, come with Henderson, Chippa, Diovalo, and me. Tao and Bailey, please stay here and help Cherie. Sophie, Jynx, Piper, and Oscar, you go with Ali. We'll get Caraway, you get the fairies, and we'll all meet back here as soon as possible so we can rescue Eddie and the fire dragons."

"We are having to ride Diovalo to Caraway." Chippa admitted with some embarrassment. "I doesn't know how to make a portal big enough for Diovalo. Only smaller portals. I am still learning."

"Then we fly." Diovalo agreed immediately. "There's no shame in not knowing yet, little one. We all learn as we grow."

"The music these kids listen to today! Terrible! What a ruckus! Woke me right up. Makes me glad I don't have my hearing aids in!" Murray stumbled out of his tent. "Sounded like a wild animal brawl! Did you hear all that loud music? Oh, you did. You're all up too. Wasn't that awful?" Murray grumbled.

"What about him?" Jynx asked Alice quietly.

"Has anyone seen my teeth?" Murray wandered toward the makeshift kitchen.

Alice sighed. "He can come with me. I don't want anything to happen to him either."

Tao leaned closer to Alice. "We will find him, and bring him back safely. Be strong and brave. That's what he needs most from you right now. Be the Alice who doesn't go down without a fight, because you are more that than anything else."

Tao's words lodged in Alice's mind and she pushed herself up off of the log. "You're right, Tao. You're absolutely right. I've never backed down from a fight, and I'm not about to start! We're going to get backup, and we're going to rescue our families!"

The rest of them cheered her, and Alice went to her tent to pack. It wasn't long before everyone was ready to go. Cherie had fed them all, including Bailey who was fed three times, and last checks were made.

Cherie stopped Ali and lowered a brow at her. "Have you eaten? You need to eat. I'll get some food for you to take with you. I don't want you getting hungry on the way."

She handed Ali a package of food, and gave one to Henderson as well. "Oh dear, Alice, you're not going without a hat. I'll grab it." Cherie hurried to Alice's tent and came back with her hat, helping her put it atop her head.

"There, that's better. Do you have a scarf?" Cherie pressed.

Henderson pulled a scarf for Alice from his black leather shoulder bag, in which he carried all the most important necessities from her pills to an extensive medical kit that he wouldn't leave behind on the second trip.

"I think we're all set, thank you. How did we ever manage without you?" He laughed quietly.

"Organization is what I do." Cherie shrugged. "Be safe and come back soon."

Alice nodded. "Yes, we will. Thank you, Cherie." She paused a moment then and took Cherie's hand in hers. "You should know, there is great value in all the work that each of us do to contribute to our collective success. Every great tapestry is but a tightly woven work of single threads. What you are doing here helps so much. Thank you."

Cherie grew misty eyed. "You are most welcome. Goodbye, Alice! Goodbye, Ali! Safe travels!"

Cherie watched with her hand on her heart as Diovalo lifted off the ground and rushed southeastward, and Ali along with her group headed south into the jungle on foot.

"I do hope they'll be all right." She worried. When she couldn't see them any longer, she turned to Tao and Bailey. "What shall we make for brunch? Fish?"

"Tao is the best fisher you'll ever meet." Bailey beamed.

"Fish it is." Tao chuckled softly and padded to the shore.

Ali, Sophie, Jynx, Oscar, and Piper were a short way from the camp when a swirl of sand appeared in the treetops above them.

Mendax lit on a branch and frowned at the group. "Going to get the fairies, are you? I don't think that's a wise idea at all. I can't have that. This time, you must fail."

He rubbed his hands together and went to work making his magic. With a few waves, he shifted the landscape just enough to mislead them, separating them into two different directions.

Ali turned a few minutes later to look back at the group, and groaned as her hand flew to her mouth.

"JYNX! SOPHIE! Where are you?"

Oscar turned with a start and checked over his shoulder. "Jynx was behind me! She's always behind me! Where did they go? Jynx! Sophie!" He called out in a panic.

Only the sounds of the jungle answered them in return.

Chapter Five

This Way and That

Baliste sat erect on her throne, her tail swaying in a slow curl from one side to the other as she gazed at the two earth dragons entering her great hall.

"You have returned to me once again without Diovalo, I see." Her voice sent a shiver over the drab green skin of the goblins on guard beside the door.

Lord Malevor lifted his long, thin snout and spoke boldly. "It is unfortunate that he has not yet been alone for us to take him, but we have just set a trap for him, and he will be captured very soon. Then, you can have him, and I can have the dragon throne."

"What is this trap that you have set for the dragon prince?" Baliste remained still; only her eyes moved as she watched the beasts come to the center of the great hall.

The earth dragon answered with pride. "We have taken the grandson of Alice. Diovalo will come to rescue the child, and when he does, we will capture him."

Lord Malevor took a few steps toward Baliste's throne. "As this capture is imminent, I request that you give me the throne of dragons now."

Baliste narrowed her eyes and raised her voice. "You will have the throne when I say you are ready for it, and not before! You continue to fail in capturing Diovalo! Give this child of Alice's to me and you will remain in my good graces, but you will not have the throne until I have the dragon prince!"

Lord Malevor peered at her and thought on her words. "If you have the boy, Diovalo will come to you. I can give you the boy now, but if I do, I demand that you make me king!"

Rising from her bench, she strode toward him purposefully, taking her time and locking her cool gaze on him.

"I do not take demands from anyone, least of all a worm like you." She snapped coldly. "You must give me more. I want all of the earth dragons to serve me. I know that there are some who have not committed to me. I want that resolved immediately. I expect you to see to it."

A glint stole across Lord Malevor's large, dark eyes and his mouth curled back against his fangs. "That was not the deal that we made, your highness. We agreed that I would become the ruler of *all* the dragons if I served you."

Baliste glared, and her intent was as solid as the stone fortress in which they stood. "You can have the sea dragons, but I am keeping the fire and earth dragons for my own."

Lord Malevor shook his head and a low growl rumbled deep within him. "That is *not* what we agreed upon! You're changing our arrangement!"

The spiked spade at the end of Baliste's tail flashed around her, coming dangerously close to Lord Malevor's head.

"I am all too willing to change our deal again and give you a more permanent ending if you don't like this new arrangement. The choice is yours." Her long, forked tongue shot out from behind her jagged teeth toward him.

The earth dragon was silent for a weighted moment, contemplating the situation. At last he spoke. "Yes, my queen."

With a hard look at her, he turned and left, and Liceverous followed him silently. When they were gone, Baliste turned to her goblin horde.

"I want you to take a squadron of goblins and trolls to Siang. Kill Alice, and capture Diovalo. Bring him back to me. I do not want to wait for this grandson of Alice's, nor do I wish to play games of control with those earth worms. Go now."

The goblins left her immediately.

* * *

Jynx froze and her fur went on end all over her body. She whipped her head this way and that, and called out loudly.

"Oscar! OSCAR!"

Sophie stood up on her hind legs, her sapphire eyes wide as she searched all around them. "They're gone! All of them are gone! Oscar, Ali, and Piper! I don't see any of them! ALI! PIPER!"

"OSCAR!" Jynx rushed back the way they had just come, sniffing at the ground and the air, but there was nothing. She stopped and faced Sophie.

"They're gone! There's not even a trace of their scent! All I can pick up is our trails. What's happening?" Jynx continued to search desperately, and Sophie helped.

Between the two of them, they covered a large area of the path they were on, and any possible way off of it, but there was no sign of their lost ones.

"I can't believe he's gone! They're all gone! Where did they go?" Jynx paced swiftly, triple-checking everywhere around them in full panic. "They were *just here!*"

"Maybe we're the ones who got lost." Sophie wondered quietly.

Jynx finally sat with a heavy sigh. "The question now is, what do we do?"

Sophie faced Jynx. "I think we should go to Lyria. Maybe the fairies can help us find them. I really don't see any other option. There's no trace of them anywhere here or behind us; it's like they just vanished into thin air. We can't go back for them, so the only thing we can do is go forward, especially if it means getting help."

Though she grumbled, Jynx got to her feet. "Fine. We go forward, but we search the whole way. Maybe they're headed that way and somehow wound up on a different path. The challenge is that Ali has the map. We don't know where we are, so how will we find our way to the fairies?"

Sophie lifted her chin high. "Oh, don't worry about that. I know the way."

Jynx's golden eyes thinned to slits. "I highly doubt that, Princess."

"I'm telling you, ye of little faith and darkest of souls, I know exactly where we are and where we're going. I have a sixth sense about these things. You're just going to have to trust me on this. I know how to get there."

Sophie headed through the trees on a narrow path, and Jynx growled low, but followed her. Sophie pushed and clawed her way through ever-thickening growth as the forest became denser, and Jynx was right behind her, narrowly avoiding getting whacked by branches and foliage that swung back toward her after Sophie had pushed them out of the way.

"Are you sure you know where we're going Sixth Sense?" Jynx shouted as she swiftly ducked a flung branch. "Because this looks an awful lot like no one in the history of *ever*, has come through here!"

"I told you I know exactly where we're going!" Sophie boasted over her shoulder as she struggled against layers of particularly large, thick, heavy leaves. "We just.. have to get… through this…" Her voice grew muffled for a moment, and then she screamed.

Jynx shoved forward in a rush to see what was wrong with Sophie, but the moment she did, her paws, like Sophies, lost their hold as the ground beneath them gave way.

Together they slipped right through the leaves, rolling head over tail as they tumbled down a sharp mountainside. Though their claws slashed through the air wildly, searching for anything to hold on to, there was no growth for them to reach. It was a steep grade of loose rock that fell with them, pelting them like hail as they scrambled, trying to stop.

Both of them howled as they crashed downward, and Jynx only barely managed to get a hold of the ledge where the hill ended in a cliff. She had just crawled up the side of it to her feet when Sophie flew past her, straight off the cliff, shrieking and twisting.

Jynx's claws shot out and she deftly snagged Sophie's diamond collar. With a deep groan, she hauled her catch back up over the ledge.

"Tao isn't the only good fisher in the family." Jynx panted as Sophie coughed and sputtered, gingerly getting to her feet.

For a long moment they were both silent as they took in their surroundings and caught their breath. A few straggler rocks bumbled down past them and sailed off the edge of the sheer stone wall into the gorge below. It was so deep that they couldn't see the bottom of it; there was only a mist, a long, long way down.

Across the abyss was the sister-wall, which looked to have been cut away from where they stood, and moved a good distance a long time before. It was lined with even more forest as far as they could see.

Jynx's voice was low and sharp. "You know what a sophomaniac is, don't you?"

Sophie turned her head to look at Jynx. "Someone who adores me?"

"No." Jynx answered flatly, staring down into the gorge. "It's someone with the delusion of having superior intelligence."

Sophie's eyes widened in anger. "This is NOT my fault!"

"It *is too* your fault, Sixth Sense! *You* said you knew which way to go! You *swore* that you knew exactly how to get to Lyria, and *now* look where we are! That's a loose rock hill behind us that we can't possibly climb back up, and that's a bottomless pit before us, and here we are with barely enough room to stand, trapped on the edge of a *cliff!* This is *all* your fault! Why did I ever listen to you! I know better than to listen to you!"

"Oh shut up!" Sophie shot back. "You're not right all the time!"

"Yes, I am!" Jynx blasted her. "I am right all the time because I stop and think about things! I think things through! I don't make rash decisions or take fly-by-the-seat-of-my-pants chances!"

"You don't wear pants!" Sophie shouted, glaring at Jynx.

"Oh shut up!" Jynx hissed at Sophie.

They turned away from each other, each of them ignoring the other one bitterly. It wasn't long before Sophie spoke over her shoulder without looking at Jynx.

"So what are we going to do? We can't stay here."

"Do you see a way out?" Jynx replied wryly.

Sophie began to wail. "We're going to die!"

"We're not going to die. I just need to think this through." Jynx grumbled.

* * *

Ali, Oscar, and Piper searched everywhere for Jynx and Sophie, but they found nothing. Oscar was desperate.

"We've got to find them! They're lost! My family is lost!"

Piper nuzzled the fuzzy orange kitten. "I know how you feel. I will help you find them!"

"Thank you, Piper!" Oscar bemoaned sadly.

"First, I think we need to find ourselves." Ali intoned worriedly. "We were just in a jungle with Sophie and Jynx. A tropical jungle. We are *not* in a tropical jungle now. Look at these trees. I've never seen anything like them before! Maybe we took a different path or something, but as far as I can tell, there's nothing tropical anywhere around us. These trees are old growth. Very old."

Oscar and Piper looked about and noticed for the first time that they were not where they had been when the others were with them.

Reaching from the ground as far up as they could see toward the sky, the friends discovered that they were nestled at the feet of giants; trees that were bigger than any they had ever seen before. Amongst the trees, there was no end of growth; flora and fauna had gone wild everywhere.

"How did we get here? When did we get here?" Piper fluttered about in confusion, trying to make sense of it.

"I don't know," Ali answered quietly, "but I think we need to ask ourselves how we're going to get out. Maybe if I climb one of these trees, I can get a better view, and perhaps see Sophie and Jynx, or even Lyria."

Ali yanked her skirt up and tied it, and then began scaling the side of one of the skyscraper trees nearby. She hadn't gotten far when the tree began to shiver. Ali held on tighter, and suddenly the tree laughed.

Ali froze and peered up at it.

"I think this tree just… laughed." She called down to her friends. "But that can't be possible…"

One of the strong branches slowly curled its way toward her, wrapped itself around her like a hand, and placed her back on the ground gently.

"OHMIGOSH!" Ali cried out, panicked as she held fast to the limb before it let her go. "What's happening? What's *happening!*"

A voice sounded from high in the tree.

"Do not be afraid. I mean you no harm." It was a pleasant voice, calming and serene.

"Who is that? Who's talking to me?" Ali called out, as the voice who had spoken to her seemed to come from somewhere far above them.

"I am! I'm a Towering Tree Nymph! My name is Phedrus." Whimsy and delight colored the nymph's voice. "It tickled when you were climbing my tree, so I had to put you back on the ground."

"What's a tree nymph?" Oscar sniffed, poking his nose up closer to the crackled old bark.

"Nymphs are spirits that live within trees!" Phedrus replied gaily. The boughs and branches of the tree began to twist one way, fluttering all their leaves, and then they swished the other way, changing direction in a graceful dance.

"Do you like my dress? I'll be changing it for cooler weather!" Phedrus' tone glowed as the leaves quivered and rippled.

"I do love autumn leaves." A grin formed over Ali's face. "Your leaf gown is lovely."

"Oh, thank you!" Phedrus swirled the leaves and branches once more for effect.

"Phedrus, did you happen to see two very large cats around here?" Ali pressed her hands together hopefully.

"What's a cat?"

"I'm a cat. The two that we're looking for are a little bigger than me, and they're different colors." Oscar answered the tree spirit.

"No, I'm sorry, I haven't. Are they lost?"

"Yes. We were on our way to the fairies at Lyria, and two of our party disappeared. It's quite distressing. We need to find them and get to the fairies as quickly as possible. We're going to ask them for help in a battle against the evil sorceress Baliste."

A soft shimmer began to emerge from the ancient, deeply cracked bark of the titanic tree, and a partly translucent figure stepped free of it, swirling into the shape and size of a young woman similar to Ali. She stood before the group of friends, and they could see features that resembled a human, as well as shape and form, though she had no actual body; it was instead a combination of silvery light and shadows.

"Phedrus?" Piper asked, hovering near Oscar.

"Yes." The spirit answered. "I can take any form, but this one looks like you." She indicated Ali. "I have heard of this evil sorceress; there are whispers, but I know nothing of her. All of the forest is abuzz with gossip about it because some of the growth at the top of Mount Jaiath, has died off."

Her voice grew deeply sorrowful. "What hasn't died off has been blackened; scorched by the deep fires that are burning there beneath the fortress that she built. She calls it Mordauz. Baliste's evil is spreading to everything around her, and everything that it touches either falls under her control or dies. It's terrible!"

"Well, we're going to fight Baliste, and we're going to win! We will save the fire dragons that she has taken, and we will stop her evil!" Piper vowed, shooting upward and flying in excited circles.

Phedrus watched the baby dragon and smiled.

Ali took a step toward the shimmering spirit. "Do you know where Lyria is? We really need to get to the fairies!"

"No, I don't know. My friends and I never leave this old growth forest. We've always been here, as long as these trees have lived."

"Maybe it's time you did leave," Ali suggested gently, "because I believe Baliste's evil is spreading, and if it isn't stopped, it will reach this place."

Phedrus was horrified. "Blackened? Here? Destroyed? That cannot happen! These trees are thousands of years old!"

Ali nodded solemnly. "If she isn't stopped, then yes. For now, I need to come up with a plan to get us out of here."

She began to pace in one direction and then another, tapping her chin in deep thought. Phedrus, Oscar, and Piper watched her and waited.

Suddenly Ali stopped and spun on her heel, facing them. "I've got it! This has got to work! It's probably the only way!"

She began to hurry about, collecting bunches of thick fallen branches, and stacking them in a pile.

"What are you doing?" Piper puzzled curiously.

"Can I help you?" Oscar offered, going to a nearby branch and picking it up with his teeth.

"Yes! Please! Help me get as many branches in this size, as you can find!" Ali was so busy bustling around that she didn't bother to explain any further.

Phedrus watched in fascination as Oscar and Piper both helped, and in no time, they'd made a big pile of branches.

"Excellent! Now I need vines!" Ali gathered as many green vines as she could, and once more, her friends helped her, though they still had no idea what she was doing.

Ali used the vines to tie the branches together, creating what looked like a large and sturdy raft.

"What are we going to do with that?" Oscar tapped his paw at the edge of the branch raft.

"Nothing if I can't find a way to make these leaves stick together." Ali hauled several giant vine leaves over to her project. The leaves were each more than five feet across in diameter.

"Oh! You could use tree sap! It's the best at making anything stick!" Phedrus bubbled happily. "I'll help you with that."

She waved her silvery-translucent hand, and it looked like water gliding through the air. Some of the bigger tree limbs leaned toward Ali, and Ali held the leaves where she needed them as sap dripped generously from the tips of the branches.

"Piper, could you please breathe some hot air onto these leaves to dry the sap? Not fire… please be careful. Just hot air." Ali held the pasted leaves up for the baby dragon.

~ 113 ~

"Sure! I can do that! I won't let any fire come out!" Piper concentrated and used all her control to do it. She held her claws together nervously. "Did I do it right? Did it work?"

Ali examined her leaves carefully. "It worked! You did it! Great job, little one!"

Piper bounced blissfully through the air. "I can't wait to tell my mom about all the new things I'm learning! She will be so proud of me!"

Everyone else watched closely as Ali put the leaves together to form a great ball with an opening at one end. Then she tied several vines into knots, forming a net that she placed over the ball, and secured tightly to the raft.

"What *is* that?" Oscar sniffed at it, trying to figure it out.

Ali stood and planted her hands on her hips, grinning. "It's a hot air balloon! We can all sit on the raft, Piper can breathe hot air into the balloon, and we can fly up over the forest. I'm hoping we will see Sophie and Jynx from above the trees, but we'll certainly be able to find Lyria this way!"

"That's brilliant!" Oscar bounded around excitedly, and Piper joined him.

"I'll make an opening for you in the canopy, so you can get out safely." Phedrus waved her hand again toward the tree tops so far above them, and they drifted away from each other, creating a circle of blue sky.

"Thank you so much, Phedrus, and you as well, Oscar and Piper, for helping me!" Ali climbed onto the raft, followed by the cat and the dragon, and Piper breathed small spouts of flame into the balloon as Ali and Oscar held it for her. Oscar's whiskers got a bit singed at the tips, but the balloon filled with hot air, and slowly the raft rose toward the sky.

They waved goodbye to Phedrus, and saw her disappear back into her tree once more. The balloon and its crew sailed out over the old growth forest.

Oscar buzzed with anticipation and curiosity, but he stayed at the center of the raft for balance, and because he had no interest in falling off.

"This is incredible!" Ali gushed with a thrill, gripping the edge of the raft as her dark brown hair danced wildly in the wind. "Everything looks so different from up here!"

"You should see it from the back of a dragon!" Oscar beamed. "But this is fantastic!"

Piper puffed a bit more into the balloon and they floated higher.

Ali glanced back at Oscar. "Put your tail down over the edge please, and we'll use it as a rudder!"

Oscar complied, and it worked.

"Now to find Lyria!" Ali peered closely at the world beneath them.

* * *

Warm sun bathed Alice and Diovalo as they soared through the skies, while Marlowe, Chippa, Henderson, and Murray rode in the hollow under Diovalo's left wing.

They'd gone a while with nothing but the wind and sun, when Alice noticed that a slight mist had begun to fill the air around them. It wasn't easily noticeable at first, but the further they flew, the thicker the mist became, until it gradually obscured the sun completely and swallowed them.

"Diovalo, can you see anything?" Alice called out to him. The wind had gone along with the sunlight, and there was nothing but dull, gray mist all around them.

"No, I can't. I'll fly higher, and maybe we can get out of this cloud bank." He rose, and continued to soar upward, but no matter how high he went, the misty fog remained.

"I can't seem to break free of it!" Diovalo told Alice. "I'm going to go back down. Maybe we can fly closer over the land, and find our way more easily."

"Go slowly, Diovalo, we can't see the ground. I don't want you coming to it too fast." Alice held tight to him and peered as far as she could, which wasn't more than a few meters.

"Watch out!" Henderson shouted up to them.

Out of nowhere, treetops and rocky hills appeared directly beneath him, and Diovalo dodged, pulling up swiftly so as not to hit them.

"I'll try to soar over it, if I can." Diovalo announced, barely beating his massive wings. "It's difficult when I can't see anything."

The dragon prince blasted a stream of fire before him, hoping to burn some of the mist away, but it had no effect.

"This is not natural mist." Diovalo told Alice. "I should have been able to clear it with fire."

"Diovalo! Look out!" Alice shouted.

They had nearly crashed right into the side of a looming hill. Diovalo stretched his feet out before him, clutching the land on the hill with his claws, and jolting to a sudden stop.

"I cannot fly through this, and to be honest, I don't know where we are. I've never flown this direction before and it's impossible to see anything. We may have to wait until it clears." Diovalo sighed heavily.

Chippa scuttled out from the hollow under the dragon's wing. Henderson, Marlowe, and Murray followed him. Alice met them on the ground, and Diovalo brought his head down close to them.

"This is magic. This is not natural mist." Chippa agreed with the dragon. "I has already tried to move it, and it doesn't go."

Murray stretched. "Oh, this is terrible London fog! It comes so fast. One minute there's sun, and the next, the fog rolls right in. Do you hear that? Must be church bells."

"Oh, Murray. Your ears are probably ringing. There aren't any bells out here." Alice patted his arm, feeling sorry for him that he'd lost so much of his hearing.

"No, wait… I hear bells too." Diovalo turned his head one way, and then the other, listening closely.

Chippa perked his floppy ears up and tilted his head. "Yes. I hears them too. Bells."

Alice strained, and then she heard them. They were light and melodic. She raised her hand, touching Diovalo's side.

"What is that?" She murmured.

Everyone looked. Soft glowing lights began to shine through the mist, coming toward them.

Chapter Six

Beyond Expectations

Eddie discovered right away that Liceverous had been right about light not getting into the tunnels where the earth dragons lived. It was the blackest place he had ever been; he could not even see his hand in front of his face.

Somehow, he realized, with his sight taken from him, all of his other senses kicked into high gear. He could hear so much around him; the quiet thumps of dragon's feet against the dirt, and their snuffling breath as they moved from one tunnel to the next.

The air was warmer than he expected, but it made sense to him; with no outward influence of other elements, nothing would really change the temperature.

He had tried to keep track of which way they turned, in case he might get free and could escape back out again the way they had come, but in mere minutes he was completely lost. All he could do was hold on to hope.

Lord Malevor had left him in some cavernous place, though he could not be certain because he couldn't see it, but the sounds echoed further than they had in the tunnels. He clapped his hands a few times to judge distance, and was surprised by his own mind, telling him the shape and volume of the cavern just by the return sound of the echoes.

Liceverous had been left to guard him. He'd heard Lord Malevor tell his underling that he was going to see Baliste, and to keep watch over the prisoner. Eddie was bitterly angry about having been stolen away from his grandmother, and terrified about what the earth dragons might do to him, but he'd said nothing to them, instead trying to get some kind of control over his fears.

In the recesses of his mind, the words his grandma had said to him that very night came back to the forefront of his thoughts, just like the echoes in the cavern.

"It's the most difficult things we go through which make us the strongest..."

He swallowed the hard knot in his throat and thought to himself, *"I'm trying, grandma. I'm trying my best to be brave and strong."*

He focused on her voice in his head, and on what she had told him only a little while before.

"Just because you can't see me in this form doesn't mean I'm not with you. Look up at the stars... they're always there, whether or not you can see them. Anytime you wish you were with me, you just look up at the sky, day or night. Look at the stars and know that we are connected by them. I will always love you, and I will always be there with you. You have a forever home in my heart, my dearest, remember that. I will never be more than a star away."

His heart ached for her, and he wished desperately that he was with her. Eddie peered as hard as he could at the pitch blackness around him, but he could see nothing at all. Then, a thought came to him.

Eddie closed his eyes and pushed his fingers against them, rubbing firmly. When he stopped rubbing, he kept his eyes closed, and suddenly he could see countless stars.

He knew they weren't real stars, but they were the closest thing to it that he could come up with so far down into the ground. He smiled a little, concentrating on them, feeling as if his grandma was right there with him, and wishing on each and every one that she would come to get him.

"The most difficult things we go through make us the strongest." He whispered to himself, feeling a little braver.

Eddie's whisper filled the space around him, as there was no other sound, save for Liceverous' loud and steady breathing.

"Then this should make you unbeatable." Liceverous taunted him smoothly.

Eddie blinked, realizing that his whisper had been loud enough for the dragon to hear. His mind raced, and he thought he might try something to change his situation.

"Liceverous, I thought we were friends. When we met on the beach and talked, you were so pleasant."

"It was the time to be pleasant." The earth dragon answered in a steady, almost velvet tone.

"But… what about being friends? We could be friends, you know. You and I." Eddie hoped, leaning forward on his hands and feeling them press into the soft dirt beneath him. It felt like his grandmother's garden when they were working in it, and he realized that it must be freshly dug; it hadn't been tamped down, hardened by feet and weight yet. He was in a place that was newly created. He wondered if it had been dug out especially for him. He also realized that as a newly dug hole at the end of long, twisting tunnels, it might be harder to find.

"I only like friends in high places." Liceverous' voice took on a chilling edge. "Some dragons have an insatiable hunger for gold, some for blood, and some for power."

"But... none of those things bring true happiness. They don't give you anything in return. That's what friends are for. I could be your friend, Liceverous. We could be... friends." Eddie tried to sound sincere, though he wasn't feeling that way at all.

"I do not need friends!" Liceverous raised his voice sharply. "Do not continue to speak to me, if you value your life at all! Continue, and I will kill you here and now!"

Eddie's heart began to race as the truth unfolded itself before him like a blossom of light in the darkness.

"You can't kill me. I'm too valuable a prisoner to kill." His fear of dying at the hands of the dragons dissipated immediately, transforming into strength and boldness. He couldn't be killed; he was their ace in the hole. There was nothing to be afraid of, but there was a good deal more hope to hold onto until he could get away or be rescued. He knew that his grandma would come for him, and he knew full well that she had several friends to help her do it.

"Your tongue is taking you too far, young one! Silence it! I may not be able to kill you, but I can certainly injure you, and if you speak so much as one more word, I will moisten the ground beneath you with your blood!" Liceverous warned angrily.

Eddie only smiled at the corner of his mouth. He had found his boundaries with the dragon, and in doing so, he had also found his own strength and determination.

* * *

Jynx tilted her head to one side, studying the rock wall to her left. It continued upward to a dizzying height, and jutted out somewhat over the gorge. There were thick vines growing down it, tangled here and there, lodged in some of the crevices within the stone.

"Hey Soph," she interrupted Sophie's pitiful wailing, "how would you feel about taking a fly-by-the-seat-of-our-pants chance?"

Sophie paused in her misery and blinked, turning to look at Jynx. "What?"

Jynx rose as high as she could on her hind legs, holding fast to the stone wall with her left front claws as she batted at the nearest vine, trying to reach it, but it was too far above her.

"What are you talking about? What are you doing?" Sophie snapped, facing the black and cobalt cat fully.

"I told you I would think of a way out of here, and I have. See that overhang above us?"

"Yes."

"See these thick vines growing on the wall?"

"Yes." Sophie frowned in confusion. "So?"

Jynx sank back down and sat, knowing there was no way she could get the vine on her own.

"Oh come on, Princess, draw a line from point A to point B. Look, we get one of those vines that's growing from the overhang, and then we hold on to it and swing over the gorge and land on the other side. Voila. We're saved."

"You want to do *what?*" Sophie gasped, round-eyed in horror.

"I'm wide open for other ideas if you have any." Jynx gave her a droll stare. Sophie looked away silently.

"Didn't think so. Listen, I'm going to need some help here. The nearest vine is too high for me to reach. I'm going to have to stand on you to get it."

Sophie grumbled low in her chest. "You are *not* going to stand on me."

"I am if you want to get out of here! Look, we've got a mission to complete. We have to get to the fairies, and then back to our family, and we're not even going to get off this cliff if we don't make some sacrifices and take some risks! As much as it makes me cringe to say it, we're just going to have to work together if we want to get anything done! Do you want to stay here on this cliff for the rest of forever?"

Sophie whined, knowing there was no way around it. "No."

"Then kindly get your high horse over here and let me stand on you so I can reach that vine. This is going to have to be a team effort. You and me. So let's do this thing." Jynx moved back as much as she could so that Sophie could get right up beside the wall.

Sophie grumbled, but she moved to her position and held on tightly to the stone beneath her. With painstaking care, Jynx crawled up onto Sophie's shoulders and slowly rose on her hind feet; her left front claws gripping the rock wall, while her right claws sunk into the thick green husk of the vine.

"How can you be this heavy! You weigh a ton!" Sophie growled.

"Be grateful, Sophie. It could be Bailey standing up here." Jynx glanced down with a wry smile. As she raised her head to focus on the vine again, something caught her eye and she looked closely at the horizon in the distance. A shining glint of white was nestled into a sea of green blanketing the ground.

"Sophie! I think I can see Lyria from here! There's nothing but green for ages, and then right in the middle, there's a big white spot! It's the White Song Forest of Lyria! It has to be!"

"I knew it! I'm sure it is Lyria! I *knew* I had us going in the right direction! I just didn't know this gorge was in our way!"

"Well, it's not going to be in our way for long. Lower me down carefully, I've got the vine!" Jynx instructed, holding it with both her front paws.

Sophie backed away from the wall very slowly, sinking down to the ground as she did, so that Jynx could step off of her safely.

"Okay. On the count of three, we both push away from the cliff as hard as we can and swing to the other side. We let go, and then we land."

"That's the plan?" Sophie's voice took on a high, nervous pitch.

"That's the plan." Jynx stated with certainty. "Let's hope it works out like that. If we can get to the other side, it will be easy, fast going from there. Are you ready?"

"NO." Sophie grew breathless.

"Sophie, the alternative is to stay on this cliff."

With a deep sigh, Sophie rose on her hind legs like Jynx, and drove her claws into the vine. "Okay. On three."

"One." Jynx began quietly.

"Two." Sophie added, just as hushed.

"Three." They called out in unison, and both of them shoved their hind feet against the edge of the stone cliff, thrusting themselves forward with every bit of strength they had.

The vine swung out over the gorge. Sophie screamed and Jynx shut her eyes tightly as she held her breath. Wind rippled their fur and tugged at them as they soared through the air.

"OHMYGOSHOHMYGOSHOHMYGOSH!" Sophie cried out as they neared the opposite bank. "JUMP!" She shouted, pulling her claws out of the vine and leaping with true feline grace to the swiftly approaching ledge. Sophie landed softly, and heaved a huge sigh of relief.

"That wasn't as bad as I thought it was going to be! I can't believe we made it! I have to admit, it was a great idea Jynx!" She smiled as she looked around.

"Jynx?" Sophie called out.

She was alone on the ledge with a massive forest spreading out behind her. Her head jerked up and she caught sight of the vine, swinging back wildly to the other side of the gorge where they had just come from. Jynx was still clinging to it; her eyes clamped shut.

"JYNX!" Sophie shouted.

Jynx yelled back, her voice bouncing off of the stone walls on either side of the gorge. "I can't let go! I'm too afraid! What if I fall?"

"Be brave Jynx!" Sophie encouraged her. "You can do this! If I can do it, you can definitely do it! I'll catch you when you come back! I promise! I'll grab the vine, and you jump!"

"Do you swear?" Jynx called back, finally opening her eyes and instantly regretting it.

"I am not going to let you fall Jynx! I promise!" Sophie vowed, and Jynx, wide-eyed with terror, met the wall on the original side. When the vine drew close enough, she used both her hind legs to kick off once again, giving herself a swift launch toward the forest side.

The vine twisted and turned, streaking back over the abyss. Jynx howled miserably, but she kept her eyes open. As it neared the far bank, Sophie stood poised and ready on her hind legs; both her front paws extended, perfectly balanced as she focused hard on the approaching vine.

"Ready!" Sophie shouted.

"NO!" Jynx answered back sharply.

"Set!"

Jynx whined.

"JUMP! NOW! JUMP JYNX!" Sophie caught the vine and held tightly to it with her claws, struggling to keep it from pulling her off the ledge.

"I can't!" Jynx cried fearfully, staring wide-eyed at the space between the vine and the cliff.

"Jynx you have to! The vine is slipping! If I don't let go now, it's going to drag me off the ground! Jump! I'll catch you! I'm not going to let you fall!"

With a growl, Jynx leapt toward the bank, and Sophie released the vine. It swung back out over the gorge, and Sophie shot her claws out, closing them on Jynx and hauling her to the ground. They lay there together for a moment, panting and staring at each other with huge eyes.

"We made it." Sophie murmured.

"We made it." Jynx answered quietly. "Thank you. I've never been so scared to jump. You saved me."

Sophie smiled smugly as she rose to her feet. "Well yes, I did, but remember, you saved me on the other side when I went off the cliff. I might be out on a vine here, but maybe, just maybe… we make a good team."

Jynx stood up and shook herself out. "Maybe." The corner of her mouth turned up just a little. Suddenly she narrowed her eyes at Sophie. "You aren't going to tell anyone about this, are you?"

Sophie lifted her chin high in the air and began to prance through the forest, tail aloft. "Oh, I'm going to tell *everyone* about this!"

Jynx groaned and padded along behind her.

* * *

Ali held fast to the map she'd made as her gaze skipped from the sketches and markings on it to the real world below them.

"I think we're about halfway there!" She held it up to show Oscar and Piper, who were tucked in together at the center of the raft.

"I wish we had a little more wind, though! I don't think we're sailing fast enough." She peered up at the balloon that was carrying them. It had been well made and was holding up perfectly.

Almost as if in answer to her request, the passing breeze ruffled the edges of her map, and then began to tug more firmly at it. She clenched her fingers around it, and the breeze became a gust, pulling even harder.

Ali swiftly rolled the map up and tucked it safely inside her dress jacket as the balloon lurched sharply to one side, heeling in the wind. Ali, Oscar, and Piper all scrambled to hold on and keep their balance.

"What's happening?" Oscar panicked, going wide-eyed as his claws dug into the branches beneath him.

"This wind is too strong!" Ali cried out, holding on to the vine ropes of the net over the balloon.

"AGH!" Piper shouted, nearly blown away, "I can't fly! It's too hard!"

"I've got you!" Oscar snapped his paw out and curled it gently around her, scooping her to safety under his arm just in time.

"Thank you!" She sighed in relief, nestling in close against him as the gusts grew even stronger.

"What are we going to do?" Oscar yelled above the howling blast to Ali, who had locked her arms around one of the vine ropes.

"There's nothing we can do! Just hold on tight until we're out of it!" She shouted back to him.

They ducked their faces and shut their eyes as the raft and balloon whipped wildly one way and then spun another, whisking up and then dropping down over and over again.

It was a long while before the gale finally began to blow itself out, and the balloon spun haphazardly toward the ground.

"Oh no! I think we're going to crash!" Ali shot Oscar and Piper a swift look through her hair as it swept back and forth around her face. "Everyone hold on!"

In a rush they pelted toward the ground. One corner of the raft jolted into the earth, slamming the friends against the branches, and then the whole thing cartwheeled erratically, sending them all flying off of it as it splintered. Shards of broken branches sprayed outward, and the leaf balloon shredded, finally collapsing onto the ground.

Oscar groaned and slowly pushed himself up, staggering to his feet and spitting sand out of his mouth. His fur stuck out on end in every direction, looking as though he'd been through a cyclone. "Piper! Ali!"

"I'm here!" Ali moaned, sitting up. "Are you two okay?"

"I'm okay!" Piper called out listlessly. She was lying flat on her back, staring upward.

"I think I'm gonna throw up." Oscar coughed several times and then heaved.

"Oh, poor things. I'm so sorry. I don't know where that wind came from, but it blew us clear off course. I'm so glad we're all okay. Are you feeling any better now, Oscar?" Ali trudged to him and patted his shoulder.

"Yeah." He answered thinly, giving himself a little shake.

"Where are we?" Piper finally got to her feet and took a look around.

"That is an excellent question." Ali murmured, as they all turned in place and stared.

They had crashed into a wide, empty valley filled with nothing but low, undulating dunes of black sand. It was bowled in by great black cliff walls standing stalwart in a ring far off at its every border.

The sky above the vast ebony sand bowl was covered entirely in storm clouds which billowed and swirled, flashing here and there with lightning.

"Oh my gosh!" Oscar shouted suddenly, picking up both of his front paws and trying to stand on one back leg. "What is that? Did you see it? What is it?"

Piper shot up off of the sand and hovered in the air. Ali gasped and jumped onto a small chunk of the raft wreckage near her.

Silver streaks of light flashed over the surface of the black sand, zipping and snaking in every direction.

"It looks like lightning! Or… electricity, which is really the same thing." Ali cried out, watching it with a mixture of awe and horror.

The three friends stared as the streaks of silvery light began to race with more intensity and speed, shooting randomly across the dunes, coming closer to one another until they coalesced. Suddenly a burst of lightning shot up from the sand, ripping through the air up to the heavy, lavender shaded clouds above.

When the bolt struck the clouds, a far-echoing shriek sounded, filling the whole valley.

"What was that?" Piper grabbed hold of Oscar, hiding behind his shoulders as he teetered on his back paws in the sand.

They gaped at the storm clouds overhead as a massive black bird with silver electricity flashing in moving webs all over its body tore out of the billowed darkness and shot straight toward them.

"DUCK!" Ali screamed, rushing to Oscar and Piper. All of them cowered down, huddling together against the sand.

With a great gust of wind, the giant bird swept onto a low dune near them, shook out its wings, and folded them carefully against its back.

"Do not fear me. I intend you no harm." It spoke with a deep and reverberating voice.

The three friends slowly raised their heads, peeking out from under their arms. Ali gradually stood and faced it, as Oscar rose to his feet with Piper still on his back.

"Who are you?" Ali swallowed the lump in her throat and asked with a quivering voice.

The great bird watched them with large black eyes as the fine lines of electricity dancing across its feathers began to dissipate.

"I am Keleon."

"Hello Keleon. I'm Ali, and this is Oscar, and Piper."

"You're almost as big as a bus! What are you?" Oscar lifted his nose and sniffed at the air between them curiously.

"I'm a thunderbird." Keleon answered evenly. "You probably wouldn't have seen one if you haven't been here before."

Oscar's eyes rounded with admiration. "Does the lightning hurt you?"

"No, I control the lightning that traverses between the sky and the land. It moves through me; it is my power."

"Wooooow!" Oscar was starstruck. Piper stayed perched on the cat's shoulders, hidden to a degree behind Oscar's ears.

"May I ask what you're doing here?" Keleon studied them interestedly.

Ali pointed to the wreckage of their hot air balloon. "We were traveling in that… flying in it, actually, and a gale blew us off course. We crash landed here. I'm not even sure where we are actually."

"You're in the Tohnar Valley in the far north of Corevé.

Ali pulled her scroll free and examined it. "It's not on my map at all."

Keleon inclined his head slightly. "Not many people come here. Where were you traveling to?"

Ali's shoulders sank as a heavy sigh left her. "We were trying to get to Lyria to ask the fairies for help. The fire dragons of Siang have been captured and are all missing, except for Diovalo; he's the dragon prince. We're trying to get help to rescue the ones who've been taken."

Keleon nodded. "I know Diovalo's mother. She's a great leader."

Ali bit at her lower lip. "She was taken as well, and killed by the evil sorceress Baliste. Baliste is behind this whole mess."

Electricity flashed across Keleon's black eyes and rippled over his body as he spread his mighty wings and beat them against the air. His head fell back, and a sharp cry sounded from him, echoing throughout the valley and returning off of the black cliffs that encircled it.

"I have felt the evil of this witch spreading slowly like a disease from the crown of Mount Jaiath. She must be stopped!" He demanded angrily, digging his claws into the sand.

"We're going to stop her, but we need to find our friends who've been lost, and get some help if we ever hope to do it. Right now our focus has changed because it seems like everything that *could have* gone wrong *has*."

Keleon's voice softened, and he folded his wings once more. "Being blown off course might not be something that has gone wrong. It has simply put you on another path; one you wouldn't have been on otherwise. You may not see that right away, but it might not be the bad luck you feel it is."

Ali pushed her tangled hair from her face and straightened her clothes, dusting black sand from them.

"Time will tell. I think at this point, the best idea is to return to our camp at Siang. We need help from the others to find our friends and regroup. Maybe Sophie and Jynx have gone back to camp looking for us. Either way, we need to find our way out of here and back to Siang to get sorted again."

"I will take you. It would be the fastest way there, and I would be honored to join you in your fight against Baliste. I am compelled to avenge my friend the dragon queen, given any opportunity, and I will not rest until the fire dragons have been rescued. They are among the best creatures living in Corevé."

Ali blinked as her mouth fell open and she turned her head slowly to look at Oscar and Piper. "Shall we go with Keleon?" She asked in an awed voice.

"Yes!" Piper and Oscar chimed together.

Keleon spread his massive wings out widely again. "I believe this young dragon will not be able to match my speed in flight, perhaps it would be best if one of you held her."

"I'll carry you, Piper." Ali grinned and Piper hugged her as Ali wrapped her arms tightly around the baby dragon.

Keleon rose into the air a few feet and tenderly closed Ali in one claw, and Oscar in the other. Seconds later they were soaring through the air again, almost as swift as lightning, leaving the electric marbled black sand far below them.

* * *

"Stand behind me!" Chippa cried out bravely as he held his paws up in the air. "I will not let anything hurt us!"

Alice smiled at the little Inkling, realizing just how much he had grown, more inside than out, since she had seen him.

"Courageous Chippa, I will stand with you." Diovalo replied respectfully.

"As will we all." Marlowe added at Alice's side.

The sound of ringing bells grew louder as the softly shining lights that came toward them in the mist swayed subtly, and Alice realized she was holding her breath. She exhaled slowly and tried to steady her racing heart.

Two figures, slender and strong, appeared almost suddenly through the fog. They weren't much taller than Eddie. They were dressed in earthy toned sheaths that reached to their hips, their legs were clad in snug material, and they wore boots that came up to an angle at their knees. Their ears were pointed at the top, and their noses and cheekbones slightly elongated. In their hands they carried long poles with lanterns; the shades of which were made of large blossoms.

"Elves." Chippa told the others, without looking back at them.

"Elves?" Alice raised her brows and peered closer to get a good look. "I shouldn't be surprised by anything here in Corevé anymore, but I'm constantly surprised by everything here."

Murray broke out in applause, walking toward the pair. "Oh what fancy costumes! So well done! I expect you're collecting for some charity or other." He smiled at them and patted his pockets, finally pulling out a pound coin. "Here you are, then. Good luck to you!"

Murray handed the coin to the elf on the left and then ambled off a short distance, on exploration.

The elf examined the coin and then stepped forward. "Who are you, and what are you doing in Mainos?"

"What is Mainos?" Alice asked politely.

"Mainos is the name of the Mistlands. It's where we elves live, mostly." The elf in back answered, coming forward as well so that he was shoulder to shoulder with his partner. "We're elven guards."

"We're here quite by mistake." Alice answered their question. "We were flying to the Light House and got lost in the fog. Might I ask your names please?"

"I am Mere, and this is Rioux." The one who spoke first answered. Mere's eyes were the lightest shade of blue Alice had ever seen, and Rioux's were jade green, with translucent depths, almost like looking into water.

A thought occurred to Alice. "Are there many elves in Mainos?"

Rioux's face, like Mere's, remained completely stoic; there was no sign of emotion, only of thought. "There are many elves, though not all of them live in Mainos."

A smile tugged at the corner of Alice's mouth. "We have come from Siang; the land of dragons. You might not have heard, but all of the fire dragons have been captured by the evil sorceress Baliste."

"We have heard." Mere replied evenly.

Alice cleared her throat; her mind humming swiftly as she considered how she would say what she was thinking.

"There is a group of us going up against Baliste. A few of our own are en route to bring the fairies in as well to help in the battle. I wonder if the elves might consider joining us. Surely you would want to protect your lands against encroachment by her evil." Alice thought that any additions to their numbers that they could get would be a tremendous help.

Rioux and Mere did not even look at one another to consider it. "We will not join."

"Do you not fear that she might come here and wreak havoc on your own lives?" Alice wondered aloud.

"It is unlikely that she would come here. We seclude ourselves, keeping to our own, mostly, and we take no interest in the affairs of others outside of our realm." Rioux answered.

Alice could see that their pragmatic and logical thinking would not allow for any kind of empathetic emotion or compassion toward others in times of distress.

"Very well then, if you will not join us, would you please tell us how we might find our way out of the mist? We have gotten quite lost in it."

"Everyone who comes into Mainos becomes lost in the mist if they have not an elven guide. It is the protective barrier we have formed against the outside world," Mere explained.

Rioux held out his hand, palm up, and a ball of softly glowing light appeared. "This will guide you to the boundaries of our land. It is bright here, where you are so far into the realm. As you near the boundary, it will dim and fade away."

"Thank you." Alice nodded to them and took the ball of light into her palm. Chippa leaned up on his toes to get a good look at it; the tips of his ears perked up.

"That's good magic." He noted pleasantly.

"We will wait here as you leave to make sure you are gone. Begin in that direction if you wish to get to the Light House."

Chippa and Marlowe watched the elves closely, waiting until Alice was up behind Diovalo's head and Henderson had Murray seated back up on what he thought was the dragon ride at Hyde Park. When everyone else was ready, Chippa and Marlowe climbed up into the hollow.

"Thank you!" Alice called down as Diovalo spread his wings with a thunderous clap.

The elves did not wave to them, or speak. They simply watched with no trace of expression, as the dragon took to the skies.

"They're so strange." Alice murmured to herself as she held the ball of light in her hand. "Hello, please leave. Who would act in such a way?"

Diovalo flew eastward, they guessed, and the ball of light in Alice's hand grew dimmer and smaller as they went.

"I think we're going the right way! This ball is working! Just keep at it as you are please!" Alice called to Diovalo. He continued onward.

The mist began to clear, and as it did, the clouds grew lighter and thinner, and sunlight began to filter through. Alice gasped as the ball in her hand disappeared altogether.

"We're free and clear!" She announced happily to the dragon prince.

No sooner had they slipped out of the fog, than a big flock of Quiri birds descended upon them, shrieking bitterly, with their claws outstretched, and their sharp beaks wide open, ready to tear the riders apart.

"OH NO! Quiri birds!" Alice yelled out, and the group below had to take action.

"I cannot abide those wretched things!" Henderson snapped bitterly. He set his hand on Murray's shoulder.

"You must stay here. Under no circumstances should you get up. Do you understand?"

"Yes, of course!" Murray beamed up at him. "I love this ride! It's my favorite in the park!"

"Well, stay in your seat then." Henderson told him firmly.

With a swift look to Chippa and Marlowe, they nodded to one another, carefully climbed out from beneath Diovalo's wing, and quickly scaled his back.

Alice waved a free hand at the birds, trying to use her Inkling powers to push them away with air, but suddenly a small cloud formed over them and burst out into a rain shower, soaking Diovalo and everyone on him.

"Drat! Am I ever going to get these powers figured out!" Alice sighed and hung on to the dragon as he began to twist and turn through the air, careful to keep his riders aboard while evading their attackers.

"Hold on everyone! I'll do what I can!" Diovalo roared, blasting the Quiri around him with giant plumes of flame. Two of the giant birds were immediately roasted to a crisp and fell out of the sky.

Alice gave up on the idea of using her magical powers and started swinging her black bag around, bashing them with it anytime they got near her. She injured one of them, and it narrowly escaped being hit a second time.

"I doesn't like Quiri! Last time I hid, but this time I will fight! I will fight the Quiri and they will not take Hesson!" The little Inkling still hadn't quite learned how to say Henderson's name, but he was determined to keep the butler and everyone else safe. In their last encounter with a flock of Quiri birds, Henderson had been stolen away, and the group had to rescue him and Diovalo from their prison.

Henderson wielded his closed umbrella, jabbing at the birds sharply as they dove in for strikes against him.

Marlowe slashed with his razor sharp claws and brought one Quiri bird down onto Diovalo's back, shredding it until there was nothing left but a few brightly colored feathers swirling about him.

Chippa moved his paws swiftly through the air, and a great wind erupted; practically a gale force. "I will send them north as far as they can go!" He pushed with all of his might, and the few remaining Quiri birds tumbled and flailed against the mighty force of the wind.

"That wind is taking them to the north edge of the world!" Chippa wiggled his furry, feathered bottom in glee with a little dance. "We is beating them! Beating the Quiri birds!"

"We did indeed. Well done, young Chippa. Of all the things in Corevé, I dislike them the most. This was a win." Henderson gave him a pat and Marlowe nuzzled him.

"Now, let's get back down where it's safe." Henderson indicated the hollow. "I'm not keen to stay up here a moment longer than necessary."

The three of them, windblown but safe, slid back to the space under Diovalo's wing with great sighs of relief, and no small amount of satisfaction.

Murray waved at them. "This ride is really spiffy, isn't it! Quite good! I might have another go after we stop!"

Henderson chuckled and nodded. "Yes, I think we all will, Murray."

A short while later, Alice recognized the small, crooked, shamble of an A-framed shack that served as the Light House. She shook her head, wondering how it was so much bigger on the inside.

It was no surprise to her that Caraway, the old man who kept the light at the Light House, was already outside, flagging them down. Diovalo landed precariously on the biggest patch of ground near the mountain peak, where the Light House stood. There was hardly enough room for both of his feet, let alone any other part of him.

"What took you so long?" Caraway asked, hobbling over and reaching a hand out to help Henderson and Alice down from the dragon. "I was 'specting you a while ago. Guess you got hung up in the Mistlands."

He rubbed his palms against the well-worn front of his multi-pocketed vest and peered out at them with his brilliant blue eyes from beneath big, bushy white eyebrows.

"If you knew why we were delayed, then why are you bothering to ask?" Alice's mouth twitched in annoyance.

Caraway shrugged. "Don't plan on staying too long. I'm not going to go with you."

"We haven't even asked you yet!" Alice frowned sharply at him.

"I already knows. I knows what the light knows, I sees what the light sees, and I knows why you're here. I'm not going."

Murray rambled past Marlowe and Chippa, and reached his hand out to Caraway.

"Ah! Another old timer! Good to meet you, sir! Are you the head gardener here for Hyde Park? I'll tell you, that's one fine garden house you've got there, and you're doing a bang up job here in the park! A bang up job! Lots of changes, but the place has never looked so good!

Caraway snorted and a chuckle escaped him. "Thank you, sir. You must be Murray."

"I am! Did Alice tell you? She's a good lady, that Alice." Murray nodded.

Alice smiled wryly and leaned closer to Murray.

"Murray, Caraway is the Light House Keeper."

Caraway furrowed his thick brows. "I keep the light, not the house."

Alice rolled her eyes and groaned. "Perhaps you shouldn't keep the house, at this point it might be more sanitary just to burn it down."

Murray's eyes widened in curiosity. "A light house keeper! Say! Do you happen to know Mr. Baxter? He used to run the North Foreland Lighthouse in Broadstairs, just east of Margate. Good man. Do anything in the world to help anyone. But I guess that's what lighthouse keepers do, isn't it? Bring light to those in the dark to keep everyone safe!"

Caraway tucked his chin and coughed quietly, looking away for a moment, pushing his hands down deep into his pants pockets. Slowly, he raised his eyes to Murray and gave him a nod.

"Good man, Mr. Baxter." He didn't quite meet Alice's steady gaze on him. "Oh all right. I suppose I can leave for just a bit."

Alice beamed with delight. "Caraway, you are our saving grace. I cannot tell you how much we need you or how much this means to me. Thank you."

He only shrugged his shoulders and gave his vest a serious patting down, checking to see if he needed to bring anything, not that there was any room left at all in his overstuffed pockets.

Bits of dust and particles puffed off of Caraway in small clouds, and a moment later, Alice couldn't help it; she sneezed three times. With each sneeze, a bolt of lightning streaked down from the clear blue sky and blasted the ground right at their feet.

Henderson, Marlowe, and Chippa nearly got hit before they managed to dodge out of the way of the first one. The second bolt almost struck Alice, but Henderson yanked her clear of it just in time. With one last sneeze, a final bolt hit the Light House and bounced off of it.

Alice saw it, and gave Caraway a pointed expression. "That's a clear sign if I ever saw one."

Caraway scowled at her. "Now, no more of that, Missy!"

Alice rolled her eyes and sighed. "I didn't do it on purpose."

Chippa slipped his paw into her hand and gave it a gentle squeeze. "You will learning eventually. Just like me."

Alice grinned and leaned down close to the Inkling, giving him a hug. "Yes, dear one. We will learn together." She reached into her pocket and pulled out a few ginger chews, handing them to Chippa.

Chippa chirped blissfully as he popped them into his mouth and savored them.

"At least start working on your aim." Caraway grumbled as he climbed onto Diovalo.

Alice lifted a brow. "Take a seat and I'll give it my best shot." She retorted. Henderson, Marlowe, and Diovalo chuckled as they lifted off of the mountaintop and soared northwestward to Siang.

CHAPTER SEVEN

MATTERS OF THE HEART

With fleet-footed steps, Jynx and Sophie made short work of their journey through the green forest, and at last they came to a place where a definitive line of demarcation changed the color of every natural thing around them to pure white.

The cats both paused, sharing a look of excitement before they stepped across the border.

"Lyria! The White Song Forest. I can't believe we made it!" Jynx sighed with relief.

"Montgomery!" Sophie thrilled beyond happiness.

"Ready Princess?" Jynx gave her a half smile.

"More than ready!" Sophie stepped across the boundary with Jynx, leaving the green trees and growth behind them. The moment both cats entered the magically protected realm, their entire bodies lost all color, and they became as white as everything around them, save for their eyes.

"You look good in white." Sophie teased Jynx.

"Thanks, I prefer being a black cat. It's the fashion that never goes out of style. Little black dress, little black cat, little black bag. You can't argue with perfection." Jynx gave Sophie a sidelong smile.

"You could not be further from being a little black cat right now."

"This is merely a brief intermission."

"Can it really be my oldest friend? Sophie! And Jynx as well!" A deep and pleasant voice caught Sophie and Jynx by surprise, and they stopped short for a moment as a big, white cat with a bit of shaggy hair at his chin and over his green eyes bounded up the path to them. He was a grandpa cat with the energy and liveliness of a kitten.

Sophie cried out with pure joy, and even Jynx beamed with love as Montgomery reached them and nuzzled them both.

"It's so wonderful to see you!" He purred loudly, shaking the trees and leaves around them some.

"You look great!" Sophie walked around him, curling her tail across his body as she came back to face him.

"I am a guardian of the White Song Forest now, and I love it. I miss you all terribly, but for all my time here, this is such a good life with the fairies!" Montgomery looked from Sophie to Jynx and back again.

"What do you mean all your time here?" Sophie puzzled. "It's only been two days!"

"No, dear one. Remember that time passes very differently in Corevé. It's been much longer for me. But tell me, what brings you back, and where are the others? Is Alice all right?"

"Yes, Alice has never been better." Jynx answered, happy to see her old friend as well. "We're here because Diovalo needed Alice's help. All of his kind; the fire dragons of Siang, have been taken by the evil sorceress Baliste. We came back to Corevé to help rescue them."

"There's more though!" Sophie chimed in. "Eddie came with us this time, and the head of the earth dragons stole him away! We have to rescue him!"

"Oh no, that's awful! Our young master Eddie? Poor thing. I hope he's not too frightened." Montgomery was deeply troubled by the news. "If anyone can save him, it's Alice."

"That's true, but we came here to ask the fairies for help. We know we're heading into a battle against Baliste, and we can't do it alone. We need numbers and power, and the fairies have that." Jynx told him earnestly.

Montgomery turned quickly and spoke over his shoulder. "Come with me. I will take you to the Fairy Queen. We have no time to lose!"

The three of them streaked through the peaceful forest like ghosts, slipping in and out of trees, and leaping over bushes.

They reached the center of the White Song Forest, which was not white, but was instead, like the outside world, full of color and magic. The barrier ring of the White Song Forest around the fairy kingdom kept evil at bay, for if anyone without good intent tried to cross into it, they would be blocked, unable to enter.

Montgomery's coat returned to its pretty sea blue with sea green circles and spots here and there. Both Jynx and Sophie regained their magical coats as well when they entered the large circle of the fairy kingdom.

He called out in a strange language; his voice soft and melodic, and then he sat to wait. Sophie and Jynx sat with him.

Moments later, a beautiful fairy at about six or seven inches tall and just a little bigger than those flying around her, came to them with a slightly smaller fairy at her side, who was armed with a bow and a quiver of arrows on his back.

All three of the cats bowed low. Sophie beamed with delight. When she had last seen the Fairy Queen, the fairy had gifted her with a star flower garland that had saved Montgomery when he needed it most. She had been entranced with the little queen right from the start.

"Your majesty, these are my sisters, Sophie, and Jynx. They've visited here once before when we all came to see the Fairy Sway." He turned to the cats. "Sophie, Jynx, this is Diantha, queen of the fairies, and Jak, the head of the guard."

"How lovely to see you again. I remember you. It's an honor to have you in our circle once more." The queen looked sincerely pleased.

Jynx smiled, loving the Fairy Queen's dark chocolate skin which gave off a honeyed glow, and almost illuminated her golden hair.

"Your majesty," Jynx began warmly, "if I may, we've come here seeking your help. The fire dragons have been taken from Siang by Baliste. We have come to rescue them, and we know there will be a battle when we do. We're here to ask for your help. We need the might of the fairies if we ever hope to win, and free the captured dragons."

Queen Diantha nodded. "I am aware of what has been happening, and Baliste is indeed an evil force that must be stopped, but I do not want to involve the fairies unless it's unavoidable. I want to protect my own. We cannot join you in your battle."

Jynx and Sophie were crestfallen, and Montgomery spoke up immediately. "Your majesty, am I not now one of your own as well? I gave my life for my family, and for this entire world. Corevé would not even exist right now if I had not given of myself for the greater good. You know that better than anyone. It was you who brought me to live within this magical place when I drew my last breath in the outside world. How can you say that only the fairies are your own? Are we not all one? Every living thing in this world? Are we not all dependent upon each other, living a symbiotic life? What affects even one of us, affects all of us at some point.

"There are no barriers or disconnects between the fairies and the dragons or the Inklings, or any other kind of creature in this world. We all exist with each other in one place. I did not give my life to save my family and this whole world so that the evil sorceress could come along behind me and destroy it. Her evil will eat away at it, decaying it until it is nothing left but a corpse. We must all come together and fight back against it to keep our world good and strong. Please, your majesty, I implore you. Help them. Help all of Corevé. How long will it be before Baliste is at the edge of the forest here? This is your chance to make a difference before it gets worse. Do not miss the opportunity to save us all."

Queen Diantha sighed heavily and nodded. "Montgomery, you are very wise. I will commit to the cause. I can see now that we truly have no choice. It is a matter of the utmost importance."

Diantha turned to Jak. "Ready all of our warriors. We are heading into battle immediately."

"Yes, my queen." Jak bowed to her and almost vanished, he flew away so fast.

It seemed only moments later that a massive army of fairies was assembled and ready to go. Diantha turned to Jynx and Sophie.

"Where are we going?"

"We need to go back to the beach at Siang." Jynx answered.

Diantha moved her wooden twig wand through the air, and created a shimmering portal for them to walk through.

Sophie nuzzled Montgomery. "Are you coming with us?"

He dropped his head a little. "No, I cannot ever leave this place, or I will die. The fairy magic here is the only reason I'm still alive."

Sophie swallowed hard and closed her eyes. "Will you remember me?"

"Always." He answered quietly. "How could I ever forget my best friend?"

Sophie lifted her head and met his eyes. "Do scars hold us fast to the past?"

"Only if we let them. Hold on to all of the good we had, and let go of the pain. The price of loss is loneliness, as well as emptiness, bitterness, and above all, tremendous weight. The weight of loss can sometimes seem to be too great to bear, but you do not bear it alone, and that makes it much easier to carry."

Jynx agreed, giving Sophie a nudge. "We hold on to those we've lost by keeping them in our memories and hearts, carrying them safely there, where they live on within us. You must remember that we were always going to say goodbye at some point, from the moment we said hello."

"Will I ever see you again?" Sophie grew teary eyed and her breath shortened.

"I don't know, but you will be in my heart forever." Montgomery nuzzled her once more. "Be safe, and be well. Give my love to the family."

"We will." Jynx replied quietly. "Come on, Sophie, it's time to go."

"But... I can't!" She stood stock still.

Montgomery gave her an understanding look. "I'll leave first. It'll be easier that way."

He turned and walked into the White Song Forest, and his coat became pure white again. Sophie watched him go, waiting for him to turn and look back at her, to flash his green eyes at her just one more time, but he disappeared behind a tree, and was gone.

"No!" Sophie cried out desperately, reaching her paw toward him. She knew that if she ran into the forest, she might find him again. Jynx nudged her gently.

"You're not alone. Come on, it's time to go. Our family needs us."

Sophie lowered her eyes and dropped her head, walking at Jynx's side through the portal as they followed the fairies to Siang.

In the span of a breath, the earthy feel of the forest beneath their paws became soft sand, and when Sophie looked back over her shoulder, all she could see was beach.

A great black bird shot out of the sky above, carrying Oscar and Ali, who had a tight grip on Piper. The bird set them gently in the sand, and then landed; its wings vibrant with ripples of silvery electric light.

Oscar raced to them and pounced on Jynx. "You're here! Oh thank goodness, you're here! We were so worried about you!"

"Oh Oscar! I was worried sick about you too! Are you okay? I'm so relieved to see you!" She checked him over and shot him a dark look. "What happened to your whiskers?"

Oscar blinked. "My whiskers? Oh! Um... they got a little singed."

"That was my fault!" Piper admitted right away.

"Well, sort of." Oscar shrugged. "Really it was the hot air balloon, so it's okay."

"The *what?*" Jynx gasped.

"How did you get here? What *is* that thing?" Sophie stared at the great black creature behind them.

Piper spun excitedly in the air. "This is Keleon! He's our friend! He's a thunderbird and he makes lightning happen!"

Sophie took a step back and Jynx eyed the bird with interest. "That's pretty impressive! Now, what was that you said about a hot air balloon?"

"I made a hot air balloon after we lost you in the forest. I used branches and leaves, and Piper blew hot air into it for us, and we flew! It worked! I'm still surprised that it worked, but it did!"

"Yeah, until the wind blew us off course and we crash landed in the black sand, and then we met Keleon, and he brought us back here! He wants to help us fight too!" The story flooded from Piper like a rushing river.

"You crash landed?" Jynx worried over Oscar and began sniffing him again. "Are you hurt? Did you break anything?"

"I'm fine!" Oscar laughed.

"Flying in a balloon is different than riding on my mom's back. I want to make the biggest balloon ever so my mom can ride in it too and see what it's like!"

"Piper, you shouldn't hope for that, your mother is gone. I'm so sorry little one, but that's the way of it." Lord Japheth tried to talk some sense into the baby dragon. He and the other sea dragons had come onto the beach to meet with the fairies.

"I don't believe that. I'm never going to believe that." Piper shook her head. "Nope! Nope!"

Oscar looked from Jynx to Sophie and then back to Jynx again. "Where did you go? Why did you leave us?"

Jynx sighed. "We didn't leave, little one. We turned around and you were gone, so fast. It was like magic."

She paused and then narrowed her eyes. Ali met her gaze, and so did Sophie.

"Like magic… I wonder if that's what happened." Jynx growled low.

"Baliste? Mendax? Who knows." Sophie grumbled.

"But where did you go? What happened?" Oscar pressed, less concerned with the why than the what-about.

Sophie grinned. "*Well*," she began dramatically, "we went through the jungle and then slid down a horrible hill and I almost went off of a cliff, but Jynx saved me. Then, she had the brilliant idea to swing on a vine, if you can

~ 152 ~

believe that, over a massive, deep gorge to the other side, and it worked! We were regular Tarzans!"

Jynx groaned, knowing what was coming. Sophie rolled on with her story, as Oscar stared wide-eyed, hanging on every word.

"We made it to the other side safely and found Lyria. We got to talk to Montgomery, and we brought the fairies back with us!"

"Wow! Jynx, weren't you scared swinging over a big gorge?" Oscar asked breathlessly.

Jynx sighed. "It was terrifying."

Sophie jumped in. "It was, but Jynx was very brave."

Oscar smiled and leapt in the air with excitement. "You're home safe! Woohoo!"

Sophie and Jynx shared a secret smile.

Diovalo landed then, and Alice, along with Henderson, Marlowe, Chippa, Murray, and Caraway descended from him.

Murray took immediate notice of the fairies and stopped short. "Now... what in the world are those things? Am I losing my mind?" He rubbed his eyes.

Alice patted his shoulder. "No, Murray. Those are fireflies."

Murray laughed heartily. "Oh of course! I don't know what I was thinking!"

Alice went to her cats, where Bailey and Tao, as well as Cherie had joined everyone.

"I see the fairies have joined us! That's wonderful! And you're all here and safe. That's such a relief! I've been so worried about all of you!"

She hugged them all closely and frowned when she saw Oscar's singed whiskers. "Hmm. You'll have to tell me about that later."

"Yes, mom." Oscar laughed softly.

Ali held her hand up to their newest guest. "This is Keleon. He's a thunderbird. He's here to help us fight Baliste."

Diovalo drew near to the bird. "My mother spoke of you to me. She held you in high regard. Welcome, and thank you for being here with us."

"It is my honor, great prince, and please accept my deepest sorrows for the loss of your mother. She was a good friend, and I was lucky to know her."

"I appreciate that." Diovalo replied. "We can do her no greater service than to save the fire dragons she spent her life caring for, and I know she would be grateful that you are here to help."

"I could be in no other place while this necessity exists. My allegiance is to you both." Keleon bowed to Diovalo.

"Thank you, my friend. Now we have a pressing and urgent matter at hand. Alice's grandson was taken captive by Lord Malevor, and we must rescue him."

Keleon cocked his head to one side and studied Mrs. Perivale.

"Alice? *The* Alice? The one from the prophecy of the mystics?"

"Just so." Diovalo answered proudly.

"I'm honored to meet you. If I may be of any help at all in the recovery of your grandson, I am at your service." The thunderbird offered sincerely.

"Thank you, Keleon. It's very nice to meet you, too." Alice gave him a smile. "I'm glad you're here with us. The biggest help that you could be right now would be to remain with Diovalo and make sure that nothing evil gets near him."

"I would be glad to do that." Keleon replied as he spread his wings and shook them out. Electric threads quivered rapidly over his feathers.

"Thank you. Now, let's get this rescue organized." Alice turned to Diovalo and looked him squarely in his bright, jeweled eyes. "You are to remain outside, here on the beach with the sea dragons, Keleon, and the fairies. If anyone untoward shows up, you go straight into the air. We are taking no chances in losing you. Right?"

It wasn't a question as much as it was a crystal clear order.

"Yes, I will do that," Diovalo gave her a smile, "if you promise to be extremely careful while you're down there. I don't want anything happening to you either."

"Thank you, dear one. I'll be just fine. Now, Cherie…" She turned to Cherie who was close by.

"Yes? How can I help?"

"Please look after Murray. If you feed him, it will distract him while we slip off."

Cherie grinned. "I'm already on it. I've had a big feast prepared, and it's a lucky thing, because now I have an army to feed!" She looked absolutely delighted about it.

Alice waved to Caraway, Henderson, Chippa, Ali, Piper, and the cats. "It's time to go get Eddie."

She led them past the beach and into the trees at its edge, until they came to the first low foothill, where Lord

Malevor and Liceverous had left a gaping hole in the ground.

"In we go." Alice intoned with deep anger. "My grandson is in there somewhere waiting for me."

They entered the great tunnel into darkness.

Chapter Eight

Alice to the Rescue

"Well, they certainly made a mess of this place." Sophie tutted disapprovingly. The massive hole that Lord Malevor had left in the hillside was skirted with torn shrubbery, scattered leaves, and broken trees.

"They were more concerned with stealing my grandson than making a clean getaway." Alice scowled darkly as the group trekked along the steep tunnel into the earth.

As they traveled down the sloping grade, Alice kept her hand on Marlowe's shoulder. She studied the freshly dug wall of the hole, and as she spoke, her words bounced off the dirt and returned to her.

"This is only one tunnel. Perhaps it might not be so difficult to find Eddie after all. I thought it would be trickier."

"I hope he's not too far ahead, it's awful in here. Poor Eddie. I can't stand to think of him in this place." Bailey worried in a mournful tone.

"It's getting dark in here!" Oscar murmured, looking around wide-eyed.

"I don't like the dark," Piper replied quietly, though everyone heard her in the subterranean silence, "you can't ever really see what's hiding in it."

For a few minutes, the light from the world outside followed them, but after one turn, it was gone, and they found themselves in absolute darkness.

Piper cried out and flew to Oscar's shoulders, settling there.

"It's too dark. We can't go on if we can't see." Marlowe peered as far as possible but could detect nothing.

"I've got it. I s'pose this is why I was brought along in the first place." Caraway lifted his hands, and light as warm and brilliant as the sun shone forth from them. He turned his hands this way and that, as if he was shaping the light and sculpting it. When he was done, there was a four foot ring of light in his hands, almost like a halo.

"It only takes a little flicker of light to erase darkness." Caraway smiled as he gave it a gentle lift, and it floated up above them, hovering overhead, spilling light everywhere, and illuminating a scene that stole away the breath of the entire group.

"I think it just got trickier." Tao sighed.

They were standing at the precipice of a great cavern; a massive hall that even Diovalo would have fit into. From it, in seemingly every direction, dozens of tunnels opened up into more darkness.

"This is unimaginable!" Alice covered her mouth with both of her hands.

"It's a maze." Jynx stared, aghast. "A giant labyrinth. I wonder if all those tunnels break off into more tunnels, and maybe those tunnels do the same as well. How could anyone find their way in or out of here?"

"I bet the big tunnels are the ones they used to steal the fire dragons through." Oscar considered, eyeing the larger holes.

"I bet you're right." Jynx agreed with him.

"How are we ever going to find Eddie in all this?" Alice choked back the fear that rose in her throat.

"EDDIE!" She called out as loudly as she could.

The word had barely left her when everyone else in the group began yelling for him as well. All of them called out as loudly as they could, over and over, until Alice held her hands up.

"Wait! Wait! We can't hear him answering us if we're still yelling. If he's within earshot, he'll have heard us."

Her heart raced and she listened harder than she ever had in her life. Only the distant echoes of their voices reverberated back to them, taunting her with their hollowness.

"Oh no..." Alice clutched her hand to her heart. "How are we ever going to find him in all this! There's no way to know where he is!"

Tears burned her eyes, and her throat tightened as she lost her breath. Turning to Marlowe, she slumped against him weakly, and a sob finally escaped her.

Chippa patted her leg with a comforting hug. Henderson held out a handkerchief to her, and Marlowe rubbed his cheek against her head.

Alice dabbed at her eyes and her nose, and then took a deep breath and lifted her face.

"No. NO. I am not giving up on Eddie just because this seems impossible. It's the most overwhelming thing I've ever seen, but I know he's in here somewhere, and we are not going to give up until we find him!"

She drew in a shaky breath and faced her family. "There are several of us here. We're just going to have to split up. Each one of us will take a tunnel and search, but if the tunnel breaks off into other tunnels, we turn around and come back to this central lair. We check all the tunnels until we find him, and we meet back here in the center. I realize that it might take a while, but it's the only way we'll ever find him."

"It would take a lifetime." A deep voice sounded nearby.

They all turned with a start and jumped at the sight of two earth dragons not twenty feet from them.

"I didn't even hear them come up, did you?" Bailey murmured to Jynx and Tao.

"I didn't hear a sound." Sophie answered.

"Get back!" Alice shouted at them bitterly, shoving her hand into her bag and yanking out two sharp knitting needles.

The cats all hissed and growled loudly, arching their backs as their fur went on end. "We are ready to fight you right here and now! Unless you want more trouble than you can handle, you'd better tell me where my grandson is right this minute! Do you hear me!"

* * *

Cherie was mildly disappointed to discover that the food she had prepared wasn't fairy or sea dragon fare, but she was pleased that Diovalo and Keleon ate heartily of it.

The fairies were talking with Callidus, Keres, and Galiphes, as well as several other sea dragons, while Keleon and Diovalo spoke of many things, when a sharp cry cut through the air, followed by a rhythmic thumping that beat out from the hills in the jungle.

Everyone on the beach turned their heads, and were stunned to see an enormous flock of Quiri birds diving from the sky like hailstones; their razor sharp claws stretched out before them, ready for attack.

From the trees, goblins and trolls spilled forth in a river, running with their weapons held high, straight for the camp.

Diovalo roared, and immediately blasted the frontline of trolls and goblins with an explosion of flames, turning them to charcoal in seconds, but the Quiri birds had already reached the camp, and the fairies and sea dragons were fighting them off. Several of the Quiri birds went straight for Diovalo.

Keleon, who was much bigger than the Quiri birds, turned to Diovalo as he launched into the air. "Go the sea. You can swim underwater for a while. It's the only safe place. You cannot be captured there!"

"I will not go and leave all of you to fight without me!" Diovalo argued resolutely.

"You promised Alice that you would leave if anyone untoward showed up. Keep your promise! You will do us no good if you are captured before we can fight Baliste! Into the sea with you! GO!" Keleon ordered.

Diovalo gave him a disgruntled nod. "You are right. I will go, this time." With that, he shot up into the air, where the Quiri birds almost blanketed him. With a mighty roar, and a blast of fire at them, he dove down into the depths of the rolling green sea.

Cherie grabbed a flaming branch from the fire she had been cooking on and swung it wildly at the goblins who bore down on her.

Ali followed suit and snatched a burning branch out for herself, brandishing it furiously at anything that came near her.

Faster than the blink of an eye, the fairies shot arrow after arrow at their attackers, and each arrow that hit a troll or goblin instantly transformed them into a flower that dropped to the sand.

Keleon rose high and spread his wings, beating them powerfully against the air. Thunder sounded all around him, and electricity crackled in every direction. His black wings went ablaze with silver streaks, and suddenly he threw his head back and a deafening shriek drowned out the entire battle.

In an explosion of energy and an earthshaking boom, the great thunderbird blasted electricity outward from his body in a sphere of blue and silver light, disintegrating every Quiri bird that wasn't on the ground.

* * *

The earth dragon who had spoken first, spoke again with a calm and steady voice. "Forgive me, Alice. We didn't mean to surprise you. I am Rhyoden, and this is Andessai. As you can see, we are earth dragons, and you have every right and reason to be furious with us, but we want to help you. We no longer wish to follow Lord Malevor. He's turned his back on the dragon ways, and we want no part of that. He became a traitor when he took the fire dragons to Baliste. He has asked us to join him in serving her. Neither of us is willing to do it. We wish to serve Diovalo. He is the true and rightful king, and it should be no other way. He is the only one of us descended from the sacred dragon lineage. Lord Malevor, Liceverous, and the earth dragons who have followed them are despicable traitors. If you will allow us, we will be more than happy to take you to your grandson."

Alice gritted her teeth. "How can I possibly trust you? It was earth dragons who took him in the first place!"

The cats around her continued to growl deeply and hiss sharp warnings at the beasts. Chippa's paws were in the air, ready for a fight, should it come to it, and Henderson had his closed umbrella pointed straight at them.

Rhyoden lowered his head. "We know where they are keeping the boy. You will never find him if you look on your own. It would take more than your whole lifetime to get through even half of these tunnels. Only an earth dragon would know how to get there. We've been watching from the shadows. Lord Malevor has left him alone with Liceverous and gone to see Baliste. Liceverous has been ordered to capture Diovalo when he comes to rescue the boy. Lord Malevor would require the work of the capture to be done by Liceverous, but he would take all the glory for it himself."

Andessai, the other dragon, finally spoke. "If we hurry, we can get there before Lord Malevor returns. I'll tell Liceverous that Diovalo went instead to the fortress, thinking they took the boy there, and was captured. I'll say that Baliste and Lord Malevor wish to see him, to honor him for what he's done in his role in fooling Diovalo. I'll say that he is to be honored above all dragons, and I am to remain behind and guard the boy. He will believe me. He will be hungry for the recognition and glory, himself. When Liceverous leaves, I will bring the boy to you."

Alice bit at her lip. She knew that there was probably no other realistic chance of her finding Eddie on her own without their help, though she still wasn't certain that she could trust them.

"And what do you want in return?" She eyed them both suspiciously.

Rhyoden and Andessai gazed at her. "We wish to become part of Diovalo's army. We want nothing to do with Lord Malevor any longer." Andessai answered.

Rhyoden gave Alice a kind of mischievous smile. "Besides, if the two of us are kept hidden, we could be used as a secret weapon if needed. No one following Lord Malevor would doubt us, because none of the other earth dragons would know we've changed allegiances."

With a heavy sigh, Alice turned and gazed at the great lair and all the tunnels. Her family and friends watched her and waited.

"We have no other choice." She admitted. "We would never be able to find Eddie in this alone."

Marlowe nudged her gently. "We've tried to pick up his scent and it's nowhere here. There is no trace of him that we can detect."

Alice nodded as she faced the two earth dragons again. "Very well. Take us to my grandson, and I will take you to Diovalo."

Chippa slipped is paw into her hand. "It is a good choice."

Rhyoden took the lead with Alice and all her company right behind him. Andessai followed them, and Jynx kept looking back over her shoulder to watch her.

They headed along a twisting path, going from one tunnel to the next, to the next after that; every which way, in circles and zig zags, and all the while Caraway kept the light with them.

At long last they finally came to a stop, and Rhyoden turned to Alice. "This is where we must remain. If we go any further, Liceverous will detect you. I will stay with you to guard you should any other earth dragons come, while Andessai goes to Liceverous to tell the lie. We will wait here for her to return with your child."

He settled himself in the big tunnel, and Andessai passed them with a look over her shoulder at Alice. "I will return as soon as I can."

Though she didn't like it, Alice knew it was the only way. "Please hurry, and please be very careful with him."

"Oh my honor." Andessai replied.

Silence engulfed the group as they waited, and the only sounds that could be heard were breathing and the soft continuous thump of the dragon's heartbeat.

Time felt to Alice as if it wasn't moving at all, and she tried to be patient, thinking of good memories with Eddie, rather than worrying about where he was or what kind of shape he might be in.

Caraway shuffled around in boredom, and as he passed Alice, his feet stirred up some of the dust in the old tunnel they were in.

Alice coughed, and the moment she did, icicles erupted all over the dirt walls around them. Everyone cried out in surprise and huddled closer together for a moment.

"I'm sorry! I think that was me." Alice shook her head as she rolled her eyes.

"Oh! So pretty!" Piper fluttered close to the walls that were covered in them. "What are they?"

Oscar took a good look too. "I don't know! I've never seen anything like them before!"

"Those are icicles, my darlings." Alice answered with the hint of a smile. "They form when it's very cold outside. Oscar, you will see them in London when winter comes."

"But it's not cold in here." Piper blinked in confusion.

"Alice is learning." Chippa told them with a gentle smile as he waved his paw through the air. The icicles disappeared. Piper and Oscar moaned in disappointment.

"Awe. I wanted to play with those." Oscar pouted a little.

Chippa moved his paw again, and a small stand of icicles appeared before Piper and Oscar.

"These are the best!' Piper bounced gleefully.

"How is it that you can make things like this?" Rhyoden asked Alice quietly.

"I was gifted powers over the elements by the Inklings. I just haven't quite figured out how they work yet." Alice shrugged.

"She will be very good with them when she is learning how to use them right." Chippa assured Rhyoden. "We all starts out not knowing."

"That is the same for dragons, and I believe, for all young ones. We all start out not knowing, and we learn as we go. There is no shame at all in that."

Alice gave Rhyoden a half-smile, but her focus was steady on the space in the tunnel behind him; the one that Andessai had disappeared down. It felt to her like years had passed.

The icicles melted, and Piper came to sit beside Alice, gazing up at her. "Are you afraid?"

Alice set her hand on Piper's head for a moment. "When I feel fear or despair, I always try to let it go. Right now we have much to gain and only a little to lose, so it's all up from here. Daylight always follows darkness, so we must look toward the coming light and focus on that."

"I couldn't have said it better." Caraway gave her a nod.

She said it as much to remind herself as she did to answer Piper's question. Even the cats began to grow restless and worry, sniffing the air for any sign of Eddie and Andessai, but there was nothing.

"This is taking longer than it should." Jynx grumbled. "Eddie had better be okay."

"I ask you for patience, please. We are not close to the place where the boy is being kept. I did not want any chance of Liceverous discovering that you were here. Andessai had a long way to go, and if I'm not much mistaken, I believe I can hear her coming back now."

Alice jumped to her feet, gripping her black bag tightly in her hands as she held her breath, waiting to see any sign of the dragon or Eddie. At long last, they appeared, and Andessai, who had been carrying the boy, set him gently on the ground.

"GRANDMA! I knew you would come for me! I just knew it!" Eddie ran to his grandmother and Alice embraced him tightly, as her heart pounded and tears rolled out of her eyes and down her soft, full cheeks.

"Eddie! Thank goodness you're safe! Thank goodness. I'm so sorry that you were taken. Are you all right?"

She held him at arm's length for just a moment and gave him a quick glancing over, and then pulled him into another hug as the cats all drew near and took turns nuzzling his back.

"We're so glad to see you! Oh it was awful watching you be taken like that!" Bailey purred loudly.

"Did they hurt you? Did they mistreat you at all?" Tao worried, sniffing at him and giving him a gentle nudge.

"He's fine, aren't you darling?" Alice finally stepped back from Eddie and took his hand in hers.

"I am. I'm just really, really glad to see all of you!" Eddie's gaze drifted from one cat to another, from Henderson to Chippa, and then it came to stop on Caraway.

"Hello! Who are you?" He asked curiously.

Alice beamed. "This is our friend Caraway. He is the keeper of the light at the Light House. This halo glowing above us is something he created so that we could find our way in the dark to get to you."

"Hello, Mr. Caraway, sir. Thank you for coming and helping my family find me." Eddie spoke gratefully as he shook Caraway's hand. The old man nodded and looked away.

"Well, I haven't gotten out of the house for a while, so it was a good time to go." He sniffed and suddenly took a great interest in the dirt wall at his side.

"I never want to be in the pitch dark again." Eddie announced adamantly.

"Me neither." Caraway agreed.

"Thank you, Andessai and Rhyoden, for helping my grandma and my family find me." Eddie faced both of the earth dragons.

"It was our pleasure to help. We're just so sorry that you were taken in the first place. Everything that Lord Malevor has done of late has been more than we are willing to stand." Andessai answered him.

Rhyoden took the lead. "Let's go, before anyone finds us. It wouldn't go well if they did."

The company trailed back up through the winding, twisting passages, and Alice realized once more just how lucky she was that the two earth dragons had come to help her. She knew that she never would have found Eddie if they hadn't.

When they finally reached the hole that emptied out into the trees on the beach, they were stunned to discover that they were heading straight into a battle.

"Oh my stars and whiskers!" Alice exclaimed in a panic, staring with the rest of her group at the chaos.

"What happened?" Marlowe growled.

"Where's Diovalo?" Alice gasped, searching the beach and skies for him. He was nowhere to be seen.

"Let's go!" Jynx shouted, and the cats followed her as Henderson, Alice, Eddie, and the earth dragons launched themselves toward the battlefield.

They hadn't gone far when Alice stopped short and held Eddie back. "Oh no. You're not going into that. You stay right here behind this tree and make sure no one sees you. I will not have you in a fight like that."

Eddie frowned. "I could help! I could fight them! You need me!"

"I *do* need you," Alice agreed, "which is exactly why you're going to stay right here and remain safe. No but's."

Eddie pouted, but he slipped behind the tree and watched as Alice whipped her knitting needles out of her bag and charged into the action.

Oscar and Piper fought side by side, as Oscar slashed with his claws and Piper bit anyone who came to attack them. She blasted fire at those she couldn't reach to bite.

Galiphes and Callidus dove for the earth dragons, ready to tear them to pieces, but Alice just barely managed to get in front of the earth dragons in time and stop them.

"NO! WAIT! They helped us! They are here to serve Diovalo! Do not harm them!"

Galiphes shook his wild mane and snorted. "If you are here to help, then help!"

"What *are* these things?" Bailey slashed his claws through one of the goblins as it came for him.

"They are trolls and goblins." Keres called out over her shoulder as she fought off three trolls.

Just then a big troll pinned Tao on her back and raised his club to bash her. Bailey arched his back and roared at the troll. It turned to face him, and Bailey vaulted straight at it, slamming into its chest and crushing it to the ground. In seconds, the troll was defeated.

Tao leapt to her feet, breathless and wide-eyed. "Thank you! Goodness, Bailey, I never knew you had that in you!"

Bailey beamed, lifting his chin. "Girl, I am *fierce* when I have to be!"

They bolted back into the melee.

With all the reinforcements that came from the company that had been in the tunnels, the trolls, goblins, and few remaining Quiri birds were beaten back. They ran from the fight, disappearing into the hills and skies.

"We'll clean up the beach." Rhyoden offered. "It's the least we could do."

Andessai agreed, and the two of them got to work.

"Where did all the flowers come from?" Sophie asked, sniffing at them.

"Fairy arrows. That's what happens to the bag guys when they get hit." Ali answered. "I have to say, I really like their style."

Chippa got to work healing everyone who was wounded, and Lord Japheth dove into the sea to go get Diovalo.

Alice plopped down on one of the logs and heaved a great sigh. "My goodness. What a day."

"Tea, Madame?" Henderson handed her a cup with a warm brew in it and her shoulders sank in gratitude as she smiled up at him and chuckled.

"Henderson, what would I ever do without you?"

"Let's never find out." He smiled in return.

Eddie came hurrying to his grandmother from his place behind the tree, gasping for breath and speaking in a rush of excitement. "That was incredible! I wish I could have fought in it, but I'm so glad that we won!"

"We did win indeed, but now there is quite a bit to talk about." Alice replied, sipping her tea as Ali, Henderson, Caraway, and Cherie sat to join them.

Alice suddenly gasped and searched all the faces coming to gather around her. "Oh my goodness gracious! Where's Murray?"

Cherie stood up and peered over Alice's hat. "He's still sleeping in his tent. I suggested he have a nap after I fed him, and wouldn't you know, he slept right through the whole battle."

Alice laughed until there were tears at the corners of her eyes. Lord Japheth and the other sea dragons came with Diovalo to the fire where everyone was gathered.

Diovalo took in the two earth dragons, who both bowed low to the ground before him.

"It is my understanding that you have both left Lord Malevor and wish to join this company in a fight against him. Is this true?"

Rhyoden rose and answered. "Yes, my prince. We will never serve Lord Malevor again. Our allegiance is to you, and you alone. You are the rightful king of the dragons."

"Thank you. Your decision shows me a great deal about you. Now, we must discuss what is to be done. Can you tell us exactly where the captured fire dragons have been taken?"

Andessai shook her head. "No, my prince. That information was given only to Lord Malevor and Liceverous."

Diovalo grew silent and stared into the fire; his jeweled eyes reflecting its bright, dancing lights. At long last, he spoke.

"Then there is only one way forward. I must give myself up to Baliste and allow her to capture me."

Alice nearly dropped her teacup and her mouth fell open. "What? NO! I absolutely forbid it! You can't go giving yourself up to her! Look at this army that we've assembled to rescue the fire dragons! We're going to fight her, not help her!"

Diovalo drew in a deep breath and his voice left no room for argument. "It is the only way. If I am captured, I can find the other dragons and help to set them free. I must be the bait. They want nothing so much as me, and it's a sacrifice that I must make. I am their prince, and any good leader should make sacrifices for those they lead."

His words rang true over the camp, and Alice gazed at him with pride and admiration.

"You'd do it anyway, even if you weren't the prince."

Diovalo nodded slightly. "Indeed, I would."

Alice set her teacup aside and raised her voice. "Then we need to come up with an unbeatable plan. We simply cannot fail."

CHAPTER NINE

THE CALM BEFORE THE STORM

"If we are going into battle, then you are our general, Alice." Diovalo stated firmly.

She rose from her seat on the log and began to pace, tapping her finger against her chin in deep thought as all eyes stayed on her.

"We know that the fortress, Mordauz, is at the top of Mount Jaiath, which is the highest mountain in Corevé. I know that our best plan of attack would be one of surprise. If our Diovalo is going to give himself up, Baliste and her hench-things cannot know that we are involved or even present. If it's a high mountain, there will be a timberline."

Piper fluttered her wings. "What's a timberline?"

Alice paused in her step and thoughts to look over at the baby dragon. "It's a line near a mountaintop where the trees stop growing, leaving the top of the mountain bare. Now, if we go to the inner edge of the timberline, where we are hidden by the trees, we can watch the fortress from afar and see where Diovalo is taken. Then, we can swoop in and rescue him and the other fire dragons. It will be a complete surprise, and Baliste won't be expecting it at all."

Queen Diantha hovered not far from Alice, and though she was small, her voice sounded out over the entire group.

"I will create a portal for the whole army here to go through at a safe place within the trees below the timberline. We will remain unseen."

"Oh good, thank you! That'll save us the hike, and I will have enough energy to fight!" Alice smirked.

She was about to continue when a loud noise drew the attention of everyone gathered, and they all turned toward the tents at the far side of the camp.

"Goodness! Murray snores quite loudly." Alice lowered a brow, and then continued.

"We need to know who we'll be facing. What kind of defense does Baliste have?"

"It's a pretty good bet that the Quiri birds, along with the goblins and trolls were hers." The firelight danced in Marlowe's golden eyes as he sat facing the fire; his mind on the battle."

"She has some earth dragons." Rhyoden added somberly.

Chippa held up his paw. "I am thinks I should better bring some more Inklings in to help fight when we doesn't know what we are fighting."

Alice gave him a smile. "That's a very good idea. Thank you Chippa. Do you think they will come?"

Chippa hopped off of the log where he'd been sitting and waddled a few steps away from it. "It is not a choice." He moved his paw through the air and created a shimmering portal, and a moment later he had stepped through it and disappeared.

Eddie, who was sitting with Piper and Oscar, leapt to his feet. "Grandma! You know I'm good at chess!"

Alice's eyes twinkled, but she groaned. "Yes, you're quite good."

"I keep thinking of this like a chess game. It's all about strategy. About where to move the pieces and when. I think that we should send these two earth dragons in as decoys, because the opposition won't know what's happening. They'll think these two are still on their side. In fact, they could turn Diovalo in! Then the earth dragons could get close to the captured dragons, and send a signal to the rest of us who are hiding so we know when it's time to attack! Maybe they can even take out the guards, if possible. Then the rest of the army will come in and help. We sneak our Chess Queen, and that's you, grandma, into enemy territory before they know what's happening!"

"Bravo, darling! That's a wonderful plan! Then we can send in the fairies and the Inklings on the ground. As soon as the dragons are released, they'll be fire in the sky for us! We can all circle in from an outside perimeter, trapping all the baddies and then take them down!"

"What's chess?" Piper asked brightly, growing excited about the plan.

Alice considered her answer thoughtfully. "It's a war game between two people; two different sides. They have to outsmart each other, and the cleverest one wins."

"Oh, that's good! I like your chess plan, Eddie!" Piper grinned at her friend.

Eddie raked his hand through his hair and sank down beside her. "Thanks! I just never thought I'd be playing chess live!"

Chippa reappeared suddenly, and with him were Bayless Grand Mari, the head Inkling warrior Jika, Oppa

Mari their healer, and Channa Mari, who looked quite pleased to be along for the endeavor.

"Oh hello!" Alice greeted them with a smile. "Thank you so much for coming. You'll all be such a big help!"

Bayless Grand Mari gave her a slight bow. "Chippa 'es telling what 'es happening, and we know you needs our help to win."

"We do indeed." Alice agreed.

"Speaking of helping," Lord Japheth addressed the gathering, "the sea dragons wish to fight alongside you, but there is one problem."

"You can't be out of the ocean for very long." Ali frowned sadly.

"Definitely not long enough to be effective in a land battle so far from the water." He replied.

Alice began pacing again and then drove her finger up into the air. "Ah ha! I've got it! What if I try to create a saltwater bubble for you to stay inside that is the inverse of Chippa's air bubble?"

Lord Japheth frowned in confusion. "Could you explain please?"

Marlowe smiled. "Last time we were in Corevé, we floated on leaves through an underground river. The water element went out of control and the tunnel we were riding through began to flood. We would have drowned, but Chippa came up with an idea; a way to save us. He created a long air bubble within the water, and we stayed safe inside it until we came out of the tunnel. I think Alice means to create the opposite of a long air bubble in water, by making a long water bubble in air for you to ride in safely."

Sophie groaned. "It was horrible! I nearly died!"

Jynx rolled her golden eyes. "Oh stop. That was after we were already out of the tunnel."

Bailey snickered. "She is the drama queen of the family."

"And what are you? The drama princess?" Sophie snapped back.

Bailey lifted his chin resolutely. "No, I'm the cuisine queen."

"Okay, that's enough." Alice leveled a stern look at them. "I think I'd like to give this a try. If you'll come with me, please." She led the sea dragons to the water's edge, and the rest of the company followed her to watch.

"Well, here goes!" Alice used her hands to try to guide the saltwater out of the sea. Slowly, some of it lifted; enough to fill a bathtub twice.

"Look! It's working!" She gushed happily, gradually drawing the water closer to Lord Japheth. Just as it was about to reach him, it crashed out of the air onto the sand.

Alice sighed and closed her eyes. "Am I *ever* going to get it figured out?"

Chippa waddled toward her with Oppa at his side. "We will helping you." He smiled. "It is tricksy."

Oppa patted her leg. "You try with us. We are all works together."

Side by side, the trio used their elemental Inkling powers to lift seawater into the air. Alice was giddy, she was so excited to see it happening.

"It's working!" She giggled.

"Keeping focus!" Oppa reminded her, and Alice concentrated harder.

Together they brought the water to the four sea dragons beside them, and all four were encapsulated in elongated seawater bubbles which floated in the air.

Oppa beamed proudly. "You is doing so good!" Then she addressed the dragons. "Bubbles is lasting until dragons go back into ocean. Wherever dragons moves, bubbles moves with them. You try." She waved at the sea dragons.

Keres took off like a shot in her bubble, racing around the camp as she floated in the air, but it was only moments before Galiphes, Callidus, and Lord Japheth joined her. They frolicked and played, learning how to maneuver their bubbles, and control their speed and direction.

"This is so much fun! Thank you!" Callidus poked her head out of her bubble and grinned at Oppa, Chippa, and Alice, before she ducked back inside it and took off again.

"They play more than dolphins do." Alice laughed. "I do love their high spirited ways!"

Oppa crossed her furry arms over her belly and gave Alice a big smile. "You is very impressing! This idea is genius!"

Alice shrugged. "It was Chippa's idea first! It's just the opposite of what he came up with."

Oppa patted them both. "Then you is both very clever."

"Thank you," Alice replied, "but I don't know if I'm ever going to be able to get a hold on my powers. It's quite frustrating sometimes."

Chippa took her hand. "You will. Comes in time. Just remember there is bad magic that is going right along with good magic. You is learning the good magic. If you keeps practicsaying, like I is, then you will get it. I is still learning, but I is doing much better. So is you too, soon."

Alice sighed. "I wish I could learn it all before our rescue in the morning. I know we could certainly use it, but I have no doubt that with all the help we have, we will be great together. Besides, worries are lighter with friends."

"This is true." Chippa agreed pleasantly.

"For now, though, we need to prepare. If we're going to fight and win, we're going to need some armor. If our battle with the goblins and trolls today taught us anything, it's that. I found some silk vines that are practically impenetrable. I'm going to knit together some chainmail sheaths. That will at least give us some leverage and some protection."

Alice sat at the fire with long sections of the silk vines, which were about the diameter of a fat pen, and she began kitting.

Bailey, who was cat-napping nearby, lifted his head and watched her bright-eyed. "Mom, will you please put some flowers on mine? It's sewing magic into armor if you pick the right flowers! And please make sure to accentuate my tail; it's my best feature!"

Alice giggled. "Yes, darling, I'll do that for you."

"Thank you mom. You're so good to us!" Bailey purred happily, and it rumbled through the air around them.

Eddie sat beside her and watched in fascination as her fingers flew. "Grandma, will you teach me?"

Alice beamed at him. "Yes, of course dear! I could use all the help that I can get! I brought extra needles. Here you go."

It took a few minutes, but Eddie figured out how to work the needles, and he was off; excited to be sharing a project with her that he had learned from her.

"Grandma, I wanted to tell you something. When I was in the tunnels, I remembered what you told me about being only a star away from each other. I was scared when I first went in, but after a while I closed my eyes and rubbed them, then I saw stars, dozens of them, and I felt so much closer to you. It made me feel brave, and then I realized that there was no reason to be afraid because Liceverous couldn't kill me. I was too valuable."

"You are such a smart young man, and I'm so proud of you!" Alice kissed his head. "You must always remember that I am never more than a star away, no matter what."

Eddie grinned and worked again on his knitting.

Chippa and Oppa sat with Alice as well, and Oppa studied Alice's work. "What is this that you is doing?"

Alice handed it to Oppa so she could see it. "I'm knitting. It's a form of weaving."

Oppa took two nearby sticks and using her magic, formed them into knitting needles. She sat beside Alice and watched and learned. When she had it figured out, she set the needles down.

"Now I is showing you how to be doing the same with magic." Oppa took Alice's needles from her and showed her how to move the silk vine through the air, weaving it into itself without even touching it.

Alice tried, and before she knew it, she had air-knitted the entire front of a sheath. "Well! Will you look at that? I finally got something magical figured out! Oh, this is so exciting! Thank you Oppa!"

Alice finished the sheath and then glanced over at Oppa, who was working on one as well. "You might want to take those knitting needles into battle with you. They do more than weave." She winked, and Oppa laughed.

When they had been air-knitting for a while, and Alice had gotten quite good at it, Alice stopped, and began rubbing her fingers and knuckles. With a sigh, she glanced up at Oppa.

"The only problem with knitting so much is that it makes my arthritis act up."

Oppa came to her and examined her hands closely, and then waddled off a short way and rooted through some of the greenery growing nearby. She returned with the leaves of a plant.

"Here. Eat this." She handed the leaves to Alice.

Alice only hesitated a moment as she glanced at them and then she tucked them into her mouth and chewed. They were sweet and soft. When she'd swallowed them, she laughed a little.

"Why did I just eat that?"

Oppa looked at Alice's hands. "Is they hurts now?"

Alice gasped as she held her hands up and moved her fingers. "Why no! They don't hurt at all now! Not a bit!"

Oppa grinned. "They is never hurts again. You is cured."

Alice's brows shot up. "Cured? Completely cured?"

Oppa nodded. "Yes, no more 'thritis."

Alice laughed loudly and let her head fall back. "Oh, how grateful I am! Thank you!"

Oppa only smiled and went back to work on her knitting.

Tao, who was sitting nearby watching, inclined her head some. "Oppa, could you tell us about the mystics? I've only heard a little, and I'm so curious about them!"

Oppa moved the vines through the air with her hands as she spoke. "The mystics happening in almost every race in Corevé. They is born special. Can seeing through mists of time to what will come. Highly respectable in this world."

Tao's eyes grew bright. "They're fascinating to me! I'd love to meet one and learn from them if I can. Do you know where any of them are?"

Oppa mused over the question. "They is in different places in Corevé."

"Then I will keep my eyes open for them. Thank you." Tao purred softly, and it rumbled the sand at Alice's feet.

Cherie came to them with a cup of hot tea in her hand.

"Here you are, Alice. I thought you could use this."

"Oh! You are an angel. I would love a cup of tea." She laughed for a moment and shook her head.

"What is it?" Cherie asked lightly.

"I was going to say that it's remarkable how you know me so well, but that's because we're the same person! Sort of." Alice sipped her tea and savored it.

"We are the same, and so is Ali." Cherie tipped her head subtly at their youngest counterpart, who was a short distance away from them, making weapons with Jika Mari.

"Jika seems to like her." Alice mused thoughtfully. She and Jika had not hit it off on her first trip to Corevé.

Cherie nodded. "Oh yes, he took an instant liking to her. She's feisty, and perhaps even a bit scrappy, and that appeals to him."

Alice laughed softly. "Do you remember how nice it was to be her, and to have that much energy, and the pretty looks?"

"I do," Cherie agreed, "but I am really glad to be who I am and where I am in my life now."

"Me as well." Alice nodded pleasantly.

"Well, I'd best get back. Channa Mari is going to teach me how to bake Mari sweet biscuits."

Henderson brightened immediately. "Oh, I love those! I need to learn to make them as well. I'll come with you!"

"Me too! I'm coming! I'll taste test for you!" Bailey was up like a shot.

Cherie laughed at them. "Then come along, you too! We've got work to do!"

"Meeeeeeyow!" Bailey exclaimed happily. "Can we make mine pink please? With little rainbow sprinkles?"

"Yes, I'm sure we can do that, Bailey." Cherie patted him. "You know, Channa is such an adorable little thing. My son Edward would love her." She hesitated a moment, and cocked her head, looking at Eddie. "I guess my grandson must love the Inklings too. This is still so strange to me, but I guess I'll get used to it."

She smiled, and they left to go bake with Channa.

A while later, Henderson returned with more tea and freshly baked sweet biscuits. Alice closed her eyes and savored them.

"They are simply divine!"

"I agree." Henderson looked happier than she'd seen him during the entire trip.

Ali marched up to them proudly, and presented an array of incredible weapons to Alice, Henderson, Eddie, and Cherie. "Here! I made these for you!"

"How in the world did you make those? I've never seen anything like them!" Alice stared, and the others did the same.

"Jika helped me make these out of sand! Just look at these things! It's beach sand that has been melted so hot through magic that it forms into unbreakable glass!" Ali hefted a sword and then handed it to Alice.

"Unbreakable glass? Who would have ever thought! Are you sure?" Alice eyed the extraordinary piece doubtfully.

"Oh yes. Definitely sure. I tested them out. And, they're unbelievably sharp. Watch this!" Ali lifted a sword above her head and sent it flashing downward through a thick log laying near the fire. The sword cleaved the log in two without leaving so much as a splinter behind. As the glass sheared through the wood like butter, it rang like a windchime.

"My goodness! These are so beautiful!" Alice ran her hand carefully along the blade and turned it over in her fingers.

Cherie frowned and cleared her throat. "I'm not so sure that giving a sword to Eddie is a good idea. That might be too much of a risk."

Ali stood up straight and met Cherie's gaze. "Isn't the reward great enough to justify the risk? Would you have him go into battle unarmed? Think about it. How does risk change us? Are we braver going in, knowing we will be different coming out on the other side? What is the risk here? What is he losing, and what might he instead gain?"

Silence filled the spaces between them.

Alice exhaled a long breath. "I agree with you Ali. I don't want Eddie in the fight, but I don't want him unarmed either. Eddie, you may choose a sword that suits you and keep it."

Eddie leapt from the log, dropping his knitting needles. "YES!"

"But, you have to learn to use it tonight."

Cherie groaned softly. "I'm still worried about that."

Henderson rose. "Eddie, I excelled in fencing. Choose a sword, and I will give you some key lessons right now. We'll have you adept in no time."

Alice grinned. "There you are. Fencing lessons. Eddie will be fine. He's in very good hands."

Tao smiled. "Confucius said, 'To lead uninstructed people to war is to throw them away'. Our young master will be better off with knowledge that may save him."

Henderson and Eddie moved to the far side of the fire, and every time their swords struck each other, they rang out with musical notes.

Bailey pouted. "I don't like swords. Swords mean gore! I'd rather have glitter than gore. Can't we just glitter bomb them? Glitter is forever! Wounds heal. Usually. The Inklings could make magic glitter that tickles when it lands, and the enemy could just laugh themselves to death. Couldn't we do that? Please?"

Tao spoke once more. "Sun Tzu said, 'The supreme art of war is to subdue the enemy without fighting'. In your case Bailey, I think glitter bombs would be perfect, but sadly, that is not part of our plan. Focus on the positive hope that soon we will have rescued the fire dragons, and be once again at a point of peace."

"Fine." Bailey sighed, rolling onto his back and looking up at the stars. "I'll settle for peace and sweet biscuits."

Everyone chuckled.

When Henderson had worn Eddie out, they returned to the fire. Henderson sat near Alice, and lifted his eyes to her.

"I think he is much better prepared than he was. Hopefully, he will see no action, but should a situation arise, he has some tools at his disposal."

"Thank you, dear Henderson." Alice nodded gratefully to him.

Henderson hesitated, and then met her gaze. "Madame, aren't you afraid?"

The entire group turned their heads and eyes to Alice.

She drew in a long breath and contemplated his question briefly.

"Yes, I am. I'm afraid something else will happen to one or more of you; my precious family. We already lost Montgomery. I'm terribly afraid, but we cannot be stopped by our fears, we cannot be imprisoned by them. It comes down to a choice; a simple choice. Do we remain shackled by fear and let it control us, or do we use our minds to stop and think, and realize that fear, real or imagined, only has the power to stop us if we let it. Once we face our fears and take them on, they dissolve like a misty fog. They are most often based on what we do not know or understand, and something I've learned in all my long years is that it's useless to be afraid because nothing ever turns out the way we think it will. Almost never. We plan, we worry, we fear, and then everything goes left anyway, and we wind up in a completely different place than we ever imagined. Fear is little more than a waste of time. Could something happen to any of us? Yes. We could be killed. But we could just as easily be killed trying to cross a busy street. It could happen anywhere, so we might as well go and do what we want to do or what needs to be done, and not concern ourselves over fear. I'll tell you this; nothing good comes of it, so let it go. It's one of my Cardinal Rules. It's fine to be afraid, but go anyway. If we make a mistake, it's fine; we learn from it and go on. Mistakes are not the worst thing that can happen; not learning from them is."

Cherie fretted. "Yes, but when is the cost of sacrifice too much? When is it enough? When do you win?"

Alice faced her seriously. "Is it a sacrifice for each and every one of us to go on this mission? Unquestionably! But every reason we are going is a reason worth fighting for! Life, love, freedom. We protect those things because they are worth the risk of sacrifice! Hope is built on them, and they must be kept safe! The greatest reward for sacrifice is love. Much like what our dear Montgomery did when he died to save every single one of us and this whole world the last time we were here. When the reward for sacrifice is love, the sacrifice is the win."

"I could not have said it any better." Diovalo gave Alice an appreciative smile.

"Nor I." Keleon agreed.

"Our Alice; a one-of-a-kind wonder." Lord Japheth smiled with his head poked out of his saltwater bubble.

Cherie sighed and gave up. "All right then. It's been a long day, and we've got a bigger day ahead of us. It's time everyone was going to bed. We all need a good night's sleep if we expect to have a successful day of fighting tomorrow."

"Madame, it's time for your pills." Henderson reached into his bag and pulled them out.

"Thank you, Henderson. You are the glue that keeps this family together and going." She took them from him with a smile.

Chippa built a new tent for Eddie that would fit Piper and Oscar as well, and they all curled up together. Tao and Bailey slept outside the tent, to keep guard.

Alice said goodnight to all her new friends, and to her family. She kissed Eddie just before he fell asleep, and gave Piper and Oscar both a pat.

When she laid on her own leaf bed, she closed her eyes and hoped with everything in her that the coming day would be a greater success than she could ever imagine.

Chapter Ten

Risk, Sacrifice, Love

Misty morning air slipped in from the sea, blanketing the beach and hanging heavily throughout the entire camp.

Alice opened her eyes. It was not yet light enough to be sunrise, but it was close. She couldn't sleep. Rising to her feet, she pulled fresh clothes from her bag and changed into them, readying herself for what she suspected might well be one of the biggest days of her life.

With a few deep breaths, she pushed all the what-if's from her mind, set her shoulders back, lifted her chin, and walked out of her tent with her black bag and her umbrella cane with the bird's beak shaped handle over her arm.

Cherie and Henderson were already up and making breakfast. Alice sat at the blazing fire, and Henderson came to her with a meal and hot tea.

"I don't know if I can eat." Alice admitted with a sigh.

Cherie wasn't far behind Henderson. "Everyone is eating before they go. I'm not letting anyone out of here without a good breakfast in them first."

Alice laughed softly. "All right, I'll eat." In a lower voice, she shot a quick look at Henderson. "Was I ever really like that?"

Henderson couldn't hide his chuckle. "I did not know you then, Madame, but I can say without a doubt that you most certainly must have been exactly like that, and thank goodness for it."

Alice laughed and shook her head. "Bless you, Henderson."

Marlowe padded to Alice and nuzzled her shoulder gently. "How are you doing? Are you feeling all right?"

"I'm good. I'm… just deeply focused on today. There can be no mistakes, and I know all too well that things don't always go according to plan. It's weighing on me."

"Do not let it weigh on you. You are not going in alone. In fact, you couldn't be in better company; you are going with all those who love you best, save for your son, who should probably never know about this."

Marlowe gave her a little smile. Her shoulders shook as she covered her mouth with her hands, chuckling.

"How right you are my darling."

Her softly lined cheeks spread in a wide smile, and she sipped her tea, realizing just how lucky she truly was.

It wasn't long before Cherie had everyone in the camp up and fed. Afterward, Ali and Jika made sure that everyone who needed to be armed was, and Oppa and Alice fitted everyone with the impenetrable silk-vine armor that had been knitted the night before.

Bailey beamed as he turned this way and that, examining his. "The flowers are *so pretty!* Thank you mom!"

"You are most welcome, sweet one." She gave Bailey's ears a rub and then strode out before everyone who had gathered, to get a good look at them.

The fairies had donned their own armor and carried their magical weapons. Piper waited with the cats, who were dressed and at attention. Ali, Cherie, Caraway, Eddie, and Henderson were all decked out in their gear, with chins held high. The sea dragons were already rollicking in their seawater bubbles; anxious to go. Keleon was rippling with electricity. The Inklings were covered in knitted armor and held fast to their weapons. The two earth dragons waited solemnly, and Diovalo stood beside them, proud and determined. Murray had been near his tent picking flowers, and he brought one to Alice.

"I keep finding these flowers. Not sure what they are, but the petals keep blowing off and flying around. Must be late in the season for them. Have you seen these before?"

The corner of Alice's mouth turned up slightly. "Yes, actually, I have. Last time I was here. Murray, let's go for a walk, shall we?"

He brightened. "Oh yes, please! I'd like that."

Alice nodded to Queen Diantha, and with a simple wave of her twig wand, a massive portal opened.

Alice and the army slipped right through it, and found themselves tucked into the recesses of the forest just inside the timberline below Mordauz.

"It's time to send in our secret weapons." Alice stated firmly. "Queen Diantha, please have all the fairies go with Rhyoden and Andessai, completely out of sight, of course. When it's time for us to go in, please come back to tell me where we're going."

"Right away, Alice." Queen Diantha nodded. "I will leave one with you to serve as a messenger, should you need it. Tansy, please stay with Alice."

A pretty young fairy warrior came and hovered near Alice's shoulder.

"Hello, Tansy." Alice smiled at the wee thing.

"Hello, Alice." The fairy sparkled.

Queen Diantha and the rest of her fairies camouflaged themselves to match the earth dragon's skin, hiding in amongst the knots and knolls along their bodies.

"Are you ready, your majesty?" Andessai asked, looking up at Diovalo.

"Yes. Let's go."

Rhyoden shook his head. "I hope Baliste believes this. There's no way that two earth dragons could ever really capture and haul Diovalo into this fortress. It would take a lot more than that."

"Nevertheless, here we go." Andessai closed several of the claws on her many legs around Diovalo's right legs, while Rhyoden did the same on his left. Together, they marched him through an area of sparse trees toward the smoldering fortress.

Inside Mordauz, Baliste paced before Lord Malevor, whose head was hung low. Liceverous had shrunk back into a corner of the great hall, staring silently.

"You have failed me yet again! I have never given a creature as many chances as I have you, and I regret that I have shown you such favor! You do not deserve it! How could you possibly expect to be king of the dragons when you can't even accomplish one simple little task?" She demanded furiously.

Lord Malevor stared at the flagstone floor.

"Tell me how you and your miserable subjects have managed to lose your quarry! How could you possibly have stolen Alice's child and then *lost* him? He was the bait in your trap, was he not? He was the only reason that you were going to be able to finally get Diovalo, and he vanished under your watch! There is no way you'll ever get the dragon prince now!"

"I am sorry, my queen. I do not know how the boy escaped. It seems impossible; he was too far underground to have ever found his way out again." Lord Malevor tried to explain piteously.

Baliste stopped her incessant pacing and stood directly before him. Her voice quieted to a deadly calm.

"You have been nothing short of a disastrous mistake from the moment we met. I have no further use for you."

Lord Malevor raised his eyes to meet her dull blood red gaze. "But my queen, if you would only give me one last-"

In the blink of an eye, she spun in place where she stood and flung her tail toward him with tremendous force. The large, spiked spade at the end of it slammed into Lord Malevor's shoulder. She gave her tail a yank and it ripped clean of him, tearing away his flesh and leaving a trail of bloody lines in its wake.

Lord Malevor gasped as blood began to pour out from every puncture in the wound. Baliste only stood there and stared at him. She spoke in a calm and even tone.

"There is a cocktail of eighty different venoms circulating through you right now. You might feel a bit weak."

Lord Malevor slumped to the floor at her clawed feet.

"You may lose control of some of your muscles."

The earth dragon's body began to twitch.

"And by now, you might be feeling some pain in every part of you."

The beast began to roar and howl in agony.

She gazed down at him. "You will most likely lose your sight."

His eyes turned a milky white and he twisted his head desperately, this way and that.

"Your flesh may begin to feel warm."

His dragon's hide began to steam, and ribbons of smoke undulated off of his writhing body.

Baliste watched him, expressionless. "You could have trouble breathing."

The torturous echoes of his roars subsided swiftly as he began to gasp desperately for air.

The corners of Baliste's mouth turned upward, almost into a smile. "And now the real fun begins as your mind starts to crash into an excruciating vortex while your body slowly decays from the inside out."

Liceverous shook with terror in the corner as he watched the slow and horrific demise of Lord Malevor.

"Your majesty!" A troll lumbered into the great hall as quickly as he was able to.

"What is it?" She demanded, flipping around to look at him. "I'm busy!"

The troll panted breathlessly as he delivered the news. "Your majesty, the dragon prince is being brought to the fortress! They're nearly at the door!"

Baliste swept across the room to a window and gazed out of it. A true smile formed on her gray, speckled face.

"It's about time."

Rhyoden and Andessai were bringing the prince right to her gate.

"Liceverous!" Baliste shouted.

The dragon crawled toward her on his belly, shuddering. "Yes, my queen?"

"Get up off of the floor and come with me."

"Yes, my queen." He slowly rose and followed her as she went to the doors of the fortress.

"Look at this! The mighty Diovalo, prince of the dragons, is mine at last!" She relished in her triumph.

Diovalo roared fiercely at her. "I demand that you release me and all the fire dragons that you have stolen! Fail to do so and you will not survive!"

An icy laugh shattered the air between them. "I am not done welcoming you to my fold! I have plans for you, young prince. You will serve me in ways you cannot begin to imagine."

Diovalo blasted Baliste with a rolling blaze of fire, and when it subsided, she gave him a cool smile. "That was pleasant." The smile faded. "Perhaps you see that it had no effect on me. Your attack is futile, my servant, for you see, fire is my element."

Diovalo glared daggers at her.

A swath of cave trolls and mountain goblins emerged from beneath the fortress and surrounded Diovalo and the earth dragons. In moments they dragged him roughly back through their door. The earth dragons remained outside with Baliste and Liceverous.

Diovalo was hauled through a secret tunnel to a massive cage behind the fortress, on the far side of it. The dragon enclosure was partly tucked into the mountain beneath Mordauz, but the greater part of it spread out into the open. One of the trolls kicked the dragon prince as he locked the gate between them.

"You won't be getting out of here. These bars are made of dark magic and cannot be destroyed!" A gravelly laugh sounded from him as he walked away with the rest of his horde.

Alice and all of her army watched anxiously from their hidden place, waiting for the return of Queen Diantha.

"Where did they take Diovalo?" Piper worried helplessly.

"I can't see him anymore!" Oscar panicked. "What if we can't find him and get him out of there! How will we be able to rescue him?"

"We will find a way. Don't you fret my darlings. We will not let him remain captive in that horrible place." Alice reassured them. "Have confidence in yourselves, and in all of our mighty friends here. We will succeed."

A shimmer flashed just off to Alice's side, and she turned with a start. Standing there near her was a translucent looking figure in the shape of a human female.

Ali clapped her hands excitedly. "Phedrus! What are you doing here?"

Alice gasped. "Who and… what… is this?"

Oscar and Piper leapt with joy. "This is our friend Phedrus! She's a Towering Tree Nymph! A tree spirit! We met her when we were separated from Jynx and Sophie!"

Phedrus waved her silvery transparent hand at the kitten and the baby dragon. "I heard through the vines and the roots from the trees here where you stand that this battle was about to happen. I've never left my tree before, not for thousands of years, but I had to come. Baliste is spreading an evil that is killing the natural world, and she must be stopped. I will not lose my Towering Trees to her! So I came, and I brought several of my friends."

As she spoke, more than a dozen nymphs appeared behind her, all taking different forms.

"My goodness, that is extraordinary! Thank you! I know that we could certainly use your help!"

"I am glad to give it." Phedrus shared a smile with Alice.

Murray stared at the fortress. "I have to say it. I don't think much of what they've done to Kensington Palace. Never looked worse, but I might as well have a peek."

Alice was busy talking with Phedrus and Ali, and did not hear Murray, and no one happened to notice when he wandered off through the trees and headed through the big rocks above the timberline toward Mordauz.

Baliste turned to Liceverous. "Go now, and find any other earth dragons that may be roaming out there. Bring them all to me."

Liceverous bowed low. "Yes, my queen. May I say how happy I am that Lord Malevor is gone. It would be my honor to serve you."

Rhyoden eyed Liceverous. "Where is Lord Malevor?"

"Our former lord is dead." Liceverous hesitated then, and stared at Andessai. "Why did you tell me to come here to the fortress when I was watching over the boy? You said Diovalo had been captured."

Andessai's voice rang with strength and clarity. "I did what Lord Malevor told me to do, but I suspect that it was a trick of the fairies. They found me and they must have made a false Malevor, because I fell under a sleeping spell as I was watching the boy, and when I woke, the boy was gone."

"Liceverous! I have already told you once to go, and yet here you stand in conversation." Baliste warned him sharply.

"Yes, my queen. I am going now." Liceverous slunk off to a hole in the ground, not far from fortress gate.

Baliste turned to Rhyoden and Andessai with a wide grin. "I could not be prouder of you both. You have done an excellent job in bringing the dragon prince to me."

Rhyoden lifted his chin. "Your plan worked beautifully. Liceverous never suspected anything when Andessai went to him in the tunnels. We were able to gain the trust of Alice and the whole of her company by pretending to help her save the boy. The ruse enabled us to get close enough to Diovalo that we could make him think that he should turn himself in to you because there was no other choice. Your plan worked perfectly; we were able to bring him here with no problem at all."

"I had to come up with it because I knew full well that Malevor and Liceverous would only fail again, but there was never a doubt that my two most trusted earth dragon servants would be able to trick Alice and all her company with the rescue of her child, and pretend to befriend them in order to infiltrate them and get close to Diovalo. I knew there would be no other way to get him; he was too closely guarded. I had to outsmart our enemy. It's all about strategy. So well done, my pets."

Baliste reached a hand up to each of them and stroked their long, narrow snouts.

"Come with me now to the dragon cage and keep guard over my quarry. Make sure that nothing happens to Diovalo."

"Yes, Baliste." Rhyoden answered.

Just as they began to go to the great door beneath the fortress, she stopped and turned, frowning sharply at them.

"What is that stench? You two stink of fairies!"

Andessai dropped her head slightly. "We were around them at the camp in Siang.:

Baliste turned away in disgust. "Pray that it wears off soon, I cannot abide the stink of fairies!"

The two earth dragons followed Baliste through the secret tunnel to the area before the holding cell. Baliste placed her hand on a lever, pulling it.

"This lever moves the door. When it is set to the left, it opens out onto the grounds around the fortress for a swift exit from the structure. When it is set to the right, it opens into the cage enclosure. It's how we put all of the fire dragons into the cage to begin with."

Baliste pushed the lever to the left of center, and a door opened to the outside grounds beside the massive cage. "Go out and guard the dragon keep."

Rhyoden and Andessai went through the door, and Baliste closed it behind them. They noticed immediately that there were already cave trolls and mountain goblins guarding the prisoners as well.

As they walked around to the back of the enormous cell, Diovalo caught their eyes and shared a silent look with them from inside the cage. The other fire dragons called out desperately to them for help, pleading with the pair of earth dragons to set them free.

Step by slow step, Murray made it to the base of the right side of the fortress. He looked along the wall and found a narrow door.

"Oh, what luck! This must be a water closet! I could do with a quick freshen up." He gripped the handle and tugged a few times, and after a solid yank, it finally opened. He stepped inside.

Queen Diantha flew to the end of Rhyoden's snout and glowed with anger. "You've betrayed us! How could you do that! You lied to your own kind; your own prince! You lied to Alice and to all of us who have come to free these imprisoned dragons and stop Baliste's evil! How *dare you!* I am going to turn you into an earthworm!"

Diantha drew out her twig wand and aimed it at the dragon, but he hushed her.

"Your majesty, wait! Everything that we told Diovalo was true! We do not wish to serve Malevor or Baliste! We had to play both sides in order to get Diovalo here so that we could free the dragons! There was no other way! You must believe me!"

"How can I believe anything you say? I saw you with her! I heard everything you said!"

"And I knew that you were listening! Did we tell Baliste about you? We did not. We kept your secret and kept you safe. Now go and tell Alice where we are, and that Diovalo is here. Bring her to us. We will be waiting."

Diantha scowled sharply at him. "I can change you anytime I want to!" She warned him. "If you are lying to me, it will be the last thing you ever do!"

"Go!" Rhyoden urged her.

Queen Diantha slipped through a small portal and vanished, reappearing a moment later before Alice at the inner edge of the forest.

Alice started when the fairy appeared, but in the next breath she poured forth a stream of questions.

"Well? Did it work? Is he safe? What happened?"

The waiting had been torturous to her, though she hadn't let it on to anyone else.

Diantha nodded. "Your plan worked. The cage is on the far side of the fortress, coming out from beneath it to the grounds. Rhyoden and Andessai are guarding it, but there are cave trolls and mountain goblins there as well."

"What does the cage look like?' Alice pressed.

"It's a great cage of metal, enchanted with dark magic. Nothing can break through it, but there is a gate outside at the back."

"Does it have a lock?" Alice nearly held her breath.

"Yes, a rather large one. Alice, there's something else that you should know. The earth dragons may have betrayed us. They spoke with Baliste after Liceverous left, discussing with her their plan to infiltrate our group disguised as friends in order to gain our trust and trick Diovalo into coming here. After that Rhyoden assured me that it was all a ruse and they're really on our side. I do not trust them."

Alice sighed heavily as her shoulders sank. She carefully considered what she had been told. "Do you know where Diovalo is?"

"Yes, he's outside in the cage. Rhyoden and Andessai are guarding him."

"Then this is a chance we'll have to take. Please bring me to Rhyoden, and make sure that I'm not seen when we get there. Good heavens I hope I don't have a fall."

Alice turned to Henderson. "Please stay here, hidden in the trees with Eddie and keep him safe, along with Murray."

She looked around then and gasped. "Murray! Where is Murray? Has anyone seen Murray?"

A chorus of no's sounded, and several of the company began to search for him. Ali came back to Alice to report. "He's gone."

Alice groaned. "Well, we'll have to find him later. He can't get into too much trouble in the woods."

Diantha opened a portal for herself and Alice, and they stepped out of thin air beside Rhyoden's leg. Alice hid on the far side of him from the cage and the grotesque guards. Setting her hand on him, she spoke softly.

"I'm here, Rhyoden. You tell me right now whose side you're on."

"I vow to you, Alice, that I am with you and I wish to serve no one but Diovalo."

"Rhyoden, if you are lying to me, it will be the last thing you ever do."

"That's the second time I've heard that in ten minutes."

"Well, I mean it. Don't you even think about testing me. Now, let me get a look at this situation." Alice peeped around him. Andessai drew near and Alice addressed them both.

"I'll go for the gate, and you take out the guards. We'll be fast enough that we'll be able to do it without attracting too much attention."

They both gave her a nod.

"Don't you let me down. I'm warning you." She whipped her knitting needles out of her purse and pointed them at both of the dragons.

Alice took a deep breath and then rushed toward the gate. As she hurried, the dragons each swung around and close their jagged teeth around a troll and a goblin, while grabbing more in their claws and crushing them.

Breathless and panting, Alice reached the gate and jabbed her knitting needle into the lock. "Come on... come on... please work." She murmured. Clicking it around a few times, she managed to disengage it.

"HA! I got it!"

Just as she was about to pull the gate open, the last mountain goblin lunged at her. Alice turned sharply on the spot and drove her knitting needle straight into his chest. The goblin keeled over onto its side.

"Ugh. Disgusting!" Alice pulled the needle free and wiped it on the grass, cleaning it. "Oh my stars and whiskers, I'll have to sanitize this when I get back to London. Never leave home without a good set of knitting needles."

With a grunt, Alice pulled the gate open. The fire dragons were freed. Not a breath later, a strange siren blared out over the fortress.

Diovalo was the first one out of the cage. He only stopped long enough to let Alice climb onto him and then he shot up into the sky. All of the other fire dragons came rushing out after him, following him like the tail of a kite, one right after the other.

The multitude of fairies that had been concealed on the earth dragons lifted off of them in an enormous cloud, zooming over the field, ready for the coming battle.

Some of the escaping fire dragons remained on the ground with the earth dragons, and together they barreled around the side of the fortress.

Baliste's form filled a window as she looked out over the back of the fortress and the cage. She saw the dragons escaping and shrieked.

"After them! Send all of my army after them now! Stop them! Get those dragons back here immediately!"

From the front of the fortress, the great doors on either side of the bridge going into the main gate opened, and goblins and trolls streamed out of them.

They headed the dragons off before they could get to the front of the castle, clashing with them at its side in the wide open space of the grounds between the fortress and the timberline.

Alice's army waited, hidden in the trees. Suddenly Chippa yelled out, "Forward! Defend!", and all of their army swarmed from the forest and up the incline to the field surrounding Mordauz.

Tao went wide-eyed staring at the mass of trolls and goblins. "Normally I'd say all creatures have a life of great value, but I think I'm going to have to make an exception today. My family takes priority!"

Oscar shuddered. 'I hate trolls and goblins!'

Tao shook her head. "Not as much as I hate Quiri birds!" As she said it, a cloud of the vicious birds descended out of the skies and into the melee.

The Towering Tree Nymphs rushed into the battle, doing all they could to fight. Phedrus and her kind swirled around their enemies, rushing against them with wind and plastering them with leaves and grasses so that they could not see. Many of them drew up the roots of the nearest trees and sent them to wrap around the legs of their foes, dragging them across the ground and down into the depths of it where they could not escape.

Keleon vaulted into the air with an ear shattering cry, and shot arcs of electric energy at every Quiri bird he could see. While doing that, he also dove down to the ground and clenched trolls and goblins within his claws, hauling them up to great heights and then dropping them to their ends.

Piper and Oscar left the battlefield and headed to the back of the grounds where the cage had been left open. "Where's my mom?" Piper cried. "I don't see her! My mom isn't here!"

Piper flew wildly all over the outside of the cage, and around the edge of the battlefield, coming back to Oscar in tears.

"She isn't here! My mom isn't here!"

Oscar nudged her gently. "I'm so sorry, my friend."

Piper dropped to the ground and sobbed into the dirt. Oscar knelt beside her and rested his head against her quivering back.

From out of nowhere, Oppa Mari appeared and knelt at Piper's other side, petting her head. "Now, now, little one. Sadness is passing. I can help." Oppa's paws grew warm on the baby dragon, and calmed her until her tears stopped, and she could breathe again.

Murray plodded along at a leisurely pace through a large, dark hallway. "Now where is that exit? There must be one around here somewhere. Can't see much in all this dark."

He stopped short in front of a large lever in the ground and brightened. "Oh! Well look at that! Must be for the lift. Not sure how I wound up in the lower levels. Had no idea Kensington Palace had a dungeon."

Murray wrapped his hands around the lever and pulled it to the right, then let it go and waited patiently. Suddenly a hoard of trolls and goblins rushed past him through the hall.

"Oh!" He tried to step out of their way. "Pardon me! I'm so sorry! Goodness, excuse me!" He apologized continuously. They rushed headlong in the wrong direction, straight into the dragon cage.

"Must be a whole busload of tourists!" Murray peered after them.

Oppa Mari heard a commotion and turned to see the swell of trolls and goblins coming out from the underground area of the cell. She hustled to the cage door and as fast as she could, she closed it and clicked the lock back on it, sealing it with magic. The trolls and goblins were trapped. They screamed and yelled, until Diovalo appeared in the skies above them and roasted them all with a tremendous stream of fire, right through the bars.

Inside the hall, Murray frowned and looked around. "Must have sent the lift in the wrong direction." He reached for the lever again and moved it to the left. The door opened to the outside. Murray beamed.

"Oh, lovely! That must be the gardens. I'll go out and have a look." He slipped his hands into his pockets and wandered outside.

Oscar saw him and went right for him, kneeling down beside him. Murray clapped his hands excitedly. "Oh, well fancy this! Horseback riding! Don't mind if I do! Good day for it!"

As Oscar passed the cage filled with the blackened remains of trolls and goblins, Murray sniffed the air and peered through the bars. "Hm. Must have done a community barbecue. That's a little too extra crispy for my taste. I think I'll stop for fish and chips in a bit."

"Jynx! Catch!" Sophie grabbed a goblin in her teeth and flung it to Jynx who caught it in the air and brought it down to the ground, shredding it.

"Good one Sophie! Here's one for you!" Jynx swiped her massive paw against the back of another goblin and sent it acing through the air to Sophie, who caught it in her claws and used her teeth to dismember it.

Marlowe launched himself onto the back of a troll and brought him crashing to the ground, where he finished him off.

The fairies were sending arrows through the air like wildfire, never missing a shot as they dropped several of their enemies onto the battlefield in the form of flowers.

"I've got another one!" Ali shouted as she fought back to back with Cherie, swinging her sword through the air and slicing her opponents to slimy green ribbons.

"Me too!" Cherie answered, halving one who had come straight for her with an axe.

"Keep going!" Ali yelled. "Keep going until they are gone!"

"Go team!" Cherie hollered, battling another troll.

Gabbrod the earth dragon who had served Lord Malevor came tearing out of the hole in the earth with Liceverous behind him. Liceverous took one look at the battle and sank back into the hole, watching from its depths.

Gabbrod dove straight for a fire dragon on the ground and sunk his teeth into the dragon's hide. The fire dragon roared and blasted the earth dragon with a stream of fire, and they tangled together, wresting and rolling wildly around the ground, ripping and tearing at one another.

The skies above them were ablaze with flames, shrieks, and roars as the fire dragons in the air blasted their flames at the Quiri birds, who attacked them viciously.

Channa Mari, Jika, Bayless Grand Mari, and Chippa were all working the elements to bring the birds down out of the sky as well as tripping up the goblins and trolls whenever they got the chance, so that the cats could have an easier time getting them.

"I'm going for another one!" Callidus cried out, diving in her water bubble toward the ground where she scooped up a goblin in her webbed claws. The moment the goblin was engulfed in the saltwater it dissolved.

"EW! That's so gross!" Keres laughed.

"It's like salt on slugs!" Galiphes told them. "Goblins and Trolls can't handle saltwater!

"Well let's give them more than they can handle!" Lord Japheth yelled, diving with them into the thick of the battlefield.

Alice and Diovalo fought against a big earth dragon who was nearly the size of Lord Malevor. Diovalo grabbed him with his claws and hauled him to a dizzying height before letting go and dropping him to the ground far below.

Caraway was blasting pure light off of both of his palms straight into the eyes of every earth dragon he could find, except for Rhyoden and Andessai, who were helping him. With the earth dragons blinded by such brilliance, they were much easier targets for the cats, fairies, nymphs, and other dragons.

When he wasn't streaming light straight into the eyes of the beasts that lived in the dark, he was taking the light from the eyes of those who needed it to see; particularly the Quiri birds and the mountain goblins. As the light left their eyes, they could see nothing at all, and were blinded with darkness, making it almost impossible to attack.

The fairies had begun turning the goblins and trolls into blossoming trees one by one, which completely horrified beasts. They began running from the fairies, but the Inklings were right there to trap them with grass shooting straight up out of the ground and twisting around their feet and legs, and gusts of wind that swept them up off of the battlefield and held them in midair until a fairy could get to them.

Rhyoden and Andessai raged through the mass of trolls, tearing them apart with their claws each time they got hold of one.

Queen Diantha saw them and gave them a nod of approval.

"We are on Diovalo's side, make no mistake." Andessai told her, and the queen of the fairies smiled.

"I'm glad to hear it. Keep on fighting!"

She took off, aiming her wand at a particularly big troll, who soon became a flowering tree.

Bailey plopped down on a goblin and squashed him. The goblin wriggled and yelled, demanding to be freed. Bailey only looked down at him and shook his head.

"Don't fuss now. Flat is the new black. Embrace change."

Piper, whose heart was still very sad, but much comforted by Oppa after she lifted a great deal of the pain away, was zipping through the battle biting as many trolls and goblins as she could get her teeth on.

"You took my mom!" She shouted at them, biting over and over again. Those she bit fell lifeless to the ground in seconds.

Oscar raced around the far side of the fortress with Murray on his back, avoiding the battle altogether as he headed for the trees to get Murray to safety. Once there, he knelt low and Murray climbed off of him.

"Well done! Off to the stables with you then!"

Oscar paused only long enough to speak to Eddie and Henderson. "I've just left Murray back there, in that little glen. I'm heading back in."

"Thank you, Oscar. Stay safe." Henderson eyed him seriously.

Oscar bolted out of the timberline, and it drew the attention of some of his foes.

Two goblins at the edge of the battlefield noticed Eddie and Henderson in the trees, and ran for them. Henderson's eyes grew wide.

"Master Eddie, it's time to put your lessons to good use. This is what you practiced for! Remain focused and remember all that I taught you!"

"I will! I promise!" Eddie vowed adamantly. Both of them had their swords raised and ready when the goblins got to them, and the fight was on.

Eddie slashed and dodged, doing his best to get away from the goblin who was after him, but the goblin was fast, and it managed to rake its claws down Eddie's shoulder and the side of his arm where his armor did not extend.

Pain shot through Eddie and it ignited a fire in him, driving him to fight better. He focused with everything in him and battled the goblin until at long last he drove his sword straight through it.

He turned to see Henderson just finishing his fight, and taking down his goblin attacker as well. Henderson drew in a sharp breath when he saw Eddie's wound.

"Are you all right?"

Eddie nodded. "It hurts, but it's not too bad. I hope grandma won't be upset about my shirt; it's shredded on this sleeve."

A laugh of relief escaped Henderson. "No, dear Master Eddie, she will not be upset about your shirt. I can promise you that." Henderson wrapped an arm around the boy and rested his cheek on the top of Eddie's head.

"I've got my medical kit with me. It will do, until we can get you healed magically." Henderson opened his black bag and got the boy patched up in no time.

When he was done, they stood together, watching from behind the trees. "It looks like we're winning!" Eddie breathed hopefully.

Just then the front doors of the fortress flew open and Baliste herself erupted out of them in a rage. She began swinging her tail in every direction, taking down anything near her, whether troll, goblin, fairy, or dragon. The cats and Inklings ran from her path, and the fairies kept more than a safe distance between her and themselves.

"What in the world..." Henderson's jaw fell open. "How can that be?"

"Grandma!" Eddie screamed, and then hesitated. "That is grandma... Isn't it?"

They stared as three women of different ages came running out of the doors of the fortress right behind Baliste. Alice in her thirties, Alice in her fifties, and Alice in her sixties.

"That lying little..." Henderson began and then pressed his lips together into a tight line. "Mendax said there were only two others! There are three more Alices right there! I wonder how many there really are!"

The three Alices began fighting fairies immediately, giving backup to Baliste at every turn.

"Missus P!" Chippa exclaimed, running toward the three Alices. "How is you getting inside the fortress? Doesn't you worry! I will help you!"

The little Inkling rushed toward the trio of Alices, and the Alice in her thirties spun on her heel and faced him.

"Little monster!" She shouted. "Horrid little thing!"

Chippa froze in place and stared at her. "Missus P?"

The younger Alice flung a blade at Chippa, nearly hitting him, but he moved his paw through the air and swept it away before it could hit him.

He choked up and blinked back tears. "I... I doesn't understand! Why is you fighting me? You is my friend!"

"I am not friends with you, little beast!" She shouted, picking up a rock and hurling it at him. "Baliste is my friend, and I am here to help her defeat you! You will not win!"

Chippa shook his head and covered his small mouth with his paws as tears rolled out of his big, dark eyes. The rock narrowly missed hitting him, and he did not bother to try to deflect it, he was too brokenhearted.

From high overhead, Alice Perivale looked down from Diovalo's back and gasped.

"NO! Oh my dear heavens... no!" She leaned closer to Diovalo's ear. "Let me down! I have to get down now!"

Diovalo was on the ground in seconds and Alice ran for Chippa. A second well aimed rock would have hit him, but Alice scooped him up in her arms and rolled out of the way just in time.

"Ali! Cherie!" Alice yelled as loudly as she could. Queen Diantha saw her and within seconds, she had portaled both ladies to Alice's side.

"What? Where are we?" Ali gasped.

"I was just about to take that goblin!" Cherie swiveled her head in confusion.

"What's happening?" Ali spun and saw Alice holding Chippa tightly in her arms.

"You is Alice!" Chippa stared and then turned and gazed back at the women who were charging them. "And they is Alice too? More of you?"

"Chippa, I love you and I would never, ever hurt you. Do you know that?" Alice asked him hurriedly.

He sniffed and nodded. "I loves you too." He buried his face in her neck and sniffled.

"Now I'm going to set you down, and I want you to back off. I don't know what's going on here, but I don't trust it, and I don't want you to get hurt."

Chippa scowled at the oncoming Alices who had suddenly stopped short. "Chippa is not letting them fight you! Chippa is protecting you! You are Chippa's friend!" He snarled bitterly.

"Uh oh. They've done it now." Alice shook her head. "He's speaking in third person. He must be really angry." She bent and set Chippa on the ground, and the little Inkling balled his paws into fists and gritted his teeth.

"Who are they?" The Alice in her thirties who threw rocks at Chippa stared at Ali, Cherie, and Alice.

"They are mirages! Magic tricks done by the opposition! They aren't real! We're the only three real Alices! Get them!"

The trio of Alices rushed at Mrs. Perivale, Cherie, and Ali with their weapons drawn, ready for a fight.

"I AM THE REAL ALICE!" Mrs. Perivale shouted. "I am no mirage, and if you come one step closer, you're going to find out just how real I am! I don't care if that lousy little djinn Mendax did bring you to life! You're not getting out of here in one piece if you come after me or these other two versions of us!"

The trio stopped again and stared.

"Wait…" The Alice in her fifties cocked her head and studied the three women facing them. "I think… I think they're real!"

"That one mentioned Mendax! If they were mirages, how would they know that Mendax brought us to life?" The one in her sixties frowned.

"BECAUSE I AM THE REAL ALICE!" Mrs. Perivale shouted at them again.

Ali nodded. "She IS the real Alice, and Mendax brought the two of us to life as well, just like he did you, but he didn't bring her to life, because she's the original! We all came from her, and if you'd stop for a second and take a good look at the six of us, you'd realize that!"

"Oh my goodness… I think we've been tricked." The Alice in her thirties gasped.

Mrs. Perivale jabbed her finger toward the timberline. "Look into those trees! You're going to see two people that at least the two older of you know!"

The three Alices looked, and the older two cried out.

"Henderson! Why, that's my butler, Henderson!"

"And… and that's Edward!" Oh my goodness! Son!"

"No, that's *my* butler Henderson, and that's our grandson Eddie; he's Edward's son!" Mrs. Perivale corrected them sharply.

The three Alices stood in shock for a full moment before they began wiping away tears and apologizing.

"I'm so sorry! We had no idea! Mendax brought us here and Baliste told us that we were the only three Alices to survive the destruction of the Illusionary Palace!" The Alice in her fifties told them.

Cherie shook her head. "Oh no. Ali and I were at Illusionary Palace too. That's where we all came from. We just didn't know that any of the rest of us existed, that is, until Mendax brought Ali and I to Alice, and I guess he took you three to Baliste."

They all frowned at each other.

"Why would he do that?" Alice in her thirties wondered aloud what the rest of them were thinking.

"Because Mendax is a rotten, lying little cheat! Chippa doesn't trust Mendax!" Chippa spat bitterly from behind Alice.

"What are you doing attacking my dear little friend Chippa!" Mrs. Perivale snapped at thirty year old Alice.

The younger woman hung her head as her shoulders sagged. "I'm so very sorry. I didn't realize that you were a friend, or that we have a grandson. We've all been lied to. Please, forgive me Chippa. If I had known, I certainly never would have attacked you."

Chippa nodded. "You doesn't hurt me. My Alice is saving me. She loves me."

Mrs. Perivale rubbed her fingers on his fuzzy, floppy ears. "That's exactly right, my darling. Now we all know the truth. There are six of us, and I'm going to tell you this right now. Baliste is evil. She's as evil as they come. Whatever she told you is a complete lie. She's only using you, or I guess us, for her own greedy, malicious purposes, and we absolutely cannot allow that."

"I've seen her evil, and she needs to be stopped!" Ali added.

"I second that! We're going to do everything that we can to stop her!" Cherie told the trio.

~ 217 ~

The three Alices looked at one another for a second and nodded. "We'll help you." Thirty year old Alice agreed.

"I'm not keen on being lied to and used, especially for anything evil!" Alice in her fifties reddened with anger.

"We have an ace up every one of our sleeves, and that is that we know each other better than anyone, because as absolutely bizarre as this is, we are all Alice. Together, we are extraordinary!" Mrs. Perivale told them seriously, and they all nodded in agreement.

"Then let's go after Baliste!" Ali cried out.

They didn't have to go far. Baliste had just turned around and seen them all talking, and realization washed over her face.

"There are more of you?" She shouted, and began to rush toward them. "You will join me, or you will die!"

Seven foot tall Baliste bent and swung her claws fiercely at them. Every one of them ducked out of the way. Ali bobbed down and then popped right back up and sent a punch straight at Baliste's rib cage.

Baliste groaned, and then drove her claws right back in Ali's direction. Ali ducked and Cherie swiped at Baliste with her glass sword, leaving a deep gash on her leg. Baliste shrieked in pain and glared at Mrs. Perivale with burning eyes.

"This is all your fault! ALL of it!" Baliste spun on the spot and sent her venomous tail racing toward Mrs. Perivale. In a flash, sixty year old Alice jumped in front of her, taking the hit as the spikes drove deeply into her flesh. Blood began to spill out of her, and she groaned in agony as she sank to the ground at Mrs. Perivale's feet.

"ALICE!" Mrs. Perivale screamed, sinking down and wrapping her arms around the woman who was her younger self. It was almost like looking into a mirror, only ten years earlier.

"You're going to deal with us now!" Ali raged as she, Cherie, and the other Alices took on Baliste, driving her a short distance from Mrs. Perivale.

"Alice what have you done?" Mrs. Perivale wept as her heart caught in her chest.

"You're the real Alice! I couldn't let you die! Take care of our grandson! He needs us!" Alice pleaded as she began to go through the different stages of agonizing death that Baliste's venom had wrought on her.

Mrs. Perivale turned to Chippa. "Do something! Can't you do something?"

Chippa trembled with fear, staring at the horror before him. Slowly he brought his paw to his mouth and trilled as loudly as he could. In a heartbeat, Oppa was at his side.

"Do something!" Mrs. Perivale pleaded as the Alice in her arms screamed and writhed in agony.

Oppa sighed, looking at Baliste's tail as Baliste fought with the other Alices. "I is afraid there is nothing to be doing. I can stop it, but I can't heal it."

"Stop it?" Mrs. Perivale whispered, shaking her head. "What do you mean?"

"Stopping her heart." Oppa answered quietly.

"Please! Please stop it! End me now! This is too much!" Alice begged miserably.

Oppa nodded and placed her paws on sixty year old Alice's chest. In the next moment, her eyes closed, and her body relaxed. She almost looked as if she was sleeping, save for the blood issuing from her wounds.

"She is gone." Oppa sighed heavily. "No more suffers."

Mrs. Perivale stared down at the slightly younger version of herself in her arms. Her jaw set into a hard line and she let the woman go, setting her gently on the earth. Turning her head, her hardened eyes met Oppa's.

"Take Chippa and get out of here. Go back to the woods with Henderson and Eddie. I will meet you there if I can. Keep them safe. I cannot bear for this to happen to you or them."

Oppa nodded, and though Chippa protested vehemently, pleading to stay with Alice, they were gone in an instant.

"This is your last chance to join me!" Baliste screamed at the various Alices she was fighting. Mrs. Perivale raised her hands and issued forth a gust of wind, trying to blow the evil sorceress away with it. Instead, it turned to fog, and then dissipated almost immediately.

"Darn it! Am I *ever* going to get that right!" She snapped angrily.

Just then Baliste whipped around again and sent her tail slamming into thirty year old Alice, killing her with the impact before the venom could eat away at her slowly.

"NO!" Cherie, Alice, and Ali yelled, along with fifty year old Alice.

"I'll kill you all!" Baliste vowed as her long, forked tongue shot out from behind her jagged teeth.

"You're going to have to get through me first!" Mrs. Perivale roared at her.

Baliste turned and grinned. "You are the one I want to end the most!"

She was about to fling her tail at Mrs. Perivale, when Ali raised her glass sword over her head and brought it down singing as it swept right through Baliste's tail, cleaner and quicker than a hot knife through soft butter.

For a moment, Baliste waivered, losing her balance and not realizing why. The spiked spade hit the ground with a thud, and Baliste blinked for a split second before wailing in agony. She turned her head and flipped her tail from side to side, spraying blood everywhere.

In a fit of rage, the evil sorceress punched her claws up into the air and electric currents began to arc through them. She turned her blood red eyes to Ali, and Alice knew that she was going to send the electric current right through the girl.

She snatched a knitting needle from her bag, but before she could use it, Mendax appeared out of nowhere.

"Oh no you don't!" He shouted. "You've already taken two of them!"

He snapped his fingers, and Ali, Cherie, and fifty year old Alice disappeared instantly.

Alice gasped. "They're gone!"

Baliste spun toward Mendax, outraged. Alice had had enough. She flung her knitting needle at the sorceress like it was a dagger.

It almost impaled her, but Baliste saw it coming and disappeared in a puff of black smoke.

Breathless, her heart racing in her chest faster than it ever had, Alice turned to Mendax. Her hand shot out as quick as lightning and she took hold of his arm.

All the emotion in her swelled up and erupted in that moment.

"What are you *doing?* Whose side are you *on* anyway?" With her free hand she yanked her umbrella cane from her belt and began bashing Mendax with it wildly.

"You told me there were only two other Alices!"

Bash!

"Ouch!" He tried to duck, but couldn't get out of her grasp.

"You lied and brought three more here to Baliste!"

Bash! Bash!

"Ouch! Stop!"

"You sent us on a wild goose chase to some island off the coast where there were no dragons at all!"

Bash! Bash! Bash!

"OUCH!" Mendax wiggled so hard to get free that he slipped right out of his flowing golden coat and once he was loose, he vanished, just as Alice brought her cane down on him one more time.

BASH!

"AGH!"

She heard him cry out as he disappeared.

Heaving great breaths, she turned in place and took in the view of the battlefield behind her. It was nearly cleared of living goblins, trolls, and Quiri birds, and there was almost a new forest of trees, blanketed in flowers and charcoaled lumps.

Two fire dragons had died in the battle, along with a good number of the earth dragons, but the greatest casualty were the goblins, trolls, and Quiri birds, who had been soundly defeated.

With the sorceress gone, all of the others ran or flew off. The battle had ended, and Alice and her army had won, though it had not been easy.

Marlowe rushed to Alice, and she let her head fall on his shoulder.

"Are you all right my dear?" She managed to ask him.

"Yes, We're all fine. Everyone is fine. How are you?"

Alice just sighed. "Tired."

The other cats came to her, along with Chippa, who rested his head on her leg and held her free hand. The other Inklings came with him, and Caraway rambled over to them as did Henderson and Eddie, who emerged from the trees and rushed to Alice.

Queen Diantha spoke, and everyone could hear her.

"The fortress is guarded by magic. She's put some kind of shield up around it now, and we can no longer break through. This is as far as we are going to get today."

"How frustrating." Diovalo growled darkly. "I wanted to stop her now."

"It will happen my friend, just not today." Alice told him, looking up at him and wiping a few last tears off of her face. "Ali cut the end of her tail off, and when she tried to kill Ali for doing it, Mendax showed up and stole Ali, Cherie, and one of the other Alices away."

"What other Alices?" Sophie's eyes grew round.

"Mendax lied to us." Alice told them. "There were three more Alices that he brought to life in the destruction of the Illusionary Palace. He brought them here and gave them to Baliste."

"Why on earth would he do that?" Henderson puzzled as Eddie closed his arms around his grandmother.

"That is an excellent question." Alice replied tiredly.

"Then I guess we'll have to fight her another day, but we will take her down." Diovalo vowed.

Oppa waddled over to the spiked, spade tail laying in the dirt, and she rubbed her paw slowly and thoughtfully over her mouth. "Hmm. Perhaps I am giving this a better look."

Very carefully, she brought big leaves from the forest on the wind to her, and without touching the dangerous tail end, she wrapped it thickly, and then vanished with it, and reappeared a few moments later.

Eddie looked about and then raised his brows hopefully at Piper. "Did you find your mom? Was she with the captured dragons?"

Piper dropped her head as she shook it, and looked down at the ground. "No. She did not come out with them. She is not here."

Eddie went to her and wrapped his arms around her. "Do you still feel her? Can you feel her presence?"

Piper raised her head and closed her eyes, concentrating. Slowly, she nodded. "Yes, I think I can. No... I'm sure of it. I'm sure I can still feel her. That hasn't changed at all!"

Eddie smiled at her. "If that hasn't changed, then I bet your mom is still alive somewhere, just not here. You keep the faith, my friend."

Piper fluttered her wings rapidly and rose into the air with a smile. "I am sure of it! So sure of it! My mom is somewhere still, and all the bad dragons are gone! That means that Diovalo will be the king now! King Diovalo!" She cried out loudly.

"Not without a fight." A deep voice lashed out at them from behind the dragon prince. They all turned quickly, and saw Liceverous rearing up on his back legs, claws out, and teeth bared. He had finally crawled out of the hole where he'd been hiding and watching.

"Diovalo, I challenge you to a fight for the throne!"

Chapter Eleven

The Dragon King

Baliste clenched her teeth tightly as two of her servant goblins who had remained in the fortress, seared the bloody stump of her tail with a hot iron from the fire, cauterizing it.

When she was able to breathe again, she walked slowly and carefully down to the dungeon, going to a different cell, far from the dragon cage.

It was a large enclosure. It had to be, in order to hold its occupant. Baliste opened the door and entered the chamber; her eyes steady on her prisoner.

She lay weak and listless on the floor of the cell, not even bothering to raise her eyes to the sorceress. She only moved one of her legs to try to get more comfortable, and as she did so, the chains that held her firmly in place rattled some.

"And how are you feeling today, my fire dragon friend?" Baliste asked coldly.

She gave no answer.

"It's important that I check on you, because you see, you are very special. All fire dragons are. I realized that after I struck you with my tail when we fought, and I injected you with my venom. My venom always kills very slowly and painfully, but that didn't happen with you. You see, because you're a fire dragon, you can't die from my venom, but you can change, and that's what happening to you right now. You are in transition. You are changing,

~ 226 ~

and when the change is complete, you will be lethal. When I bring the dragon prince here to you and change him as well, the two of you will become the parents of a race of the most dangerous dragons in the world, and they will become my new army. Then nothing can stop me from moving forward with my plans."

Baliste walked back to the door and glanced over her shoulder. "Now, imagine the kind of honor that would bring you, being the mother of the most lethal dragons ever to exist."

Baliste walked out, closing the door behind her.

The fire dragon closed her eyes and murmured, "I already am."

* * *

Diovalo rose up on his hind legs and roared. "Come to me then, worm, and we will see who is fit to become the king of the dragons!"

Everyone in Alice's army and all of the freed fire dragons were gathered at the edge of the timberline, well out of the way of the fighting circle.

Liceverous snarled at Diovalo, snapping his long, thin snout at him. "Lord Malevor is dead, and now I am the lord of the earth dragons! I want to claim the throne as king of the dragons!"

Diovalo's voice reverberated off of the ground, the trees, and even the fortress walls. "You are no lord of the dragons unless I give you that honor myself, and that will never happen!"

"Then I shall take the honor of king from you, and leave you dying in your own blood!" Liceverous shot straight forward, turning on his back as he reached Diovalo, biting and clawing at the bigger dragon's underbelly.

Diovalo blasted him with flames and reached his claws toward the earth dragon, but Liceverous was too fast, and escaped, circling behind Diovalo as the great fire dragon turned to face him again.

"You may be bigger, but I am faster, and I have more claws!" Liceverous raced around Diovalo and scampered up his tail to his back, ripping and biting at the great dragon, slicing his hide open with every chance he got.

Diovalo turned and rolled on his back, smashing Liceverous before the smaller dragon could get away. As Diovalo got to his feet, he shot his front claws out and managed to catch Liceverous by his long, spaded tail.

Holding fast to the end of it, Diovalo drew the dragon up into the air over his head as Liceverous screamed, and then slammed him down on the ground with every ounce of force he had left in his body.

Liceverous coughed and sputtered, but managed to get up and run before Diovalo's hind foot and claws came crashing down where he had just been laying.

"You're going to have to do better than that, weak prince! Perhaps it will be as easy to kill you as it was to kill your mother! I was there and I watched it happen. She died horribly and painfully, and I will watch you die the same way today!"

Liceverous rushed at Diovalo, crawling up the front of him and closing his jaws tightly on Diovalo's neck. The dragon prince gripped his enemy and pulled him free, though the earth dragon left a few deep gashes in Diovalo's throat.

Diovalo roared again, and closing his claws around several of Liceverous' feet, ripped them off of his body and tossed them aside.

Liceverous screamed in pain, and Diovalo threw him to the ground and placed his hind foot across the earth dragon's neck, almost crushing him.

Liceverous wriggled and cried, struggling to breathe.

Diovalo brought his head down close to his foe. "I am not like you. I could kill you right now, but I won't. I'm going to let you live with the shame of your defeat. Go and hide in your hole, worm, and never let me see you again, because this is the only time I will let you live."

Diovalo lifted his foot and Liceverous scampered off as best he could, whining and whimpering.

A great cheer sounded from the onlookers at the forest's edge, and Diovalo went to them, bloody and spent. "It is done now. Let us go home."

Queen Diantha waved her wand, making a portal, and a heartbeat later, they were all gone.

Liceverous watched them disappear from a shadowed corner at the base of the fortress and growled deeply. He sniffed around the walls until he found a door that he could fit through, and he beat on it until a troll opened it.

"I must see Baliste, right away." He insisted.

The troll let him in.

* * *

The wide swath of beach at Siang flooded with the members of Alice's army, and the fire dragons they had rescued.

Chippa went right to Diovalo. "Rest in the sand, and Oppa and I are healing you." He spoke with a gentle, comforting voice.

Diovalo pulled away from the Inkling. "No. There are others injured worse than me. See to them first."

Alice cleared her throat. "They are being seen to, dear one. The healers amongst the fairies are out helping, as are Henderson and Caraway. Eddie and I are doing all that we can as well. These dragons need a king who is strong and healthy. Please let Chippa and Oppa help you now."

"Very well, but only on one condition. Take my tears and use them to help heal the others."

Alice nodded and gave him a wide smile. "I'll do that." She used a bowl and collected a few of the massive tears he shed for her, as Eddie stared in wonder.

"Why are you doing that?" He peered into the filled bowl.

"Dragon tears have healing power." Alice explained. "All right now, Diovalo, I have what I need. I'll come back if I need more. You let our little healers help you."

Diovalo resigned, slumping down into the sand. The two Inklings got to work caring for him immediately. "

Eddie and Alice visited the most seriously injured first, using the dragon's tears and practically erasing their wounds altogether, before moving on to those who had come out of the battle better off.

Henderson found Alice and cleared his throat. "It seems as though everyone who was in need of care has been attended to. I thought I might begin cooking a meal for us."

Alice frowned. "Look at us, missing Cherie already. She'd have had it whipped up in no time."

"Indeed, Madame. I'll do my best in her stead."

Alice smiled. "You do very well on your own, in no one's stead. Thank you, Henderson."

With Channa's help, he took to Cherie's makeshift kitchen, cooking a meal for them. Henderson created different fares for the variety of different friends within the company, and when they were all seated together with their repast, a few of them began to share stories, and then a few more did the same, and it wasn't long before the whole group was piecing together their experiences in the battle, and painting a much larger picture of it.

The telling and sharing of it brought them closer together, bonding them through a trial by fire.

Late afternoon light colored the sky in myriad tones of gold and red, orange and pink, with a dash of hues in green and blue at the edges. Alice gazed at it, painting the memory in her mind to keep it always. Honeyed light washed over the beach as the sun sunk near the tops of the mountains.

"I will never get over the fact that the sun and moon rise in the west here, and set in the east. It feels so backward to me." Alice shook her head, and Henderson agreed.

"I suppose it's like driving on the other side of the road or reading a book from right to left rather than left to right. It takes some getting used to."

Murray got a second plate of food and rejoined them. "This is a fun event! Theatre festivals are a hoot! All the best costumes, you know. I haven't seen this production before, but I am enjoying it! It's quite good!"

Alice laughed. "I'm glad to hear that you're enjoying it, Murray."

When the meal was finished, Lord Japheth rose and spoke to the gathering.

"As this significant day draws to an end, all of the dragons of Siang are home where they belong, and we are honored to share this momentous night with the friends gathered in our midst."

A great cheer rose, and Lord Japheth continued. "This evening we will remember our lost queen and celebrate her with the coronation of her son, Diovalo, the prince of dragons, and his ascension to the throne."

He turned to face Diovalo.

"Do you, Diovalo, prince of dragons, accept the throne of the dragons, and take it as king?"

Diovalo stood tall, looking proud, and mighty.

"I will."

"Speaking for the sea dragons of Siang, we pledge our oath of alliance to you."

Andessai rose and spoke clearly over the gathering. "Speaking for the earth dragons, such of us which remain here in Siang, we pledge our oath of alliance to you."

Lord Japheth addressed the fire dragons who had all been rescued. "Do you, fire dragons of Siang, pledge your oath of alliance to Prince Diavolo?"

A hearty chorus of, "I will" echoed out over the beach.

Lord Japheth faced Diovalo. "Then I present to the world of Corevé, King Diovalo, ruler of the dragons of Siang."

The gathering erupted in cheers, applause, howls, hoots, cries of joy, and sparks of magic light. Alice leapt to her feet, cheering amongst the loudest of them with her entire family at her side.

"Fireworks!" Murray cried out excitedly. "Brilliant!"

Diovalo waited until the uproar had quieted before he spoke. "I accept the throne of the dragon king."

Every guest there bowed low to him as a sign of respect and allegiance.

"I will reunite the dragon realms, so that we are all one again, balanced and equal. We cannot defeat the evil in this world if we are divided. Only in unity can we be strong enough to take down the wicked one who wields too much power and should not be where she is."

Another resounding cheer filled the air. Diovalo looked straight at Alice then.

"I know now what my mother meant when she told me that the one who restored the Blue Fire Crystal would save the dragons from themselves. We would have been lost to Baliste without Alice, because of a terrible betrayal, but Alice Perivale returned to Corevé when the call for help went out to her, and it is because of her that we are all here tonight, gathered together as we should be. We owe you a great debt, dear Alice. Thank you."

Alice held her hands up to her cheeks as they warmed and turned pink, and once more the crowd erupted in joyous celebration.

* * *

Baliste stalked unevenly into the great hall where the mystic sat motionless upon the mat on the floor. The sorceress was still learning to walk with imbalance after part of her tail had been chopped off.

Outrage burned in Baliste's eyes as she glared at the mystic.

"Mystic!" She accosted with a harsh shout.

The mystic merely stared straight ahead, almost as if oblivious to the being before it.

"You said that the prophecy of Alice was supposed to end with the recovery of the Blue Fire Crystal! Obviously that has not happened!"

The mystic spoke evenly, and her eyes remained closed. "I said that Alice was prophesied to find and return the Blue Fire Crystal. I did not say that it ended there. To the contrary, the prophecy of Alice only began with the Blue Fire Crystal."

Baliste growled deeply and began to pace.

"I can't *believe* this. All this time I thought it was done. All this time I thought she was out of my way! And all this time she has been the very center of the storm around me and I had no idea!"

Continuing in her uneven pacing, Baliste concentrated. "I've been focusing on the wrong things. I tried to bring about my plans with the Blue Fire Crystal, and then the fire dragons, but I've been going about this all wrong. What I really need to do is capture and kill the real Alice. Then, and only then, all of my plans for Corevé can come to fruition!"

"Your highness…" A goblin announced from the corner of the room.

Baliste turned in place and shot him a dark look. "I'm busy! What is it?"

"You have a visitor." The goblin ducked away as Liceverous crawled into the room, beaten and broken.

"My queen, I have come to offer my services to you."

Baliste narrowed her eyes to slits and spoke with an icy tone. "Why would I ever want a pathetic failure like you in my court?"

"Perhaps you already know, my queen, that only the Inklings and the fairies can open portals."

"What of it? If you have nothing useful to tell me, then be gone. I will not have my time wasted!"

Liceverous grinned coolly at her. "We don't need the fairies or the Inklings to travel. I know a secret way to Alice's real world."

CHAPTER TWELVE

HOME AGAIN

Eddie rode on Oscar's back in the early morning light as they traveled along the edge of the shoreline, with Piper flying idly beside them.

"Piper," Eddie asked gently, "can you still feel your mom?"

Piper didn't even pause to think about it. "Yes. I'm certain my mom is alive, no matter what anyone else says."

Eddie nodded. "We all lose people we love, but they live on in our hearts all of our lives."

Piper spun in the air and fluttered her wings. "My mom isn't lost for good. She really is still alive, and I'm going to find her!"

"I'll do whatever I can to help you while I'm here." Eddie promised.

Piper beamed. "I'm so glad that we're friends! Thank you!"

"Best friends!" Oscar added with a little skip to his step that made Eddie hold on tighter and laugh.

"Best friends." Eddie and Piper agreed together.

As they headed back to the camp, they were caught by surprise.

"Where is everyone?" Eddie called out, searching the beach and the camp.

"Most of our army has gone home darling. Chippa and Caraway are still here." Alice answered as Henderson helped Eddie down from Oscar's back.

"All of the fire dragons are on the beach!" Eddie grinned, letting his eyes rove over them.

They stood in many sizes, and in many colors; blues and greens, blacks and purples, burgundies and browns, and more. They were stretching their wings and seemed eager to be up in the air.

"Are they going?" Oscar asked with more than a hint of disappointment.

"No, young one. We've been waiting for you! We are taking you to see the blazing monoliths of Siang where the fire dragons live!" Diovalo smiled widely.

"Oh! I want to see! Let's go!" Oscar scrambled up into the hollow under Diovalo's wing, and found half of his family of cats there, along with Murray, who was delighted to be going for another ride. The rest of the cats were nestled into the hollow under the dragon's other wing.

"Are you sure you'll be all right up there?" Alice held her hand to her hat as she looked up at Caraway, who was perched on top of his own fire dragon, and looked ready to leave them all behind without waiting.

"Yes! I'm fine! Let's go already! We're losing daylight!" He shouted back.

She shook her head and turned to two more fire dragons nearby, who had each offered to carry Andessai and Rhyoden.

"How are you doing? Everything okay?" Alice checked with a smile and a wave.

"We've never been off the ground before." Rhyoden groaned.

"Never?" Alice raised her brows as her eyes widened.

"No. I think I might be sick." Rhyoden closed his eyes.

"Oh calm down." Andessai almost bounced, she was so elated to be on the back of a fire dragon. "I've never been so excited!"

Diovalo brought his head down low to Alice. "Are you ready?"

"I am!" She answered gaily, and she, along with Eddie, climbed onto the back of his neck.

"Are we going?" Keres called from the shallows just off of the beach.

"Yes!" Diovalo announced loudly. "Let's go!"

He lifted off of the ground, followed by more than a dozen fire dragons flanking him as they rose into the sky.

In the rushing green and dark blue ocean below, the sea dragons in all their numbers coursed through the waves, ducking, racing, and playing as they skimmed over and under the surface like lambent streaks of light.

They headed west of the beach, into the warm light of the morning sun, and out over the ocean waves for a long while, until at last the dragons slowed.

Before them, hovering a good distance above the sea, were giant monoliths of blackened rock reaching thick and high up into the air. Each of their tops were crowned with blazing fires which consumed so much of the upper monoliths that nothing could be seen within the flames.

The sea dragons swam in circles beneath them, and the fire dragons who bore passengers flew a moderate distance from them.

"This is where you live?" Alice cried out in wonder.

"It is. I was born here. All of the fire dragons were."

"And me too!" Piper twirled happily through the air. "I was born here too!"

"I'm sorry I can't get any closer; it isn't safe for you." Diovalo explained.

Alice shook her head. "Don't you worry about that! I'm just amazed to be able to see it! There's really no way to get here other than flying, is there!"

"No. No other way at all." Diovalo spoke proudly.

They watched as the fire dragons who had been freed and carried no one with them, sailed into the blazing flames, vanishing from sight; each of them going to their own monolith.

"They are going home." Alice held her hand to her heart.

"Yes, thanks to you." Diovalo spoke gratefully. "I'll go around a few times, so you can see them all, and then we'll return to the beach."

They circled, and the other dragons who carried their friends followed them, weaving in and out of some of the monoliths, getting a good look. Then, along with the sea dragons, who were having a rollicking good time below, they headed back to the beach.

As the monoliths disappeared behind them, and the beach grew bigger before them, Alice spoke into Eddie's ear.

"Hold on to more than just the dragon, and more than me. Hold on tightly to every single precious passing moment, and never forget this; never forget anything about this, from the scents in the air, to the colors we can see in everything, and the sounds of these wings beating against the sky. Hold fast to the taste of the salt on your lips, the feel of the rush of the wind in your hair, and the heat of the sun on your skin. Capture every bit of these things and hold on tight to it. Never let it go, for it may never come again. Let every thought in your mind slip away and be present, right here, right now, soaking up all of this to carry with you in your heart forever."

"I will grandma!" Eddie promised, and he did as he grinned from ear to ear.

After delivering their passengers, the rescued fire dragons left the beach, and returned to their monoliths. Rhyoden tottered a little unevenly in the sand.

"I'd better get him underground. I think the height and the light has been too much for him." Andessai laughed. "Alice, and all of you, it has been a great honor. Thank you for all that you have done for us."

"Thank you both." Alice waved to them as they headed for the hole in the hill.

"Everything is packed, Madame." Henderson had the bags sitting in the sand, ready to go.

Chippa's face fell.

Alice knelt beside him and wrapped an arm around his shoulder. "What is it? What's wrong?"

"I doesn't like it when you leaves." He sighed, and then sniffed.

"I doesn't like it either." Alice gave him a smile and drew him into a big hug. "You are missed when we are away. I love you."

Chippa closed his small arms around her neck tightly. "I loves you too." He replied, muffled in her ear.

"I have something for you." She stood and reached into her bag. "Just promise me you won't have them all at once. Perhaps it would be best to enjoy one each day."

She handed him three packets of ginger chews, and he chirped, growing so excited that a small wind rose beneath him and nearly toppled him over.

Alice took his paws and settled him back on the ground. He patted her hand. "See? We is both still learning."

"Indeed." She laughed.

Eddie hugged Piper tightly, and Oscar nuzzled the baby dragon. Eddie let her go and gave her a sad smile. "I hope I get to see you again sometime. I'll miss you. Good luck finding your mom."

"Thank you. I will always keep looking." Piper vowed. "I will miss you both."

"Thank you for your help, Caraway." Alice smiled at him earnestly.

"Well, someone had to get the light going down there in the dark. You'd never have seen a thing." Caraway sniffed and looked away.

"Not without you, we wouldn't." She admitted easily.

"Well, I'd best be going. The Light House is probably falling apart without me."

Henderson cleared his throat and shook his head at Alice when she opened her mouth to say something. She smirked instead, and kept her mouth shut.

"Best of luck to you all." Caraway nodded to them, and then in a flash of light, he vanished.

Sophie eyed her rough worn paws. "The first thing I'm doing when we get back is getting a pawdicure. I'm a mess!"

"It's true." Jynx gave her a light appraisal. "You've looked better."

Sophie rolled her eyes.

"When we get back, will you please make sweet biscuits for me, Henderson? Please?" Bailey practically begged.

Henderson patted his bag. "I have what we need right here."

"I'll be relieved that Alice is in far less danger in London. There aren't any battles being waged there, other than the one with that woman from the group you joined." Marlowe narrowed his eyes some.

"I wish I could stay and learn more about the mystics here! I'm so intrigued by them." Tao smiled a little.

Oscar looked over Alice's shoulder at the waves. "I wish I could stay and be a sea dragon with Piper!"

Eddie cocked his head to one side and gazed at the cats. "It will be so strange seeing you all as normal cats again."

"I'm not normal. I'm rare and special." Bailey announced with a flip of his pink tail.

"I'm certainly not normal either." Sophie pointed out.

"That's the truth." Jynx smirked.

Eddie laughed at them and Alice leaned close to his ear. "Actually, now that you know what they're really saying, you can almost hear their voices when they're in London at your ankles."

Keres, Callidus, Galiphes, and Lord Japheth came out of the sea and stood beside their king.

"It's difficult to say goodbye, my dear friends." Alice blinked back tears as she gazed at them. "But it seems it's time for us to go."

"We owe you a great debt." Lord Japheth spoke from his heart. "If ever we may be of help to you, we are your servants."

Alice nodded. "Thank you. I do hope that I can see you all again someday, perhaps under better circumstances."

"Do you still have my vial?" Diovalo asked quietly.

"Yes." She patted the black bag on her arm. "I have it, and I'll keep it safe."

"Use it anytime you need it."

"I'll remember that, thank you."

"Where's Murray?" Eddie gasped, and Henderson inclined his head a short distance away.

"I suggested he might collect a few more seashells. He's been preoccupied with it. I'll get him."

"Thank you, Henderson." Alice sighed.

With tears and good wishes, they said goodbye, and Alice made a silvery green arc with seawater, opening a portal for them there on the beach.

Murray beamed. "Oh! I think that's part of the Princess Diana Memorial Fountain! Hadn't seen this end of it, I suppose! Quite good!"

Taking Eddie's hand tightly in hers, Alice somehow made herself walk through it, and her family went with her.

An instant later, they were standing in the dark in Hyde Park, drenched in the pouring rain. Eddie gasped and clutched Alice's arm.

"Where... where are we?" He blinked rapidly as Henderson opened an umbrella above them.

"Hyde Park darling." Alice checked the clock on a pin she wore at the breast of her coat. "We've been gone about a minute."

"One minute? That's it?" Eddie gaped.

"Yes. Remember, time is different there."

"My goodness, the weather certainly changed fast, didn't it?" Murray's shoulders slumped in disappointment. "What a pity after such a fun day. Long day though, goodness. I feel like I've been up for a week! I think I ought to get back home. Can I give you a lift?"

"Yes, please Murray. Thank you." Alice chuckled.

She wasn't in the car two minutes when she twisted her head to check on Eddie.

"Is your seatbelt on? Tight?" Her eyes were wide.

"Yes." Eddie answered, more afraid than she was. "I wasn't even this scared in the battle!" He gripped the armrest on his door and Henderson looked green in the face.

"Oh thank goodness. We made it!" Alice almost leapt from Murray's car, and her family made as hasty an exit as she did.

"Please let's never do that again." Eddie begged.

"Corevé?" Alice asked in surprise.

"No. Get into a car when Murray is driving!"

Alice laughed and they headed for their door.

"Thank you, Murray!"

Murray stood in the rain with his umbrella open, and shook his head.

"Thank you! That was a nice visit to the park, and they've sure done a lot to it, but I think I'm going to have to phone the authorities tomorrow. I think some of the animals from the zoo have gotten loose."

He patted his pockets and frowned. "Uh oh. I think I left my glasses on that fancy dragon ride at the park. I'll have to go back in the morning and see if someone has turned them in."

Murray looked up at them with a tired smile. "Well, I could do with a hot cup of tea and a nap. Good night, all." The old man waved one last time and ambled down the sidewalk to his home.

"Let's get inside. I could do with some tea as well." Alice led her family up the steps as Henderson held the door open for them.

It wasn't long before Henderson had a fire crackling in the hearth, and they were all seated together with a cup of hot tea. The cats were curled up in their baskets, snoozing and warming themselves, and Eddie shook his head in disbelief.

"I'm so amazed that it was all real. It feels like a dream now, but being there felt more real than anything here, almost. It's so strange."

"It is indeed." Alice replied. "But we have the wonderful memories to cherish, and some to let go of as well, I think."

Eddie's hand dropped to his side, and he gasped as he realized what it was he was touching. From a tree bark sheath that Ali had made for him to fit on his belt, he drew out his glass sword.

"I still have my sword!" He marveled at it. "I got so used to wearing it that I forgot I had it!"

It had been no longer than his hip to his knee, and once strapped into the sheath, it had become part of his attire; unnoticeable.

Alice's eyes grew wide. She rose to her feet and held her hand out. "Your parents may not understand my letting you have a sword, and there's really no explaining to anyone in this world what it's made out of. You're welcome to keep it here. It will be safe, and you can have it anytime you like when you visit."

"Oh, you're right about that grandma. My parents probably wouldn't approve." Eddie gave the sword to Alice, and together they hung it above the fireplace.

Alice placed Diovalo's glass vial near it on the mantle and then turned to face her grandson. "You do realize that you mustn't share any part of this adventure with anyone, right?"

"I do, and I promise it will be kept a secret." Eddie smiled at her. "I do want to learn more about knitting, though, if you don't mind. That was terrific armor!"

Alice frowned. "Except where that goblin got your sleeve. I should have made sleeves for you on the sheath. I'm sorry about that. In any event, we can take up knitting tomorrow. I think we could all do with a good night's rest."

Henderson bid them good night, and Alice and Eddie headed upstairs to their respective rooms. Eddie paused in the hallway and touched Alice's arm. She turned to him and his eyes glistened.

"I know that someday you will go. Nothing can stop that, but no matter where you are, you will always be with me in my heart. I'm not afraid of losing you anymore."

Alice hugged him tightly. "I will always be in your heart too, and remember-"

He smiled wide. "I can find you in the stars."

She nodded proudly at him. "Just so."

Sunday afternoon came much sooner than any of them wanted it to, and afternoon tea had barely been finished, complete with Inkling sweet biscuits, when Ed and Annabel knocked on the door. Henderson invited them in, and they were all smiles until Annabel saw the sleeve of Eddie's button up shirt in shredded tatters.

"What happened to you?" Annabel rushed to him and ran her fingers over the torn cloth.

"I told you not to wear that." Alice murmured.

Eddie chuckled. "I'm quite proud of it, actually." He looked at his mother. "It happened while I was... playing chess."

He shared a swift wink with his grandmother, and Annabel scowled.

"That must have been some match!"

"The most challenging I've ever been involved in." Eddie answered as Henderson and Alice tried to hide their smiles.

"Thank you for visiting. We've loved having you here." Alice hugged Eddie tightly, and Henderson gave him an earnest nod.

"I'll come back much more often, and soon. I can't wait to see you all again."

Oscar stood on his hind legs and pawed at Eddie's knee. Eddie grinned and bent over, picking the kitten up. They snuggled closely and Eddie whispered in his ear.

"You watch over this troop, Oscar. Keep them out of trouble, who knows what could happen." Oscar purred, and Eddie set him back down.

They all walked out onto the step in the sunlight, to say goodbye, and Eddie was about to take the stairs when he happened to look across the road and his whole body froze.

A woman in dark clothes was standing near a pole, watching Alice with a cold, strange stare.

TO BE CONTINUED...

Journey Blue

By Dash Hoffman

Chapter One
Geniss

Step, step, step, step. Walking, walking, walking. Turn. Turn. Going. All of them; going. Step, step, step, step. Walking, walking, walking. Turn. Turn. Going. All of them still going.

People passing in one direction; most of them tall, most of them staring straight ahead. Most of them dressed in coats and hats. Coats and hats and walking shoes. Walking, walking, walking. Going. People passing in the other direction; walking, turning, going.

Vehicles rolling down the road; going and turning, turning and going. They all move, and they keep moving, and the buildings squeezed in too tight together, rising high above the street, looking down sternly and silently at all of them moving; all of them going.

Going with their mouths set in thin lines. Going with their eyes staring straight ahead. Going without seeing, without hearing, without speaking, without stopping. Going and going.

The girl watched all of it in consternation; standing alone at the corner of a building where one side of it faced the street, the people, the traffic, all of it going, and the other side of the building faced an alleyway; dark and gritty, narrow and unwelcoming. It wasn't a space; the alleyway; only more of a happenstance between buildings, and there she stood, still and watching, in the happenstance.

She watched the city as it moved past her; its veins coursing with rhythmic regularity, never changing, never stopping. She didn't understand it. She wasn't much a part of it; little thing that she was, though she was in it.

Lifting her hand, she set it on the brick corner of the building beside her and saw that her fingers didn't fit it; that it wasn't made for her hand to be there. Looking from her hand to her arm and then down at the rest of her body, she frowned slightly, wondering if any of her fit it, or fit the alley where she was standing, or the street she had been walking on when she stopped to look at it, because no one stopped. No one ever stopped.

The girl wondered at being alone in such a place, and she considered that in the grand scheme of things, as she stood there at the base of it all, that she didn't really matter too much. She was only *there*; a fragment, with no place or belonging.

Looking back out to the street, she thought of a word. It came to her mind and stuck there. Methodical. Operating with a method. It was like a puzzle, she thought, all of it together; all the little pieces.

The people, the streets, the cars, the buildings, the darkness above; always the darkness above, far and out of reach, mysterious and soundless, formless, going on forever. Always there, always dark, but not black.

The darkness was gray; not light and not ebony, but something in between that never changed. Something that let nothing out and nothing in. Grayness.

She peered up at it and squinted her eyes. Dark grayness. She thought to herself that she might well be the only person in the whole city of Geniss that was looking up, or that had ever looked up for all that she knew.

A tapping sound touched her ears, and caught her attention like a fish at the end of a hook. She turned her head swiftly and looked. An old man with a cane was walking slowly down the street in his old coat and his old hat, staring straight ahead; his mouth set in a thin line, his eyes distant.

Tap, step. Tap, step. Tap, step. The girl raised her hand and waved a little at him, shy to do it, but giving in to the glimmer of hope inside of her. He did not see her, and he kept going. Tap, step. Tap, step.

With a resigned sigh, she left the corner and stepped back into the slow, methodical, rolling current of people along the sidewalk. She returned to being one of them; going.

The girl closed her hands into small balls and pushed them down into the two pockets on the front of her baby doll shirt. It looked something like a short dress, with dark blue straps over her shoulders, a white shirt beneath it, and a flare of material from the chest going outward and downward. If she twirled, it looked almost like a dress rising on the air, but she almost never twirled. And there were pockets. Two pockets on the front of it that were just right for her hands to be pushed down into, or to keep things in, if she found anything she might like to keep, or both, if she was lucky. Beneath her baby doll shirt, she wore soft matching blue pants, and little black shoes with a fat strap and a buckle on each side.

The girl liked the color of her clothes, mostly because it matched her. She had navy-blue hair, medium sea blue skin, and light sky-blue eyes. Most of the people in the city were one color or another, though nothing bright or cheery; never. There were grays and beiges, dusty sages and puces, and some other colors that she didn't know, but none of them were bright or lively.

As she walked along the sidewalk, trying to match her steps to the same rhythm of the grown-up walking near her, she wondered why there weren't more children in the city. She wasn't the only one; not at all, but babies and children weren't common in the city, and she thought how she would like to see more of them, and perhaps make a friend of one of them someday.

The girl was just coming to a corner when she felt a tug on her shirt, and she turned to look behind her; curious as to who might have wanted her attention.

She saw no one standing there, but there was an older woman a few feet off who looked down at her and shook her head, and then turned away.

The girl bit at her lower lip a moment, thinking perhaps it had been the old woman who had tugged at her, but the old woman left her, and she was alone, save for all of the people around her who were going and coming and coming and going. With a shrug, she joined them all again, returning to the stream.

She walked a long while; sometimes trying to keep her eyes straight ahead like the people around her, but more often looking around to see what was happening.

She noticed an old man sitting on a bench against the wall of a building. He was staring straight ahead, but he was sitting and not moving, and she decided to sit with him and see if he would talk to her.

At first, the old man did not look at her when she sat beside him. Her light eyes examined his old weathered face, and she lifted her chin a little and spoke loudly so that he could be sure to hear her above the noise of the city.

"Hello!" She waited hopefully.

The old man blinked as if he might be coming out of a reverie of sorts, and he turned his head very slowly toward her; his deep set gray eyes finally finding hers. "Did you say hello?"

The girl smiled and nodded at him. "Yes, I said hello. My name is Blue."

He seemed confused that anyone would sit beside him and talk with him. "Oh... hello Blue. I'm..." He paused a moment and thought carefully.

"I'm..." He thought harder. Blinking his eyes again, he pressed his lips together as he searched his mind. After a moment stretched so thin that it broke, he looked back at her shook his head slowly.

"I'm sorry, I don't recall who I am." The man looked disappointed about it.

Blue tapped her toes together on the cracked concrete pavement beneath them. "Oh. Well, that's okay. I can call you somebody, because you are somebody. We know that, at least. I saw you sitting alone and thought you might want some company for a few minutes. Have you been here long?"

Somebody furrowed the thick, long, gray and white hairs of his wrinkled brow. "Been where?"

Blue fidgeted with her fingertips a little bit, not realizing that she was doing it. "Um... on this bench. Have you been on this bench for very long?"

Somebody nodded like molasses then, finally understanding her question. "Yes, I guess I have. I've been sitting on this bench for a very long time."

Somebody turned his head and looked at the city and then sighed. "The city was only half as big as it is now when I sat down here, but now it's twice the size that it was then."

Blue tilted her head in wonder and turned her eyes to the city. She couldn't imagine it half the size that it was just then. "Will it keep growing?"

"Yes, it will." He replied tiredly. "How long have you been in the city? You're quite young, aren't you?"

She shrugged. "I've been here a little while. I'm old enough. I'm ten." Blue gave him a proud smile.

Somebody smiled back at her. "Ten is good. Old enough, I guess."

Blue wanted to talk more, but the old man closed his eyes and seemed to drift off. She didn't want to disturb him, so she stood up again and gave him a little wave of her hand, though he didn't see it. She turned and stepped back into the stream of people going by.

Passing building after building, and crossing street after street, she finally came to a stop before a structure that was made of large metal boxes. She had heard once that at one time they had been train cars, and then they were stacked all together and made into a building where people lived. The cars were set at varying angles, so that some of them went one way and others went another way, but they all went up, and so did a rickety old metal staircase, right up the side of them, so people could get to any of them.

The girl lifted her foot to place it on the first step at the bottom of the staircase, when she felt something tug lightly at her.

Surprised, she turned and looked over her shoulder. There was no one. She looked around her carefully, in case someone might have just stepped back or ducked aside, and she thought maybe someone was playing a trick on her, but there was no one. She pursed her mouth and looked down at the railing on the stairs beside her. There was a corner on it, and she realized that her baby doll shirt must have gotten caught on it and that was what tugged her. Keeping clear of it, she took the steps one at a time until she reached the fifth car from the top. It was a blue car, though it was faded and rusted in many places.

Hanging over the opening of the doorway was a curtain made of light material. She pushed it back and stepped inside. There was nothing really in the rusted, grungy, old metal box, other than an open window, and she walked to it and looked out of it.

A narrow view of the city stared back at her. It was all the same things that she had been looking at earlier, except that she was a bit higher off of the ground, though not high up enough to see over any of it. It looked dim to her, and she had never seen it look any other way. Dim and gray.

Something tugged at her shirt again, and she knew instantly that she wasn't imaging it. She turned sharply to see what had pulled at her, and she drew in a sharp breath at what she saw.

There was no tangible thing there, but for the first time there wasn't nothing there, either. A few feet behind her there was a shimmer of light; iridescent and beautiful, like a rainbow mixed with light shining on water, or through it, and it looked like a translucent wall; thin and small, almost like a window that wasn't really there.

Blue stared at it and tried to make out what it was, but she had never seen anything like it, and she had no idea what it could be. Her mind zoomed with questions, and she found that none of the answers that came with them fit the questions at all; square pegs and round holes, none of the answers she could come up with fit any of the questions that she had.

"Dojie." She murmured as she watched the shimmer window fade and disappear. "I have to go ask Dojie. She will know."

Blue hurried from the metal box house and went up the old staircase to another box car two levels up and to the left. There was a beaded curtain over the doorway, made of wooden beads, colored red, tan, brown, and yellow. It went well with the brown, rusted box car, and it was the only colorful thing that Blue could remember seeing that wasn't a machine shade.

She knocked and called inside softly. "Dojie! Dojie, it's me." Poking her head in the doorway, she smiled and stepped inside.

The box car had a few things in it. There was an old picture frame on the wall, though there was no picture in it. It was made of wood and had a thin wire on the back of it, which allowed it to hang on a piece of metal that was poking inward from the wall.

There was a chair; old and wooden as well, that faced the window, and over the window were two worn lace curtains open wide and gathered like skirts at the sides. In the chair was an old woman with a round face, big round eyes, a round nose, and a full round mouth, which had been closed and still. The mouth widened into a smile at the sound of the new voice in the room.

"Blue, is that you? Come in, child, come in." The older woman stared straight ahead, but she lifted her hand and waved in the direction of the door.

She was wearing a great red turban, wound round and round so that it was tall; like a pillar coming off of the crown of her head. Some of her gray and white hair showed around the edges, perfectly complimenting her dark brown skin, which was smooth in some places and wrinkled in others.

Her body was large, and time had made it hang here and there just a bit, shifting her shape so that there was more of her in the middle than there had been when she was younger.

She was dressed in what were once vibrant colors; her large tunic in reds, yellows, greens, blues, and browns, all forming strange and beautiful patterns. Her skirt beneath it had also been bright once, matching some of the colors in her tunic, though it was faded as well. Time had washed over the woman and she looked worn, but pleasant.

"It's me, Dojie." Blue answered, going to the floor at Dojie's feet. The old woman reached her hand out and let her fingers move gently over the young girls short cropped hair; wavy with round curls, just reaching her small shoulders.

"Well look at that, it is you." Dojie's wide smile remained. She continued to stare straight ahead, her silvery eyes locked on nothing, seeing nothing. "What brings you by here?" She asked curiously, as her fingertips moved delicately over Blue's face.

Dojie frowned. "Something's bothering you." Her fingertips felt the furrowed brow over Blue's eyes. "What is it?"

"How did you know that Dojie?" Blue asked incredulously. "You know everything."

Dojie laughed softly. "No, I don't know everything, but being blind lets me see just about everything. I can see so much, child. You could never imagine it. Now, what's biting at you?"

Blue chewed on her lower lip and twisted her fingers together. "Well, I was out in the city today and I thought that someone was tugging at me, you know, pulling on my clothes. So I looked, but there was no one. Then I felt it again a few times, but there was never anyone there."

Dojie frowned slightly. "Is that so?"

"When I went to my box it happened once more, but it was stronger than all the other times today, and when I turned around, I saw something." Blue thought back to it and her mind grew ever more tangled with numerous questions.

"Well that's a curiosity. And what did you see?" Dojie asked intently, listening to Blue as if every word she said was the most important thing that Dojie would ever hear.

Blue looked up at the old woman and studied her face. There was kindness in every line and curve.

"I saw a shimmer… thing. Kind of like a wall or a window, but I could see through it, like it wasn't really there. I never saw anything like that before. It was so strange. It was kind of… colored. The colors moved, going back and forth."

Blue moved her hand up and down, and Dojie felt it with her fingers. "Like a wave?"

The little girl lowered her hand and watched the old woman. "Yes, like that. Have you heard of that before, Dojie? What was it? What did I see? Why is it pulling at me?"

Hope lit the girl's eyes somewhat, and the old woman sat quietly for a moment as a thoughtful expression came over her face. "So many questions." She said quietly. She thought longer and then spoke again.

"When we have more questions than answers, then the best thing to do is to look more closely. Do you know about windows?" Dojie asked, a strange smile turning up at the corners of her mouth as her silver eyes glittered with intrigue.

Blue frowned and pushed her lips out a little. "Like the window right there in the wall? That kind of window?"

Dojie rocked in her chair and chuckled. "No, child. A window to the mind and soul! A way to see inside. You see, we spend our lives looking outside of ourselves; looking at everything around us in the wide world, but hardly anyone stops to look inside of themselves and honey, that's where most of the answers are."

Blue was amazed. Her wide eyes were locked on the old blind woman in the chair. "I don't know how to do that. Can you show me how to do that please?"

A deep laugh sounded in the old woman; a belly laugh, and Dojie reached her hand out and found Blue's shoulder, giving it a gentle pat. "You bet I can. You just watch me, and listen. Pay close attention, now."

Blue had never concentrated so much as she did watching Dojie, who leaned forward in her chair and raised her hand before her.

The old woman closed her eyes and drew in a long breath, holding it for a moment and then letting it go.

As she exhaled, she traced her fingertips in the air before her, creating the invisible shape of a box, like a window. As she moved her hand along, she spoke.

"I am focusing with all of my mind on what I want to see, on what I want to connect with and touch, on what is already inside of my head and my heart. I'm calling it up from my depths." Dojie began to hum in a low voice, almost imperceptibly.

Where her fingers moved, there were trails of light, like shimmering strings; a single thread of a spider's web, and then more threads, thin and iridescent, which stayed where she had drawn them, until at last there was a glimmering square before her.

"Do you see the square? Like a window?" Dojie whispered adamantly.

Blue nodded, gripping her fingers tightly around the arm on Dojie's chair. "I do! I see it! It's so beautiful!"

"Look inside it." Dojie told her. Blue did as she was bade, and stood up beside the chair, peering eye level into the window.

"I see... I see a building. It looks like a house, and there's a lot of land there with no other buildings on it, like a farm. Is that what a real farm looks like? Is that right?"

Blue was confused and fascinated all at once. The imagery in the illusion window was transparent but colorful; more colorful than she had ever seen anything be.

The window wasn't really there, and she could see the wall behind it, right through it, but the scene in the window looked more perfect to her than anything she had ever seen before.

Grass grew on the land, and flowers were sprinkled all through it. There was a wooden porch with a rocking chair and a small table. On the table was a book and a glass with dark amber liquid in it. The grass seemed to waver a little, as if the picture was moving some.

"It is a farm. It's pretty, isn't it?" Dojie smiled and nodded, leaning back in her chair. "You just looked into a window in my mind; in my soul. Now, I want you to concentrate as hard as you can, and you ask yourself about what's in your head and heart, ask yourself the question about what it is that's tugging at you, and I bet you'll find out what it is that you want to know."

Blue lifted her hand and moved it in the shape of a square. "Nothing's happening." The girl mumbled with a lowered brow.

"Keep on at it." Dojie encouraged her. "No one is going to get it on the first try. Go on now. Do it again, and then do it again after that."

Biting her lower lip, Blue traced her hand through the air over and over again, and even though nothing came of it. Dojie sat patiently and waited.

"Are you still going at it?" The old woman asked with a sweet smile.

Blue sighed. "Yes. Nothing is happening though. I don't think I can do it."

Dojie shook her head. "That's why nothing is happening. You aren't going to see anything until you know that you can do it. You have to believe it deep inside. Know it without an ounce of doubt, and it will happen."

Taking a deep breath, Blue pursed her lips tightly and concentrated with everything inside of her. She focused on the questions in her mind. What was the light she had seen? What was tugging at her? Why was it tugging at her?

A gasp escaped her, and Dojie beamed and chuckled. "It's happening?" She asked, already seeming to know.

"Yes! There are strings like you made! Now... now they're bigger! I'm doing it, Dojie! I'm really doing it!" She moved her hand faster and concentrated even harder, and the box appeared.

Dojie leaned closer to Blue. "Look inside your window. Look! What's in it? What can you see?"

Blue stared at the window before her in confusion. "I see... I see... a boy!"

Inside the square was an unclear image of a dark-haired boy, sitting still with his hands in his lap. His eyes were closed. Nothing seemed to be moving in the picture.

"Really? Is he older or younger than you?" It was the old woman's turn to be fascinated.

"I think he's older. He's bigger than me, but not too much." Blue studied him curiously.

"Do you know him?" Dojie urged.

With a slight shake of her head, Blue knit her brow. "No, I don't know him."

"What is he doing?" Dojie asked with a grin.

Blue watched the boy and spoke with a note of uncertainty in her voice. "He isn't doing anything at all. He's just sitting there, with his eyes closed. He's not moving."

Dojie's smile faded a bit. "He is?" She was quiet a moment, and then she reached for Blue's hand. "What can you feel right now?"

Blue drew in a new breath and thought about it. "I feel the tugging. It's stronger now than it was before."

With an understanding nod of her head, Dojie closed her fingers gently around Blue's hand. "And what direction is this pull going in?" She asked quietly.

"Toward the window. Toward the boy." Blue blinked and frowned. "I... I think he is pulling me. I think he wants me to go to him."

Dojie nodded slowly. "Focus on that pull. Focus with everything in you. Does it feel like you should go to him or stay away? Now think hard on that! Which is it?"

Blue's eyes widened. "It feels like I should go to him. I think… I think he needs me. I think he needs my help, maybe. The pull feels really strong."

Blue reached her hand up slowly, almost as if she was in a trance, and she hesitated only a moment; her fingertips nearly touching the image in the square. She moved her hand forward to see if she could reach into it, and the square along with the image inside of it, disappeared altogether.

"It's gone!" Blue gasped, startled as she turned quickly to Dojie.

"Did you try to touch it?" Dojie asked quietly.

"I did. How did you know that? You know everything, don't you." Blue smiled a little, though confusion flooded her thoughts.

"I don't know everything." The old woman replied kindly. She was quiet a moment and then she turned her body toward Blue, though she still looked straight ahead, blind to what was right in front of her.

"Will you go to the boy?" Her voice was solemn.

Blue looked down and thought about it for a long moment as Dojie waited. Finally she looked up at her friend.

"Yes. I think I have to. I think, maybe if he needs me, then I should go. I don't think the pull is going to go away." Blue hesitated for a moment and worry filled her eyes.

"Dojie, what will happen if I leave Geniss?" Blue searched the old woman's eyes, though she knew she would find no answer there.

Dojie pressed her lips together and shook her head. "What, this old city? Nothing happens in Geniss. Everything keeps turning while nothing much changes. You know that. If you go, nothing here will really change except that you'll be gone."

Blue spoke just above a whisper. "But Dojie... I'm not sure I can go to find this boy on my own."

Two weathered dark brown hands reached out and closed tenderly around the young girl's hands.

"I am sure that you can. The emptiness inside of you will be rewritten if you find someone who needs you."

Blue slowly took in a big breath. "But how do I get to him? How do I find him to help him?"

Dojie gave her a little smile. "You know how to create the window to the mind and heart now. You know how to look for him. You just follow that pull and it will lead you to him. It will guide you. You can make it. I know you can. You're a strong girl."

Blue rose to her feet and the old woman let her hands go. "Okay, Dojie. I will go to him. Where do I start?"

Dojie stood up from her chair; her red turbaned head much higher than the young girl before her. "You start here, and you start now. When you leave the box cars, go toward the pinpoint of light. I can tell you at least that much. Go to the pinpoint of light, and take this with you."

The woman reached into the folds of her tunic and pulled out a cloth bag of faded red and gold with elephants marching in procession around it, trunks up, frozen in mid-step. She handed it to Blue.

"What is this?" Blue asked curiously, taking it and running her fingers over it. It was soft cloth, but strong.

"It's a bag. Never go a long way without a bag." Dojie grinned.

Blue raised her eyebrows. "Do you think this is going to be far away?"

"I don't know, but it is beyond the pinpoint of light. That I am certain of. Now hug me, and then you be off."

Dojie hugged the girl and then let her go, and Blue walked to the doorway, holding the beads back as she turned to look over her shoulder at the big, elegant woman behind her.

"Thank you, Dojie." The girl gave her friend a wave, knowing she could not see it, but doing it anyway.

Dojie waved at her. "You're welcome, honey. You go on now, and you have a safe journey, Blue."

Chapter Two
The Graveyard Ship

Blue had never seen any pinpoint of light in the city, but she knew that if Dojie told her to go to it then it must be there, and she would have to find it.

She took the old metal staircase up to the top of the box cars. The stairs ended suddenly at the edge of a car, and Blue stepped out onto the surface and squinted her eyes, peering carefully in every direction, hoping to see the pinpoint of light.

Everywhere she looked there seemed only to be the same dim grayness of the city; the buildings, the concrete, the grime and dirt, the *machineness* of it all.

She tried to ignore it and focus on what it was that she wanted to see, and when she had stood in one spot and turned in a slow circle two and a half times, she finally stopped, frozen in place as she held her breath and squinted just a little more.

There at the furthest distance, tucked secretly into the razor thin crevice of space between two tall, dark buildings, was a pinpoint of light. It was so tiny that she had missed it the first two times around, but she had looked hard enough that she had found it at last.

A jolt shot through her, and she knew that she had to get to it. Keeping mind of where it was, she headed back down the stairs again, going as quickly as she could without falling until she reached the bottom. From there she headed out onto the sidewalk, and joined the river of countless people walking and going, and staring straight ahead.

Blue quickened her step, wondering how long it would take her to get to the pinpoint of light. She went, and went, and went on still, and her stride slowed after a long while, and she wondered whether she was there yet, or even close to being there yet.

Stopping and looking up, she found a tall building that she could get to the top of. It was twice as tall as the stack of box cars she had stood on, and she hoped that she would be able to see everything better than she could before.

The stairs she went up this time were zig-zagged instead of spiraled, and they were made of metal as well. It took longer to get to the top, and when she got there, she walked out onto an empty space with no railing and nothing on it but grime in the corners.

Blue had expected to see the pinpoint much closer and perhaps bigger than it had been when she had seen it earlier, but she couldn't see it at all.

She scanned the horizon carefully, her eyes taking in every part of the city around her that stretched out as far as she could see, and at long last she found the pinpoint.

Her shoulders dropped. It looked exactly the same size and distance away as it had when she had seen it the first time. Blue frowned a little and turned to go, when she stopped short at the sight of something not too far off. Tilting her head slightly, she gazed at the strange view before her.

Floating just above the buildings a few blocks away from her, was a row of ships. They bobbed and swayed in the air, each one tethered by a thick, long, rusty chain that stretched down to the ground where big iron anchors were hooked into crusted metal rings.

The ships were all made of wood; though they were partly rotted here and there, broken in some places and in others, most of them leaning quite a bit to one side or the other.

Tattered sails hung almost in shreds on partial masts, tied with fraying ropes and held loosely by tarnished rings. Railings were broken off in odd sections, while remaining in some spots. Some of the ships had holes in various places in the sides of them, and holes where there were once windows, though some of the dirty glass panes in the windows were still intact.

Off to one side of the ships was a dilapidated dock built of wood and ropes. It was barely more than a simple platform of logs bound together with weathered rope. It stretched a short distance, barely long enough for all of the ships to be secured to it.

Decrepit planks lay haphazardly between the dock and each of the ships, shifting left and right as the ships swayed slightly and floated above the city.

Blue saw one old ship coming in toward the dock as it arrived, and another leaving; drifting out over the city, still leaning to one side as it coursed along steadily.

She looked back at the pinpoint of light and then turned her gaze once more to the ships, realizing that the fastest way for her to make her way across the city would be to travel over it, not through it.

Scrambling from the rooftop, she hurried down the stairs and out of the building, rushing through the mass of people walking along the sidewalks and streets. She turned right and left, then left and right, her eyes raised now and then to the ships above as she drew nearer to them.

The girl came around the last corner and stopped all at once, blinking and staring upward at the mighty old ships far above her in the darkened grayness. The dock, also far above her, was positioned on extremely long wooden posts that reached all the way down to the ground.

Blue could see that they only way to get up to the dock was by way of a rickety staircase that looked as if it might be swaying right along with the ships above it.

It went up one way, and then after twelve steps or so it turned and went up another, and then did the same again, another fifteen steps up. Back and forth the thin and half broken boards went, with no more railing than a sagging and weary rope draped from section to risen section, all the way to the top.

"Bit fearsome up there, isn't it?" Came a low voice near Blue. She turned with a start and blinked, not having realized that she wasn't alone.

Sitting on a shabby box was a bit of a time worn man with a floppy brown hat and an ancient, crusty coat. He had long, stringy silvery hair and his face was thick with a ragged beard. His left eye was shut tight, but his right eye peered up at her, glinting dark from beneath a wild, bushy eyebrow.

"What... what is that place up there?" Blue asked, wondering how long the man had been sitting there.

"It's the ship graveyard, where all old and sunken ships go. There's some right impressive wrecks up there. The only voyage they make now is back and forth over this city." He was pensive a moment and studied her with his one good eye. "You goin somewhere?"

Blue drew in a slow, deep breath as she looked up at the graveyard. "Yes, I am."

"Then it's up the stairs with you, isn't it!" A sound similar to a rattling laugh, or perhaps a cough, echoed in his hollow chest, and he lifted a half-gloved hand a few inches off of his knee, pointing in the direction of the staircase.

Blue gazed at it for a long moment and then nodded her head. "I guess it is." She replied quietly, and she walked over the dusty ground to the first step. Giving a glance back to the old man who was watching her with curiosity, she bolstered herself and began to trek upward.

At first the going was fine, but the higher she got, the more the stairs wobbled and rattled, swaying beneath her slight weight, and the height began to worry her.

When she was a little more than halfway up, she sank down and began to crawl up the stairs on her knees, gripping each piece of wood ahead of her with tight fingers.

As she neared the top, wind began to blow around her, pushing and pulling at the stairs. It seemed the further she went, the windier it grew, which was strange to her because as long as she had been in the city of Geniss, she could not remember ever feeling wind; and yet there it was, swirling around her, blowing and blustering against her with every new step she took until she finally reached the top.

She could see then why and how the great ships in the sky, which were much bigger up close, could be shifting and drifting in the air, and why they needed to be anchored down to the ground.

"You lookin' for a ship to board, little missy?" A wide old man with several missing teeth and a scruffy chin leered at her, leaving the stack of boxes he had been standing beside on the dock.

He walked slowly and heavily, lumbering toward her, reaching out his great, meaty hands. He wore a dark bandana around his head, but it didn't hold in the mop of greasy brown hair that stuck out from under it.

"I... I don't know it..." Blue began as her body stiffened, and she felt frozen in place. She realized then that she might be in a great deal of danger.

"Got no one with you, do you?" The man sneered with a broad grin. "I've got space for you on my wreck. Why don't you come aboard with me, and I'll look after ya!"

Blue was stunned. She couldn't seem to think or make herself move, or even try to figure out what to do. The hulking man reached her and closed his fingers around her arm snugly. "You're quite the little prize! Aren't ya! You're going to be worth a pretty penny to me!"

Blue wanted to scream but the sound stuck in her throat. Suddenly another hand closed around her other arm, and she jerked her head up to see a tall, broad shouldered, dark haired man with dark eyes. There was a long silver sword on a belt at his hip and a pistol in his hand.

He glared hotly at the other man. "She's with me, Farin. You take your grubby meat hooks off of her and let her go, or I'll relieve you of your hands and you can make do with stubs on your arms."

Farin growled low and deep, but he let go of Blue's arm and flung her roughly toward the tall man who still had her in his grip. "Fine then, Captain, have it your way. She probably wouldn't have sold for much anyway." He grumbled bitterly and turned away from them, trundling back to his stack of boxes.

The man let go of Blue's arm and she turned to look up at him. He gave her a roguish but friendly smile.

"The ship graveyard is no place for a young one to be, now off with you. I'm not keen on babysitting; I've a voyage to undertake." He turned to leave, and Blue rushed to him and took hold of his black coat.

"Sir! Wait!" She pleaded, and he stopped and turned to her again, his eyes curious.

"Yes? What is it then?" He asked, giving her his full attention.

"I… I need to get on a ship. I don't know which ship to ride, though." She admitted shyly.

The man pursed his mouth thoughtfully. "You do, do you? Well now, that's a different kind of story. What direction are you going?"

Blue turned and pointed to the gray horizon. "To that pinpoint of light. I must get there, it's very important. There's someone who's trying to reach me. I think he needs me. I think I have to go to him, and he's that way."

The man drew in a breath and considered her plight. "That's a long way from here, are you sure that's where you need to go?"

Blue nodded; her eyes locked on his seriously.

He exhaled swiftly. "Well then, all right. I'm going that way. You can ride with me." He held out his hand to her. "I'm Captain Caribou."

Blue smiled. "Captain Caribou. I'm Blue." She replied happily, relieved that she had found some way to get where she was going. "I like your name."

The corner of the Captain's mouth went up. "I like yours too. Come on with me. I was just heading to my ship."

Blue walked beside him and tried to keep up with his long stride. "Why did you stop that man back there?" She asked interestedly. "I didn't like him, so I'm glad you did, but… why did you?"

The Captain looked down at her with a dark expression. "He's not a good one. He would have taken you off to the slave traders, and you'd have been sold on the underground market and become a slave. It's no kind of future for you. I didn't want to see that happen."

"So you helped me?" She asked with a grin.

Captain Caribou nodded. "I did. It was the right thing to do. Now, we'll get aboard, and you will be in good company. I'll take you to the far end, and you can find the friend you're looking for."

Blue pushed her hands down into her pockets. "I'm ready. Let's go."

The Captain chuckled and held her shoulders from behind as he walked up the plank with her in front of him, making sure she didn't fall off before they got to the ship.

She stepped off of the plank onto the deck and surprise overtook her.

She wasn't sure how it would be, standing on the deck of a boat that was leaning so far to the side. Captain Caribou picked up one of many ropes that was laying over the side of the railing close to the boarding plank. In a moment he had it tied snug around her waist.

"That's to hold you until we get going." He gave her a wink and a smile, and headed toward the wheel, hollering out to the deck crew. A small group of men dashed about the deck, avoiding the rotted out holes and missing boards, grappling with half worn ropes and streamers of what were once sails. Two of them turned a battled crank together, and the massive chain secured to it began to clank around the spindle it was on.

The heavy iron anchor was loosed from the hook on the ground, and hauled upward until it hit the side of the boat with a thunk. The deck hands worked hard, and in almost no time, the ship began to move slowly away from the dock.

Blue rested carefully against the railing; her rope tight on her waist, and her hands planted firmly on the time worn wood. The further they sailed, the more the ship picked up a little speed. It teetered a bit, and then began to right itself; not coming vertical, but listing only a bit to one side, so that it was easier to stand on the deck without concern of falling over the edge of the railing if one was not careful.

The sail rags fluttered in the wind as the vessel moved slowly over the city toward the distant pinpoint of light. Blue felt the tug on her again, and it was as if she was being pulled toward the pinpoint. She knew that she had to be going the right way.

Blue stood at the railing, gazing down at the city below and ahead of them. It looked strange to her to see it all that way; the tops of the buildings were only a short distance beneath the ship, but the streets at their bases looked like vast canyons so far away.

Something caught Blue's eye as she watched, and she leaned back and blinked in surprise, realizing that there was a baby blue ribbon hovering near her face. It was tied in a bow at the top, and the ends trailed a few inches down from it.

She looked around and saw no one near her. Turning back to look at the bow, she wondered what it might be, and if she should touch it. She lifted her hand slowly toward it and it came to her, as if it knew her.

The moment she closed her fingers around it, it no lingered hovered in the air, but instead lay still in her hand. With her brow furrowed in curiosity and confusion, she brought her other hand to it and untied it carefully.

As the knot in the middle came undone, a sensation swept through her fingers and all over her body, flooding her mind, her heart, and her soul.

It was a laugh. A deep, joyful, blissful laugh, and she loved the feeling of it. She laughed out loud herself, and realized that she had not ever laughed that genuinely before. It felt good to her; real and amazing.

The ribbon floated up a few inches from her hand and then vanished slowly, as if it was dissolving before her. She wondered for a moment if the laugh had gone with it; she had enjoyed it so much that she didn't want to let it go, but she laughed again, and she knew that it hadn't. It was inside her, in every part of her, and it was hers to keep and hold on to.

Blue looked up at the vast expanse of space above them and saw that the grayness faded into darkness with no light. She had never realized that there might be anything beyond the grayness, and it was surprising to her to discover that there was a tremendous and seemingly unending place of nothing but darkness in the beyond.

"Are you doing well, Blue?" The familiar voice brought her back to where she was. She turned and looked up at Captain Caribou.

"Yes, thank you." Blue gave him a smile. There was a twinkle in his eye, and it gave him a friendly and mischievous look.

"I thought you might like a friend to talk with on the journey, as it will be a long one. This is a stowaway we've acquired at some point or another. His name is Shuffle." The Captain turned and there was no one behind him. "Ah. He's a bit shy." The tall man laughed softly.

"Shuffle, come along now. We're waiting." Captain Caribou looked at the base of the main mast; a great round wooden beam standing erect in the middle of the ship, which was busted in half partway up, and hung at an angle to the listing side.

Blue watched curiously as a small creature peeked around the wooden pole, and then slowly made his way out, shuffling as he came.

He was almost two feet tall, with a smooth and flowing form, as if someone had draped material over him all the way to the ground, except for his face, his paws, and his feet. Those were draped in long thick fringe which covered his big round eyes, and part of his nose, though the tip of his nose and his mouth poked out from beneath the fringe. His paws were also covered with the same fringe, showing only when the fringe fell away from them, which it had as he held his two paws together anxiously, looking up at Blue. His feet were also covered by the thick fringe, and as he moved toward them, his body shuffled, and the quiet sound his feet made was a shuffling kind of sound.

"Hello." The creature murmured, with his nose poked out. He gazed up at Blue from beneath the fringe. She liked him right away.

"Hello!" Blue replied, kneeling down in front of him. "I'm Blue. I guess you're blue too," she said, meaning that his body was a light periwinkle blue, "but you have a different name."

Shuffle smiled at her and she smiled back. Blue knew that they were going to be friends. "Would you like to come to the railing with me and watch the city while we sail?"

Shuffle nodded and his fringe swayed back and forth. "Yes, please."

"You two seem to have hit it off. Good." Captain Caribou said with a grin. He left them, and Blue looked back at her new friend.

"You're a stowaway on this ship? And the Captain knows about you?" She asked, completely curious about him.

Shuffle moved forward and put his fringe covered paws on one of the planks holding the railing up, as he was too short to reach the railing. His voice was soft and friendly.

"I am. I came on thinking no one would notice me if I was very quiet, but the Captain notices everything. He let me stay."

"Where are you going?" Blue asked, sitting down beside him so that he didn't have to look up at her.

The little creature shrugged. "I'm not sure, actually. I am seeking my purpose."

Blue peered at him in confusion. "Seeking your what?"

"My purpose. You know… my reason for existing. I… I don't have a purpose right now, and I want to find one. I want something special to do; to be useful." Shuffle grew quiet and watched Blue, as if waiting for her to understand.

The girl gave him a smile and patted his back. He was very soft and warm to her touch, and she liked the way that he felt.

"That's a good thing to look for. I'm looking for a friend. I haven't met him yet, but when I do I will help him. I think he needs me. I think that must be my purpose."

Shuffle smiled then too, feeling some comradery between them. "I hope that you find your friend."

"Thank you!" Blue beamed at him. They sat together and talked a while, watching the city go by as the ship sailed. An idea formed in her mind and began rolling around in her thoughts, and when it came to the tip of her tongue, it sounded as good as it had seemed inside her head.

"Shuffle, I was thinking that if you want to, you could come with me when I get off of the ship. Perhaps your purpose will be on my way, and it could be our way; together."

Shuffle considered it a moment and then brightened, giving her a nod and a smile. "Yes! I think that would be good! I've been on the ship and haven't found any purpose, so maybe it will be on your way!"

Blue hugged him and he patted her arm with his thickly fringed paw. "On our way." She told him, and he agreed.

The ship docked, and two women came aboard, both of them arguing and talking so much that Captain Caribou could hardly get a word in edgewise. He looped a rope around each of their round bodies and sailed the ship away from the port.

Blue held Shuffle's paw in her hand and waved her free hand at the ladies. "Hello!"

They paused in their arguing to look at her. "Oh! Hello! Aren't you a small person." One of them said in slight confusion. The other one sighed and rolled her eyes.

"What my sister means to say is that you aren't a tall person, like we are." The second one seemed exasperated.

The two of them looked startlingly alike, and even their dresses were the same style, made of floral material that draped all over them and hung to the deck.

"What I mean to say is precisely what I said." The first sister announced irritably. "I always say precisely what I mean to say, and you always think that you have to correct me. I don't need correcting, Mimsy!"

The second sister rolled her eyes again and planted her hand on her hip. "Now Whimsy, you know that's not true.

You always need correcting, which is why I always correct you! That way you won't be wrong!"

"But I'm not wrong!" Whimsy scowled. "That's what I'm trying to tell you!"

"You're right! You're not wrong because I corrected you, which makes you right, and that makes me right." Mimsy tittered lightly and set her fingers on her rotund chest.

Blue stared at them. "Do you two always argue like that?" She asked disapprovingly.

They both turned to look sternly at her. "Of course we do, we're sisters!"

"If you always argue, then why do you stay together?" Blue frowned, trying to work out some sense about them in her mind.

"Oh we could never do without each other!" Mimsy laughed and waved her hand. Whimsy swatted her sister's hand.

"You mean to say that you could never do without me!" She corrected Mimsy.

"I did say that!" Mimsy shook her head in exasperation. "You could never do without me!"

"But you meant that I could never do without you!" Whimsy insisted.

They bickered ever on, and Blue quietly turned and slipped away from their company, unnoticed, with Shuffle in tow.

They went to the front of the ship, and there they saw an old woman sitting up straight and properly in a chair. She was dressed in what might have been fine clothing at one time, a very long time ago.

Her jacket and skirt were faded purple velvet with lace trim, but the lace was faded and falling off here and there. She wore gloves that had once been white, but were discolored and slightly misshapen. On her head was a wide violet hat that might have been grand in its day; high in the middle but dented here and there, with a graceful feather that arched over it limply. Fastened to the side of the hat was a pin that was missing half of its jewels.

Her hair was white, and it seemed to have been pinned up carefully once long before, but straggling pieces of it had fallen out, and wavered wispily about her weathered and wrinkled face.

She rested her hands on a fancy old cane, chipped in places, and set firmly on its end against the broken deck. She seemed to be covered in a fine dust, as if she had sat too long in one place and no one had bothered to clean her off.

"Hello!" Blue waved at her with her free hand while her other hand was held fast by Shuffle. Shuffle stood behind Blue's leg as much as he could.

"Hello." She answered, and then she looked away from Blue, turning her attention to the next port that they were coming to.

Chapter Three
Ports Aplenty

The port looked very different from the one where Blue had boarded the ramshackle ship. The place they docked this time looked like a black pyramid, and around the pyramid, a little way down from the top point of it, was the dock made of iron grating.

There was another ship anchored beside them, and it was quite different as well. It was long and wide, appearing to have once been a fine and fancy riverboat, but experience had left it in a seriously derelict state.

Mimsy and Whimsy departed the ship and Captain Caribou waved at Blue and Shuffle. "I'm going into the port. Would you like to come with me and see it?"

Blue nodded. "I will. I'd rather see it than stay on the ship." Shuffle immediately pressed his paw into her hand and looked up through his thick fringe at her. She knew he was going to stay at her side. The ship was already leaning heavily to one side, and Blue thought it might be nice to walk around the port and see it.

The first thing they walked into off of the dock was a bazaar. It was filled with sagging tents and tin shanty roofs. People of all shapes, sizes, and colors were meandering through the place. Some of them talked, some called out to others, some were standing in groups of three, or five, or eight here and there; each of them vying for the attention of the others.

Blue tugged at Captain Caribou's long black coat. "What are they doing?"

The Captain leaned down closer to her. "They're trading."

With her head cocked to one side, she watched for a moment, but saw no goods between any of the groups. Curiosity took hold of Blue. "What are they trading?"

The Captain smiled and set his hand on her shoulder, speaking into her ear. "They're tale traders. They trade stories. They're all trying to have the best one. You can listen here if you like. I'm going to see about picking up a few passengers. I won't be far off. Stay put here with Shuffle and you'll be fine."

Blue nodded at him and then turned her attention back to the tale traders before her. There was a group of six of them, and all of them were speaking loudly and pointing, trying to talk over the rest of them.

One of them; a large fellow with a funny looking pointed and faded green hat, managed to speak louder than the rest of them, and all eyes turned to him.

"There was a man with a train high in the mountains, and he would drive his train out along the sheerest edge of the mountain, so far down that you couldn't see the bottom! Always in danger of an avalanche, he were! He would drive the train down the side of the cliff of the mountain all the way into the valley below, where the track nestled into hills. At the far end of the valley there were a city, and he would take that train to the edge of the city and then go right underneath it! Right under the whole city through great holes in the ground! Then, before you know it, he is back out and taking that train right through the valley and straight back up the mountain once more!"

Another storyteller wearing an ancient purple vest, raised his hand and waved it importantly through the air.

"There was a woman who made a balloon which had a basket connected at the bottom of it; a big basket, big enough and strong enough to hold her! She got into the basket and loaded it with gear for an expedition, and then she headed out, and she sailed that balloon over seas and over cities, to the farthest known reaches with nothing more than a single companion and a book!"

Blue was fascinated with the tales that the traders were telling back and forth, and she would have stayed to listen longer to them, had the Captain not come back and startled her with a pat on the back.

She looked up at him and he tipped his head toward the ship. "Time to go if you're coming along." He spoke with a twinkle in his eye, and a friendly smile.

"Did you find anyone to get on the ship?" Blue wondered interestedly.

Captain Caribou nodded delicately to a few people standing a short distance away. There was a man, a woman, and a very small child. They all got on the ship, and Blue introduced herself to them.

"Hello! I'm Blue, and this is Shuffle." She indicated her friend, hiding behind her leg, peeking out at the new passengers.

"Hello!" The woman answered. "We're the Dawson's."

Blue furrowed her brow in confusion. "You all have the same name?"

The woman nodded and smiled. "Well yes, you see, we're a family."

Her reply made no sense whatsoever to Blue. "What's a family?"

The Dawson woman looked surprised then. "It's... why, it's the people that you care most about and live with or spend the most time with."

Blue thought that she understood then. "Oh, I see."

The Dawson man chimed in then. "Don't you have a family?"

"Well I guess I do. Dojie is my family." Blue replied, thinking about it carefully. Then she gazed down at Shuffle beside her. "Shuffle, would you like to be my family?"

The little blue creature nodded and the thick fringe over his eyes swayed. "Yes, I do not have a family."

"I will be your family, Shuffle." Blue promised him warmly. He gave her a smile and laid his head on her hand affectionately.

The ship sailed on and on, and all the while the city beneath it seemed to shift and change, with tall buildings here and there, and smaller ones amongst them, but always there were streets far beneath them, and everything and everyone on the streets was going; always and constantly going.

After a while, the ship stopped again, and the port was once more something the likes of which Blue had never seen. There were two towering metal box buildings, both enormous in size, and the ravine between them seemed to go down forever, where even the grayness faded, and it became black in the depths.

The dock was nothing more than a platform sheet of rusted metal, barely big enough for a few people to stand on, with no railing on it whatsoever.

Blue wasn't even sure that it was a dock, and she began to wonder if they weren't just stopping at some random place to pick up a straggler, as she saw a single rope with a knot at the base of it lowered down past the platform into the black abyss below.

A few minutes later the rope was slowly hauled upward by the deck hands as Blue and Shuffle stared through the railings on the lower side of the listing ship.

The rope came and came, and a long while later they could see a young man holding on to the rope. His feet were set against the big knot at the base of it, and he was the only person on it.

He had wild, pointy black hair that stuck out all around his head in chunks and half obscured his face. He wore all black, from his form fitting long sleeved shirt to his pants and boots; all of it was dark black, though there were thin strands of silver across his chest and arms, and around his back; as though he had walked through a spider's web and then decided to continue wearing the web.

The older boy said nothing to anyone; he merely stepped off of the knotted rope onto the deck and moved to a corner where he sank down with his knees up to attempt to block the view of his face. He laid his arms over his knees, and effectively closed himself off from everyone else on the ship, though Blue could see that he was watching all of them just over the top of his arms.

Blue looked away from him, but she found that she was enormously curious about him, and she kept glancing back at him. He watched her, too, though he made no move to change his position or say anything to her. They only watched one another.

It was strange to Blue that they would not greet each other, as they were both passengers on the same ship. The more she thought about it, the more she realized how ridiculous it was that they would not speak, so she stood up and Shuffle followed her as she walked to the older boy and sat near him.

"Hello, I'm Blue, and this is Shuffle." She told him, introducing them both with a friendly smile.

He lowered his arms and legs slowly, like he was coming out of a shell, and eyed her curiously.

"I'm Jaron." He told her in a solemn tone.

"Why are you traveling on the ship? Where are you going?" Blue continued, trying to make conversation.

Jaron only stared back at her with dark, still eyes. "I have no destination. I am only going."

Blue was surprised by him. He was speaking with her, but he didn't seem to have much to say. She wondered if she could fill the dark void in their communication.

"Well I'm going to the pinpoint of light at the end. It's the strangest thing. I wouldn't have left, only I started seeing shimmers of light, and I have been feeling this tug; a pull, I guess, is more like it. Anyway, I just knew that I had to follow the pull. I think it's leading me to someone who needs me." Blue kept her tone friendly and gave Jaron a smile.

Jaron shook his head and looked away from her, lowering his eyes to the broken deck. "Nothing matters. I don't know why you think leaving Geniss will change anything; it won't. You're probably just imagining the pull. It's probably not even real. You know, if you leave the city then you're only going to wind up coming back to it. That is… if the Shadows don't get you first."

Blue frowned and eyed him suspiciously. "The Shadows? What are those?"

Jaron sat up and looked sharply at her. "The Shadows! You've never heard of the Shadows? You're leaving Geniss and you've never heard of the Shadows. Well Blue, you've got a big, scary surprise waiting for you! I'll tell you about them."

He leaned forward on his knee and held his hand out before him as if he was about to snatch her up in his outstretched fingers.

"The Shadows wait until you aren't paying attention, and then they sneak up on you! They capture you when you aren't looking, and they drag you down to the dark core of the world, and there they imprison you forever!" His voice had grown menacing, and his dark eyes glittered.

Suddenly another voice cut into Jaron's. It was a strong and comforting voice. "Don't tell her such things!" Captain Caribou spoke firmly so that everyone heard him.

The old woman in the violet hat turned her head and peered at them from her perch on an old bench.

"And why not? They're true! If the girl goes out of Geniss, she will certainly be facing things like the Shadows and worse! They're no myth, you know, they're real! If she's going to be brazen enough to go out of the city and get herself into trouble, then she ought to know just exactly what kind of trouble she will be getting herself into!"

Any ice chill moved over Blue's skin, and she turned to Shuffle, who was sitting beside her. "Have you ever heard of the Shadows?"

Shuffle shook his head slowly, his fringe shifting some. "No. I haven't ever heard of them, but then I've never left the city, so I don't know about them."

Captain Caribou spoke gently to Blue. "Just ignore them. You don't need to think about things like that, or worry about them."

Blue nodded to him, but she wasn't so sure that they weren't real. Both Jaron and the old woman knew about them, and Captain Caribou hadn't said that they didn't exist, only that she didn't need to worry about them.

"Well, we'll watch out for them, won't we! We'll just pay attention, and nothing will happen to us." Blue told Shuffle quietly. Shuffle agreed with her.

"Don't you pay them any mind, Blue. You just go on about your way and don't listen to the terror tales of others. You'll be fine, little one. Just fine." Captain Caribou told her encouragingly.

Blue gave him a smile, but in her mind she was already making note to keep an eye out for whatever the Shadows might be, just in case they were more than a scary story.

Shuffle and Blue went to sit at the side of the ship, looking down through the railing at the city beneath them as the ship continued sailing with a heavy tilt toward its side.

Jaron watched her and Shuffle quietly, and a while later, he left his spot in the corner and went to them, sitting beside them as he spoke to her again.

"I didn't mean to frighten you before. I was only trying to warn you. There's a lot out there that can hurt you."

Blue watched him and spoke evenly. "I'll be careful."

Jaron stared down at the city along with them. "What do you see when you look out at Geniss?"

Blue frowned and considered it; her eyes moving over the city as she examined it with an open mind. "I see repetition. Consistency."

"What do you see?" She turned to him inquisitively.

Jaron shook his head in disgust. "I see ruts. I see a stifling place. It's all industrial; all of it. The air is still here, except when you get up out of the city and you can actually feel the wind. You can't feel the wind in the city; it doesn't exist there, because the air doesn't move. It's stale and still. There's no water. There is no nature… no real light." He sighed and his shoulders slumped. "There's no deep breathing." He was quiet a moment, and then spoke with a saddened voice.

"Everyone has empty eyes. Have you ever noticed that?" Jaron turned to look at her.

Blue nodded emphatically. "Yes! I have noticed that! It seems like they all do; staring all the time with nothing in their eyes at all. Empty eyes." She pondered it, and looked back down at the city.

"This city is nothing more than a maze, with no real way in or out. Just a continuing maze." Jaron pointed to it and she looked out and gasped.

"I see it! It does look like a maze!" Blue marveled at the new realization she'd had.

"The streets are all going one way, then they turn, they stop, they start, they go again. All the walls of the buildings block it all off and go straight up. There's no way through; only around and around, forever. All going and no direction, just turning corners over and over. No destination; only cycles." Jaron's voice went monotone as he spoke.

"And ruts." Blue added. "Cycles and ruts." She gave him a little smile of understanding.

Jaron nodded at her, and she wasn't entirely certain, but she thought that she might have seen a smile crack at one side of his mouth. "And consistency. No change. It's a machine."

Blue agreed, knowing that he was right as she looked back down at it, and as she did so, Jaron stood up and walked across the deck, looking over another part of the railing.

The ship docked at a small hill where the houses were a little more scattered, leaving empty space between them. There wasn't much else around, save for the few residences.

It was there that the Dawson family departed the ship, and Blue waved at them and called out a goodbye. They waved back and wished her well, and then they left. As they waved at her, she looked at them and for the first time she could see that their eyes were empty. Jaron had been right. So many empty eyes, but she just hadn't noticed it as much before.

The ship left the dock and moved on again, sailing out over the city, and trying to right itself just a little as it went.

They sailed on for a long while, until at last Shuffle brushed his paw over Blue's hand and she raised her head to see that the pinpoint of light which had been so very far away, was no longer a pinpoint of light, and it was quite close indeed.

The pinpoint of light was in fact a massive opening; bigger than anything that Blue had ever seen. The edge of the opening was rough-hewn stone and jagged dark rock.

Outside of the opening, there was such brilliant light that it was nearly too bright to look at, but she could make out an endless sky, and beneath it were mounds upon mounds upon mounds of sand, as far as the eye could see.

"What is this?" Blue gaped in awe.

Captain Caribou came to stand beside her. "Geniss is inside of a cave. We are in a cave right now. Did you know that?"

Blue blinked at him in utter shock. "We're… we're in a cave? The whole city? This whole big city is inside of one cave?"

"It is. It's a very big cave, and this is the mouth of the cave, or really, if you want to think about it like this, it's the only way in or out." The Captain rested his hand on the silver hilt of his sword, and gazed out of the huge hole in the cave before them.

The Captain raised his hand and pointed to the dunes outside of the cave. "That's a desert. That's known as The Shoghal. They say it has no end. I don't know, I've never left Geniss," He looked down to her and an expression of concern formed over his face.

"Are you sure that you want to go? Do you really intend to leave Geniss and head out into The Shoghal?" Captain Caribou asked worriedly.

Blue closed her eyes and focused on the feel of the pull. It had gotten a bit stronger the closer that they had gotten to the opening of the cave. It pulled even more in that direction, and her body tensed as she opened her eyes and pressed her lips together into a thin line before she spoke.

"Yes. That's where I need to go, I guess." Blue turned to Shuffle, beside her. "Are you sure you still want to go with me? Don't you think you'd rather stay in Geniss?"

Shuffle shook his head. "I have always been in Geniss, and I have never found my purpose, so maybe my purpose is out there. Maybe my purpose is in the desert. I will keep going with you. You are my family."

Captain Caribou sighed and hung his hands on his hips as he frowned. "All right then. The last port is coming up. That's as far as I go in this direction. From here, I turn and head toward the other side of the city. I hope that you will be very careful out there. The Shoghal is a wide open wasteland, and there is nothing beyond it. I don't think that you should enter it, but your way is your own to make."

Blue gave her head a shake as she shrugged. "That's where the pull is taking me, so that's where I have to go."

The Captain squatted down so that he could look Blue in the eyes. "Then I shall tell you what I know about it. That desert has shifting sands that can change your path and you might lose your way. They are always shifting, so you can't rely on the hills to know where you are going or where you've been. There's Swallowing Sand. It's places in the desert that suddenly open wide, leaving a hole, and everything is sucked into it, and then the hole just closes back up suddenly, as if it had never opened, but whatever was sucked into it is gone forever."

"Shifting sand and swallowing sand." Blue whispered. "Okay."

The Captain kept his eyes on hers. "There's more."

Blue drew in a breath and her brows lifted. "More?"

"Yes. There are Swirling Sand Towers. They spiral up from the desert to the sky and they are anchored in place, so they don't move unless the base breaks, and then they blast themselves all over the dunes wildly until they blow themselves out."

The pull inside of Blue felt stronger, and she knew that even though there were real dangers ahead of her, she had to go. "I understand." She told the Captain quietly.

"There's nothing more I can say to dissuade you." He sighed and stood, gazing down at her. "Then be safe, small one. I have warned you. Keep mindful of everything that I have told you."

Blue nodded in silence and held fast to Shuffle's paw as the ship came into view of the last port.

The Captain left her to go and take the wheel to dock the vessel. The port was wide open, with no buildings around it. There were no buildings around much of the area there. It was as if the city had made its biggest splash at the center and only a few drops had reached the mouth of the cave, where a modest sprinkle of structures stood alone against the great wide open just outside.

The port was one of those. It was a platform half the size of the ship, newer looking than any of the other ports in the city. It was constructed of wood and tied together with rope. There was a railing around the edge of it, and there was a good staircase that led down from the platform, zig-zagging to the ground which wasn't too far below. The ship was able to get much closer to the ground without buildings all over the place.

Blue and Shuffle watched as the old woman in the violet hat disembarked the ship. Jaron sat in his corner and stayed. He did look up at Blue and wave, and she waved back with a smile to him.

Blue thought that she might have seen the corner of his mouth rise ever so slightly into a smile as well.

Captain Caribou waved Blue and Shuffle to the plank. He walked with them off of the ship and to the platform, and there he shook Blue's hand.

"I hope that you are careful, and that you find whatever or whomever it is that you're looking for. You and Shuffle take good care of each other." He advised her with serious eyes.

Blue and Shuffle both agreed. "Okay. We'll be careful. Thank you for everything." She replied.

Captain Caribou looked for a moment as if he wasn't going to let go of Blue's hand, but then he sighed and nodded. "You're welcome. Have a successful journey, Blue."

With that, he turned and walked back up the plank to his ship, where he boarded without looking back. He made himself very busy, and Blue turned away and was about

~ 297 ~

to walk with Shuffle to the stairs when she stopped short and blinked in surprise.

"Oh look! There's another one!" Blue gasped.

"Another one what?" Shuffle asked, looking up at her questioningly.

"Another ribbon... floating in the air..." Blue reached her hand up and touched her fingertip to the soft yellow ribbon that was hovering in the air just a few inches beside her face. She narrowed her eyes and studied it hanging there, and as she touched it, it slipped gently from where it had been floating and slid itself into her hand.

"I didn't see a ribbon until you were holding it. Was there a ribbon in the air?" Shuffle puzzled.

"Yes, it was just there, and when I touched it, it came into my hand." Blue lowered her hand to show him.

"I didn't see that before." Shuffle shook his head, swishing the fringe over his eyes.

"I saw a ribbon on the ship, and I pulled it, and it made me laugh so much! Let's pull this one and have a laugh, shall we?" Blue took the ends in her fingers and giving them a tug.

As the ribbon came apart, a strong sensation moved through her fingers and up her arms into her body as it raced for her heart, her mind, and her soul. Just as the sensation in the previous ribbon had done. A smile made its way to her face and became a grin. She felt as if sunshine was rising inside of her and she gasped, beaming as she never had.

"It's not a laugh!" Blue exclaimed in utter joy. "It's... it's happiness!" She squealed. "I can't hold it in!"

She began to turn in place, spinning slowly as she let her head fall back and her arms go out wide from her. Her babydoll shirt flared out, and she giggled with glee as she turned and turned, her eyes closed, her heart overflowing with happiness.

"Spin Shuffle! Spin like me! It's so wonderful!" Blue laughed as she twirled and twirled around. Shuffle had been staring at her in astonishment, but he nodded and called up to her.

"Oh... okay! I suppose that I can do that too!" He replied uncertainly, and then he began to turn slowly as well, in his wobbly shuffling own kind of way. He moved his head back a bit and turned around and around, and a soft chuckle sounded from him.

"Oh! Oh my! This is quite enjoyable, isn't it!" Shuffle agreed, and together they spun for a few more long moments until they were both laughing and breathless, and then they slowed down and stopped; their chuckles softening as Blue took Shuffle's paw in her hand.

"Thank you, that was so much fun." She said quietly and contentedly. She sighed and began to walk toward the stairs. "I guess it's time to go."

Shuffle swished along at her side and followed her down the stairs carefully, as he was nearly too small to reach them all, though he managed. Soon enough they made it to the last step and saw that there was a narrow stone trail that led away from the port, going to the mouth of the gigantic cave.

Blue took a deep breath and walked along the stone trail, following the shallow steps gently upward.

The path led to the cave opening, and there it stopped abruptly. The mouth of the cave was one whole ring of chunky, rough-hewn, broken looking dark stone, going all the way around.

The stone boundary between the inside of the cave and the desert outside was about twenty feet in width. Blue and Shuffle struggled to make their way over the knee high crumple of rock, but at long last they made it to the far side, and the rock stopped, and the sand began.

It was colored sand; all dark burgundy, very fine and soft, and Blue discovered that it was easy to sink down into a little, which made walking difficult. She took a few steps and held her hand up to her forehead, shielding her view from the brightness as her eyes grew accustomed to it, and she gazed out at everything she could see before them.

"My goodness, Shuffle. Would you look at that." The girl breathed in awe. In every direction that she could see were dunes of different sizes, and all of them were different colors. Each one was a solid color, and at the bases of them, where the dunes met, the colors mixed together and made new colors.

Blue could see the Swirling Sand Towers that Captain Caribou had warned her about. They were sparse; one here, one there, and they were all on their own, without other Swirling Sand Towers around them.

They were made of whatever color sand they were tethered to, so Blue saw a green tower in one place, a blue one in another, a red one on that dune, and a pink one on this dune.

All of them swirled powerfully up into the sky so far before dissipating back into themselves again. What struck Blue the most wasn't the sand, or the Swirling Sand Towers, or even the vast desert stretched out before them as far as the eye could see in every direction. It was what was above it.

"Is that… is that the sky, Shuffle?" Blue stared in amazement, trying to comprehend the greatness of it.

Shuffle gazed at it too, lifting his paws to pull the thick fringe out of his eyes so that he could see it properly.

"I don't know. I haven't ever been out of Geniss. I guess that means I've never seen the sky before, since we found out that we've been in a cave this whole time, but I think that must be what a sky is! I don't know what else it could be."

They watched it in wonderment for a while and then Blue spoke quietly. "I didn't know that there was so much light, and I never knew that there was so much sky before. It's so… blue. I didn't know it could be so bright and pretty. What have we been looking at for all this time up until now?"

Shuffle was disgusted. "We've been looking at the inside of a cave. Grayness everywhere, and all the time this was right here."

Blue lifted her chin and felt determination rise in her. "Well let's go see it then. There's nothing else here for us!" She marched off down a slight hill toward the first dune; a purple one, and Shuffle followed along at her side as they entered The Shoghal.

To read all of
Journey Blue
and many other exciting
Dash Hoffman stories,
please visit the official website:

www.got-moxie.com/bookshelf

OR

www.amazon.com/Dash-
Hoffman/e/B06XDMMQTJ

Follow Dash!
Instagram @dashhoffmanbooks
Twitter @readdashhoffman
Facebook @DashHoffmanOfficial

Mrs. Perivale and the Blue Fire Crystal
Journey Blue
The Starling Chronicles
The Wish Weaver
Voyager: The Butterfly Effect

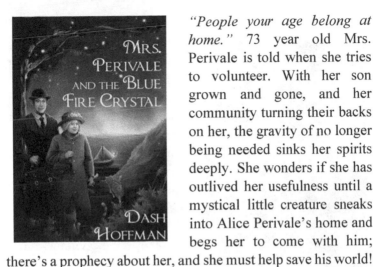

"People your age belong at home." 73 year old Mrs. Perivale is told when she tries to volunteer. With her son grown and gone, and her community turning their backs on her, the gravity of no longer being needed sinks her spirits deeply. She wonders if she has outlived her usefulness until a mystical little creature sneaks into Alice Perivale's home and begs her to come with him; there's a prophecy about her, and she must help save his world!

Finding herself in a magical place she had no idea existed, committed to a dangerous mission far more vital than helping out in her neighborhood, Alice dusts off her courage and bravery, rediscovering the feisty, sassy, powerhouse woman she is deep inside. She is determined to find the stolen Blue Fire Crystal before the imbalance between elements destroys all of the magical land of Corevé. Together with her extraordinary family of six cats and her skeptical-yet-devoted butler Henderson, she takes on the tremendous challenge.

With time running out and the world falling to pieces, Alice's precious companions are pulled away from her, and she is faced with impossible choices. Does she choose what she wants most of all, does she rescue her family, or does she save the world that will not survive without her?

Mrs. Perivale and the Blue Fire Crystal is the first book in the enchanting *Mrs. Perivale* YA fantasy series. If you're looking to escape reality for a while with a laugh-out-loud, heart-touching adventure, discover the heroine you never knew you needed today!

The Wish Weaver

Amias and his young friends enjoy simple lives in their village at the foot of the Kamado mountains, though there are circumstances for each of them that they wish they could change; a family member with ill health, a love unrequited, a life debt that cannot be repaid, and more.

A traveling stranger passes through the village and enchants them with a tale of the Wish Weaver who lives far up the mountain and weaves wishes into being. When his friends decide to go to the Wish Weaver to change their lives, Amias determines to go with them, though he is skeptical about anyone granting wishes freely to one and all. Along the journey the friends face tremendous hardships and when their quest takes a dark turn, Amias becomes the only one who might be able to save them all. If he is very clever and very lucky, his sole wish might come true.

This book is written in the style of an old Grimm's Bros fairytale and an Aesop fable. It is light and dark, and there are many moral lessons to discover woven deftly into the story. This tale takes a hard look at choosing what is right over what is easy, at moral value over material value, at self-love over infatuation, and at strong, true friendships.

YA+

Journey Blue

Blue is an unusual girl living on her own in a strange world. It is a place of consistency and method; seamless and cold, and she thinks she knows her world until the day she feels something, or rather someone, pulling at her from far away.

Visions of a mysterious boy intrigue her, and she is unable to ignore the magnetic draw within her to him. Even though Blue doesn't know him, this remarkable girl sets out to find the boy, traveling through what she believes is the monotonous machine of a land she lives in, only to discover that it's nothing at all like she ever imagined.

From giant white turtles and glowing bridges of light to colorful sand dunes and bottles of wishes, Blue's journey becomes a bizarre twist of terrifying danger and delightful fun. With the help of extraordinary and dear friends that she makes along the way, she discovers the highs of happiness and hope, and the lows of fear and sadness.

It isn't all fun and games; dark and dangerous forces come after her, doing everything to stop her from going onward. Her courage and determination are unbreakable however, and Blue refuses to give up on finding the unknown boy, no matter what it takes, how surreal the world around her becomes, or how impossible it may be to get to him. This journey straight out of reality will leave you reeling. YA+

The Starling Chronicles
Book One ~ The Starlings of Ramblewood

Daring and clever fourteen year old Jules Starling has just lost her mother and met her twelve year old bookish brother Henry for the first time. Before she even has a chance to get settled into her new home at Ramblewood with Henry and their aunt Vianne, every part of the real world they know begins to unravel swiftly!

When Vianne goes missing and they begin a search for her, traveling through time by accident is only the beginning of a series of unimaginable surprises and wild adventures for the Starling children. After a dreamlike visit to the Time Palace and a strict warning not to do anything or go anywhere, they are shanghaied onto a fantastical ship by a rogue pirate and a world class crew, traveling through oceans, air, and space.

Their new friends are a tremendous support, but the search for Vianne takes them on a dangerous quest much further than they ever dreamed they could go. Jules and Henry soon discover that they'll have to find courage, bravery, and strength in themselves and in each other if they ever hope to overcome the formidable challenges they must face and succeed in their vital mission!

This is the first book in the Starling Chronicles series, which takes the Starling children on many extraordinary adventures through space and time! YA+

VOYAGER:
THE BUTTERFLY EFFECT

Audrey Bennet and Jude Harper have just lost their dear friend Daniel, but Danny shared an un-believable secret with them before he passed away. He invented a time machine. After finding it, they decide to leave it untouched and under coded lock and key in Harper's basement, but fate brings about necessity.

Just when they need him most, Danny is there to help them. Audrey is working hard on a case that should not be happening; she's the unlucky police detective tasked with putting an old woman in jail at the insistence of a heartless tycoon.

When she hears Ruth Harrison's story, she knows she must do everything in her power to help Ruth win her freedom, her life, and get back a bit of her past so she can find peace in her future. Even if it means dragging Jude Harper back in time with her to uncover the truth.

This is a tale of enduring love; love between friends, love between lovers, and the strength that it takes to bind them all together. Harper and Audrey discover that everything that happens in every life, no matter how small, can have a powerful effect; a butterfly effect, that ripples throughout the rest of time.

CPSIA information can be obtained
at www.ICGtesting.com
Printed in the USA
LVHW021913270921
698837LV00003B/289